sprawled across her bed . . .

Amy swallowed and thought about screaming. But she was only human and he was gorgeous. She swayed, peering down at the nearest part of him—his feet—and letting her gaze run slowly upward. It was a fabulous journey. Oh yes, he was impressive in every way.

Amy knew she'd had far too much to drink and her good-sense meter wasn't working, but this seemed special. There was something about Rey, something that made him different from other men. Not just his appearance, but the way he spoke and behaved. The way he looked at her. She knew such a thing was impossible, and yet . . .

It was as if he really came from another time.

Maybe it was just that she wanted it to be true. Amy wasn't such a cynic that she couldn't enjoy a little fantasy and romance, but this time fantasy and reality seemed to have fused.

Was the Ghost really asleep on her bed?

By Sara Mackenzie

PASSIONS OF THE GHOST
SECRETS OF THE HIGHWAYMAN
RETURN OF THE HIGHLANDER

SARA MACKENZIE

PASSIONS
OF THE
GHOST

AVON BOOKS
An Imprint of HarperCollinsPublishers

This is a work of fiction. Names, characters, places, and incidents are products of the author's imagination or are used fictitiously and are not to be construed as real. Any resemblance to actual events, locales, organizations, or persons, living or dead, is entirely coincidental.

AVON BOOKS
An Imprint of HarperCollins*Publishers*
10 East 53rd Street
New York, New York 10022-5299

Copyright © 2006 by Kaye Dobbie
ISBN-13: 978-0-06-079582-5
ISBN-10: 0-06-079582-4
www.avonromance.com

First Avon Books paperback printing: December 2006

Avon Trademark Reg. U.S. Pat. Off. and in Other Countries, Marca Registrada, Hecho en U.S.A.
HarperCollins® is a registered trademark of HarperCollins Publishers Inc.

Printed in the U.S.A.

10 9 8 7 6 5 4 3 2 1

To Emma,
who helps me in so many ways.
A big thank you!

Prologue

The Sorceress strode through the great cathedral, enjoying the sense of space around her. Incense burned, flowers bloomed, and there was a deep, ancient silence.

She smiled, congratulating herself. Everything had gone very well with her past two attempts at improving history, and she hoped for more success again this time.

She entered a white marble chapel bleached by the light of many beeswax candles. The man in repose upon his tomb was big—he'd once been called a giant among men—and his powerful arms and chest proclaimed him a warrior.

But Reynald de Mortimer had been far more than that.

With his white-blond hair and gray, almost

colorless eyes, he was well named the Ghost. He was a brutal and powerful lord who lived on the Welsh Marches in the thirteenth century, and he'd had to be strong in mind and body to hold on to his lands while both English and Welsh tried to take them from him. Yes, he was feared in his day, but even his enemies said of him that when the Ghost gave his word he kept it.

That was why it was so strange that he hadn't kept his word the day he died. Afterwards his lands had fallen into chaos, with people dying in the slaughter that seemed to go on endlessly. The Ghost could have prevented that if he had lived. If he had opened his eyes to what was happening within the safety of his walls.

Well, this was his chance now to make amends, and the Sorceress had found a particularly interesting mortal to help him out. She smiled. Yes, there'd be some fireworks between them, but that was all part of their journey.

She held her hand over his face, not touching him, but close enough to feel the stir of his breath. There was an ugly scar on one side of his throat where someone had tried to kill him long ago, although the rest of his face was unmarked. Handsome, but it did not look as if he smiled very much.

"Your chance has come, Ghost," she murmured, and her voice caused the walls of the chapel to vibrate. She raised her arms and the heavy wolfskin cloak rose about her, the strands of her long red hair writing like serpents around her face. She looked frightening, like a witch from the days of old.

She began to chant, and the man on the tomb moved restlessly, as if he were fighting against some imaginary foe, and then his eyes sprang open. They were of the clearest, palest gray—almost the color of water. And he spoke one word.

"Run!"

One

*The Welsh Marches—the border lands
 between Wales and England
Winter, present day*

Reynald stood perfectly still. Despite the darkness and the dank underground smell, the castle enclosed him, welcomed him, embraced him with familiar arms. One moment he'd been in the great cathedral with the redheaded witch, and the next he was here. In the deep tunnels beneath his own castle.

Slowly he oriented himself. The tunnels were here prior to the castle. They were the remains of some Welsh burial chamber or sacred building— no one knew. They were useful for storage of

foodstuffs and weapons, and sometimes prisoners, but even he who knew every inch of his domain did not venture down here very often.

Reynald bent low, awkward in his coat of armor—the garment was thick and heavy, made of
steel plates and chain mail—only just avoiding
knocking his helmeted head against the jagged
ceiling. At first he'd thought he was back in the
between-worlds, that fearful place he had inhab-
ited before the witch took him to the cathedral for
his long sleep. But this was different, this was familiar. This was home.

He realized he was still holding his longbow
and a couple of arrows clasped in his hand. In his
heart he had always believed that the task of striking down his enemy was his alone, but he hadn't
trusted his feelings and had allowed himself to be
persuaded otherwise. He shivered with a mixture
of guilt and regret. He'd failed his people when
they needed him most.

Reynald bumped his head and swore.

Moving about in the constricted space in his coat
of armor, and with his sword strapped to his side,
was difficult enough without the longbow. What
use was it to him anyway? As he passed a niche in
the wall, he paused long enough to place the longbow and arrows within it, for safekeeping, until he
sent someone back for them later.

Was it still 1299, the year of his death? Were the

men of his garrison still up above, in disarray and awaiting his orders? His servants would weep with joy when they saw him again. Somehow he would change history and turn defeat into victory.

There were steps, narrow and dusty. As he climbed them he saw a light ahead, but it wasn't the uncertain flare of torch or candlelight, this was brighter . . . steadier.

He paused to stare at the strange burning globe. The steps continued up, toward the armory, and he climbed on, refusing to listen to the increasingly uneasy voice in his head. Was the battle still going on outside? It was very quiet.

The armory wasn't there. No weapons cleaned and shining, no dented coats of armor or well-used chain mail. Instead, there were some boxes and chairs stacked against the wall.

More stairs, and a door that no longer had a latch or a bar, just a round knob that he gripped in his big hand, and turned.

Reynald stepped out into a world run mad.

All about him were colors, frenzied discordant colors. Yellow and red and pink. Everywhere his eyes rested they were assaulted by a rainbow of different shades and hues. How could his good stone walls have been so vandalized? A half-sized tree stood in an enormous barrel, its branches hung with many sparkling balls, while ropes of glittering gold were wound about and through them. As he stared, eyes began to wink at him from the greenery. Many-colored eyes. Shocked, he forced himself forward and peered closer. The eyes were in fact small balls with colored lights inside them that flashed on and off.

"Jesu . . ."

His voice sounded deep and rusty from disuse. A moment later all thoughts left his head as a terrible whiny noise burst forth. He spun around, and found himself confronted by a fat, bearded creature in a red gown.

"Jingle bells!" it shrieked.

Reynald lurched back as the creature began to swing its hips lasciviously at him, the reddened lips pouting as it sang. He drew his sword and brought it down on the creature's head, splitting it asunder. There was a smell of burning, a whirring groan, and it slumped into silence. Reynald could see within the bearded head. This was no flesh-and-blood being but a man-made abomination, full of cogs and thin steel wires.

He backed away, sheathing his sword, bewildered and afraid.

This was his home, and yet it wasn't. Something was very very wrong.

Striding quickly, ignoring the jarring changes—telling himself that perhaps if he ignored them they would go away—he made his way toward the thick iron-studded door. Where was his garrison? Surely they were as keen to find him as he was to find them? he told himself as he flung it open.

Outside it was nighttime, and cold. Far colder than the air behind him in the castle. There was a flurry of snow, and he could see that white flakes lightly covered the surface of the ground and sparkled on top of the castle walls. There were winking lights here, too, stretching along the battlements and hanging from the towers, flashing on and off jauntily and seeming to mock the blood that had been shed in this place.

The gatehouse rose grimly before him, and beneath it the heavy doors were open wide to the drawbridge and the moat beneath. His enemies could walk in unopposed!

Angrily, Reynald de Mortimer strode forward, calling for his men, calling for the gate to be closed and the drawbridge lifted. His voice echoed back mournfully, and the snow swirled about his feet. He might have been all alone in the world.

Perhaps I am all alone. Perhaps there is no one left but me.

The thought was so horrifying, he went to step outside the gates . . . and found he couldn't.

His body simply refused to pass over the threshold.

Frowning, he tried again, moving forward, pushing hard. And couldn't. It was as if there was some invisible shield between him and the outside world, something he could not feel or see, and yet it held him captive. Frustrated, he raised his fists, but

again he could not move beyond the gates. Whatever it was, he could not push through it.

I am a prisoner here in my own castle.

If it is mine, he added bleakly. This place was very
different from the world he had left behind in 1299.
The witch had brought him back to life, yes, but it
was not the life he knew and understood.

With a groan, Reynald turned and made his
way across the bailey, toward the winding stairs
of the infamous north tower. He needed fresh air.
He needed to look out over his lands. He needed
to think.

Amy Fairweather lifted the hem of her long, gauzy
skirt as she negotiated the narrow stone stairs that
circled around and around to the top of the north
tower. The castle was full of passages and steps
leading up and down, and sometimes nowhere at
all. It was easy to get lost. And stairs like these certainly weren't made to be climbed in four-inch
heels, but Prince Nicco had insisted. And the prince,
she had learned, was used to getting his own way
in all things.

It was possible that in some men this might have
been exciting and macho—not many, but some. In
Nicco it just seemed spoiled and petulant. And
when it came to Nicco that said it all, really.

He'd made it more than clear that he expected
Amy to accompany him to his private suite and
into his luxury-sized bed. Not that she was averse

to some hot quick sex. She wasn't a prude, and it was true Nicco would be far more pliable if she gave him what he wanted. But when it came to the point, Amy couldn't bring herself to do it. Didn't want to.

No matter how much she owed Jez.

In fact—Amy paused as she stepped out of the stairwell and onto the roof of the north tower— she really didn't want to be here at all.

"Ah, magnificent!" Typically, Nicco was making a grand gesture, sweeping his arms at the view.

As far as Amy was concerned there wasn't much to see. Cold, dark countryside and some bulky hills against an only slightly lighter line of sky. It was beginning to snow again, and as she picked her way over to the crenelated wall the roof felt slippery beneath her shoes.

She shivered, clasping the thin, gauzy cloak around her. Jez said she was meant to look like a medieval lady of the manor, and although the costume was very flattering and feminine, Amy was pretty certain no medieval lady had ever worn something like this, unless she was the Barbie version.

Thanks, Jez, for the hypothermia . . .

For a moment the height made her feel quite dizzy, and she reached out to clutch at the cold hard stone before her. Down below was a deep ravine and the sparkle of a frozen river. The sense that this was a big mistake and she didn't want to be here was suddenly so strong she felt sick. She should have told Jez "no" once and for all. But even now the thought of facing him, of explaining to him, made her flinch. She owed her brother . . . more than she could ever repay.

"Nicco likes beautiful women," Jez had told her. "Red-heads, in particular—so no need to color your hair, sweetheart. Women and jewelry are his top picks. And he likes to boast. A woman like you, Amy. He'd be putty in your hands. I need to know where the Star is."

"Why wouldn't it be locked up safe and tight in a bank vault?"

Jez grinned. "The Star of Russia? The diamond ring of Catherine the Great? Come on, this bloke likes to feel it against his skin. Owning it isn't enough. He has to see it, touch it. The Star is hidden somewhere accessible— probably in one of his houses. I just need you to find out which one."

"I wish you'd stuck to stealing cars."

Jez laughed.

"Jez—" She tried to tell him, she really did, but the words stuck in her throat.

"Don't worry, it'll be a walk in the park. I trust you, Amy. You always come through for me."

But maybe I'm tired of coming through for you, she'd thought. *Maybe I want to put the past behind me. Maybe I want to put you behind me.*

"What have you been up to anyway?" he said. "It took me ages to track you down. You've moved, sweetheart."

*"I know. Sorry, I meant to tell you. I've been studying.
I went back to school to get my degree."*

*Jez laughed, just as she knew he would. "You don't
need to go back to school. How daft is that? What do you
want to do that for?"*

For myself, Jez. For myself.

Nicco's hand closed over her arm, and Amy came
back to the present with a jolt. She was standing on
the freezing roof of a castle in winter in a dress
more suited to a harem. Still, she was here now, and
the sooner she got Jez the information he wanted,
the sooner she could be gone.

Amy turned and gave Nicco her most winsome
smile. "I'm sorry."

"You were certainly far away. What were you
thinking of, Amee?"

She stopped herself from cringing at the way he
drew out her name. "Diamonds," she said truth-
fully. "Sapphires, pearls, emeralds, rubies . . ."

His smile was indulgent. She'd already told him
of her passion for jewelry. Jez had got her a cache
from somewhere or other to wear this week. It was
all part of the character she was playing. The
spoiled darling who was never satisfied.

"One day I will show you my Star," he said
softly.

Amy felt her heart beat a little faster. "I wish
you would," she pouted.

"I will place it on your finger, and you will never be the same again."

"Where is it? Perhaps we could go and see it?"

Tell me, tell me . . .

But he gave her a secretive smile. He trailed his fingers up her arm and fastened them on her shoulder. It felt uncomfortable, as if he was arresting her. His face was pressed close to hers, his breath panting against her frozen cheek. "You are very beautiful, my Amy."

I'm not yours . . .

She let him kiss her. He was an experienced kisser, she'd give him that; but despite his skill something was missing. She didn't feel special. It was as if she was just another body to add to his list of conquests. The thought made her feel icky. She leaned back with a gasping laugh, pretending to be overcome with the heat of passion. He came after her, pressing his body to hers, pinning her to the battlements. Behind her the world fell away dizzyingly.

There was something in the guidebook about a girl falling off here, hundreds of years back.

"Nicco," she said, trying to wheedle, but he ignored her. She'd kept him at arm's length too long, while making too many promises with her lips and eyes. He pressed his hips against hers, and she could feel his erection. "Please, I don't like heights."

"I will make you forget about such things, Amee," he said arrogantly.

Amy mentally gritted her teeth as he came in again, all hands and tongue. She was going to have to stop him. Jez would be furious with her, but she couldn't stand this pawing another moment, even for the Star of Russia. Amy clenched her hand into a fist and drew it back for a hard, sharp jab to His Highness's midsection.

A deep soft voice came out of the darkness, full of threat, and something more that made the hairs stand up on the back of Amy's neck.

"Unhand the woman, or I will spit you like a pig."

Two

Amy felt the prince's hands drop away from her. He turned, his profile stiff and outraged against the light from the stairwell.

"How dare you," he began in his most regal voice.

But Amy wasn't listening. She was too busy looking. There was a man, a huge man. He must have been here all along, seated in the shadows farther along the tower. Now, as he stood up, she gasped. Amy wasn't someone who enjoyed violence or the threat of it, but the moment seemed so unreal . . . She had to admit to a primitive thrill of feminine excitement.

"She wishes you to let her go," the giant said, in that soft deep rumble. "Could you not hear her? Or are you as deaf as you are lacking in wits?"

Nicco made a choking sound, and for a moment she thought he was going to launch himself at the bigger man. But Nicco was no fool. "Come, Amee," he said, his voice trembling with rage, "we will go back downstairs, where we won't be insulted by riffraff."

"I'm not insulted," she heard herself say.

Nicco turned to stare at her. He reached out an imperious hand, and she knew she should put her fingers in his and let him lead her, meekly, back to the party. That was what Jez would want her to do. That was what she was here to do. Win him over, learn his secrets . . .

"I think I'll stay for a bit," she said, trying to make light of it. "I'll be down in a minute."

He stared at her incredulously, then his mouth hardened. With a regal shrug, Prince Nicco turned and walked away.

Amy gave an inner sigh as he clattered down the steps. Jez would be furious, and rightly so. She was reneging on her promise. But just for a moment she wanted to be free of Nicco and the complications of her brother's schemes.

"He is not happy with you, damsel."

"Well, that's his problem."

"You are unhurt?"

She frowned at the dark shape. He was very big, but he didn't sound frightening. Amy trusted her instincts—they'd never let her down.

"Yes. Thank you for your help, but I could have managed."

She felt his skepticism. He shifted his feet, and there was a clank of armor. She realized he was wearing some sort of medieval costume, too. That probably explained why he looked so big. Padding could do a lot for a man.

"You don't have to stay here with me," she said. "Go back to the party if you like. Just keep away from Nicco," she added. "He can be dangerous when crossed."

"The party?" he sounded confused. He spoke with a very slight accent, as if English was not his first language.

"The fancy dress party. That's what you're here for, isn't it?"

"Fancy dress party," he said it slowly, as if he'd never heard of such a thing before.

"Yes, you know, for the guests who are here for the Medieval Long Weekend." Jez had taken a look at the guest list; businessmen and their women, foreign royalty, a couple of Hollywood actors and a few British theater and television personalities. Minor celebs. Which one of them was he?

"There are guests here?" He glanced around suspiciously. "I have invited no guests."

"No, well, you can attend on your own if you like. I meant the guests who are staying for the weekend. We're all paying for the privilege."

"But . . . this is Reynald de Mortimer's castle."

He seemed very confused. Maybe he'd drunk too much mead.

"It *was* Reynald de Mortimer's castle, before it became a first-class resort hotel. Only the best people here, no riffraff, despite what Nicco says." She heard the cynicism in her voice and bit her lip, but he didn't appear to notice. Her eyes had adjusted to the darkness, and she saw he was wearing some sort of metal helmet, with a vertical piece to cover his nose.

"You are mistaken." He said it arrogantly and turned to stare out over the frozen landscape. Something metallic struck the heavy stones of the wall. Amy's eyes widened. There was a sword fastened about his waist, and it looked as big as him.

"You've certainly gone for authenticity," she said, gesturing at his costume. "You look like the real thing. Isn't that armor heavy?"

"I am accustomed to it."

"Oh, so you come to lots of these weekends?"

He ignored her question. "Tell me, damsel, is the battle won?"

"Ah, you have me there." Maybe it wasn't such a good idea being alone with him. Some of these medieval reenactment enthusiasts were weird, so dedicated to their hobby they convinced themselves they actually were the characters they played. She'd already met a couple of Reynald de Mortimers downstairs at the party, as well as a King John, a

William the Conqueror, three Robin Hoods, and a Friar Tuck.

The man on the battlements was staring at her, and it seemed to her that his eyes had no color. She knew it must be an illusion, but it gave her a shock. Wasn't that why they called Reynald "the Ghost"? Because of his pale ghostly hair and eyes? Suddenly she wondered what color this man's hair was beneath his helmet.

"What is your name, lady?" He spoke with a peculiar intensity.

"Amy Fairweather. Lady Amy," she embellished, with a grin. "And you?"

"I am Mortimer," he said.

"I meant your real name . . ."

"Lord Reynald de Mortimer."

Amy sighed. In the circumstances it was only polite to go along with him, but she really wished he'd said "Fred Smith" or "Jack Brown" or someone real rather than someone who was dead.

"How do you do, my lord?" She'd been practicing her curtsy, and she was proud of it.

He stared down his nose at her as she wobbled, then his mouth twitched.

It wasn't the reaction she'd expected. Friar Tuck had said it was the best curtsy he'd seen since Maid Marian. How dare he laugh at her after she'd been so tolerant of him?

"Who is your father, damsel?"

"None of your business."

His mouth twitched again. "I would determine your bloodline. Are you from Norman stock or English?"

"Oh, right. English, then. My father is Lord Larry of the Parkhill Housing Estate. Block B, Flat Five."

Again he looked puzzled. Good. It served him right for laughing at her curtsy. He obviously didn't know Parkhill was one of the most notorious housing estates in outer London, where no one went out after dark but the pushers and the thugs.

"Not as nice as your place," she had the grace to add.

"My castle is altered since I left it." Was that a forlorn note she heard in his voice?

"Well, it would have, wouldn't it? How many hundreds of years is it since you were last here?"

"I . . . left this place in 1299."

"That's seven hundred years, give or take."

This time he didn't say anything, his expression stony as the battlements. Again the hairs rose on the back of her neck.

"Of course, there's the legend," she went on. "The one in the guidebook."

"Tell me."

She tried not to resent his arrogant tone. "Well, the legend says that if there's ever danger to the castle or anyone in it, then the Ghost will come back to life and save the day. A bit like a comic book superhero."

"And is there danger to the castle or anyone in it?" he asked.

"I don't think so. Not in the way you mean, anyway. Some of the guests are pretty dreadful, but I don't think they're actually dangerous."

He almost smiled.

"Although you did save me from Nicco. Not that I needed saving. All the same, I don't think you'd have returned from the dead for that, do you?"

He wasn't listening. He was gazing toward the keep, where lights sparkled, and the faint sound of music drifted through the snow. "I am back," he said, and there was triumph in his voice. "I live again. Maybe there is more to this than the witch told me."

When the hairs on the back of her neck prickled for the third time, Amy decided she should heed them and leave.

"I need to get back to the party," she said. "It was nice to meet you. My lord."

She began to pick her way carefully over the icy stones. When she was safe in the stairwell, she turned. He was watching her and there was *something* about him . . .

Amy hurried down the stairs as fast as her four-inch heels would allow her.

Reynald did not go after her. There was too much to consider. He'd known as soon as he stepped

into the armory that this wasn't the same world
that he had left behind him, but he'd hoped that it
was a matter easily put right. Now those hopes
were well and truly dashed.

Seven hundred years!

It was beyond his comprehension. What changes
had been wrought, what lives had been lived, what
wonders had come and gone in that time?

He shivered, numb with cold, despite his heavy
clothing. The woman had not been like the women
with whom he was familiar. Though French was
his everyday tongue, he recognized the English she
spoke, but it was a peculiar sort of English. And her
behavior was strange. She lacked the modesty he
was used to in the blue-blooded females of his own
time. But while she was with him here on the roof-
top, he hadn't felt quite so alone.

Reynald was a Marcher Lord, one of the most
powerful men in the land, a king within his own
kingdom. Unlike other landholding lords, the
Marcher Lords did not answer to the king; they
ruled their people and made their own laws. And
now *he* had come to this.

It was his fault.

Guilt crept into the solitary silence around him.
He had failed himself and his men; he had failed to
keep the promise he made to bring peace to his
lands. The Welsh had declared themselves willing
to lay down their weapons, and he had been happy

to meet them halfway. Angharad, with her clever tongue, had brought them together. That final day was meant to be a celebration, and he had arranged for a great feast, with a mock battle and music and players. Some of the most important men on the borders had come to see the signing of the historic document.

Aye, peace had been so close, he could taste it.

And then, in an instant, it was snatched away from him. He remembered the stench of blood and death, the shrieks of pain as people were dying all around him. Burning, everything burning. He had looked for Angharad, the old wisewoman, but she had vanished. *Run!* he had shouted, in the hope she could hear him. His last thought had been for her welfare, then there was only darkness and death, as the between-worlds swallowed him up.

"I gave my word that there would be peace. That the bloodshed was ended," he whispered to the soft-falling snow. "And I did not keep it."

A flap of wings, and a large bird settled beside him. It was an eagle, and its blue eyes were fixed unwaveringly upon him. With a ruffle of its feathers it began to speak in the voice of the witch.

"Feeling sorry for yourself, Ghost?"

"You have brought me back to life seven hundred years too late!" It burst out of him, with all his fury and pain, and he couldn't stop it.

"It was necessary to wait," she replied calmly.

"How can I help anyone now, after so long?"

"You can help by learning from your mistakes, Ghost."

He looked down his nose at her.

"You are a powerful man, Lord de Mortimer, but I could turn you to dust with a flick of my fingers."

"I always did what was right."

"But how did you know it was right?"

"My advisors . . ."

"Hmm."

He frowned.

"The answers to all of your questions are to be found here, in the castle. You must look for them in the right places."

"And then?"

"Then you can ask me again to take you home."

"I can go back to the past and remake history? I can save my people?"

"Find the answers, and you will be capable of anything, Reynald. You were a great man, but you can be a much greater one."

"Take me home now, and I—"

"You're not listening." Angrily, the eagle flapped its wings, rising slowly from the battlements.

"I am listening. The woman . . . Amy . . ."

"Amy Fairweather." The bird chuckled disturbingly.

"Is she my friend or my enemy?"

"Well, that is something you're going to have to

work out for yourself, Ghost. This time without your advisors."

The eagle sped away, growing smaller, until it was invisible against the dark sky. *What do I do now?* he asked himself grumpily. In his own time he could have shouted, and men would have come to serve him and obey his orders, but here . . . He knew that he could shout all he wanted, and no one would listen.

"I am Reynald de Mortimer," he reassured himself. "Surely, even seven hundred years into the future, that means *something.*"

But there was no one to answer him.

Three

*Reynald stood in the antechamber and glow-*ered at the big oak doors that led into the great hall. There was a tremendous noise coming from behind them—voices and laughter and music. If it *was* music! His ears hurt from the pounding of the drums and droning chant of the singers; the very stones around him were vibrating as if several battering rams were crashing rhythmically against the outer walls of the keep.

Who were these people? What were they doing here in his stronghold?

Reynald strode forward and, reaching for the doors, threw them open. The thudding of drums rolled over him, momentarily numbing his senses. It was like walking into the full force of a gale.

He gritted his teeth against the cacophony and

looked around. His magnificent hall was full
of strangers in strange garments. His elaborately
carved lord's chair was gone from the dais, as were
the trestle tables and benches used by his people,
and his fine tapestries from the walls. There were
no serious men in serious conversation over roast
beef and ale. No dogs wrestling in the herb-strewn
rushes over scraps, and no serving wenches giggling as they carried in the meal. Instead, the long
room was filled with interlopers, some dancing as
if they had fleas biting them, some standing with
glass receptacles in their hands, sipping miserly at
the liquid contained inside, and some shouting at
each other to be heard above the music. The air was
full of sweet perfumes, and the coloring and styles
of their clothing were made shocking by the fact
that it was almost familiar . . . while at the same
time there was something very wrong.

Reynald narrowed his eyes and waited for the
silence that always fell in his presence. To his amazement, a small man in a fool's colorful clothing came
up to him, holding a tray of food—tiny bits and
pieces that would be barely a mouthful for a child.
He gave Reynald a simpering smile.

"Medieval canapés, sir?"

Reynald gave him a murderous glance, and after
a tense moment the fool backed unsteadily away.

Others in the room were becoming aware of
him, stopping what they were doing to turn and
stare. The music stopped, too, and the ensuing

quiet was shocking in its intensity. Reynald cast his eye about the room, trying to find where the musicians were placed, but he could not see them. Instead, he caught sight of a man in armor very much like his own, and of a similar size and shape. He, too, wore a helmet. The man was glaring back at him, his hand resting menacingly on the sword at his side.

"Do you dare to challenge the Ghost in his own hall?" Reynald shouted, and drew his own sword several inches free of the scabbard. He saw the other man do the same.

"So, you want a confrontation, do you? I will teach you a lesson, lout!"

Reynald took a menacing step forward, but so did the other man. With a ringing sound, he drew his sword out completely and swung it in a wide arc.

A gasp sounded from the people nearest him, as they stumbled back, out of range. He ignored the reaction; he was busy watching the other man. Who did exactly the same thing as he and was now standing, glowering, daring him to move forward. Reynald showed his teeth. So did the other man.

And that was when he understood.

He was seeing a mirrored reflection. The glass was enormous, larger than any he had ever seen, and it was hanging upon the far wall, facing him. The man he had been about to fight was actually himself.

Shocked and embarrassed, he gazed into his own eyes, and roared, "Leave me! I wish to be alone."

Someone in the crowd let out a shrill shriek, which was followed by a growing swell of uneasy murmuring. No one moved. Frustrated, Reynald ran his gaze over them and noticed several more men in armor. One of the knights had pale hair that was obviously a wig. Was this sorry creature meant to be him? Under his incensed glare, the man began to shuffle uneasily.

His gaze moved on. He spotted ladies in elaborate gowns, some with wimples or veils upon their heads, and several men dressed as kings, which was strange, because he knew very well in his own time there had been only one King Edward upon England's throne.

Who were these people? Was this a game? The woman on the tower roof—Amy—had said it was a fancy dress party. But why were they aping him and those he had known? A tightness was forming in his chest as he contemplated this world gone mad. What must he do now? What was required of him?

And then he saw *her*, Lady Amy Fairweather, and a calmness settled over him.

He held his breath as she wended her way through the tightly packed crowd. In the bright light he could see what he had not seen before. Her gown consisted of layers of fine, sparkling cloth that was almost transparent. He could see the curved shape of her body, and her legs as she walked. She had red hair, bright as flame, that curled in clusters about her head, and her eyes were as green as spring grass.

She was smiling at him, and Reynald felt his heart start to pound in a way it had never done before.

"My lord Mortimer," Amy said, in a loud, gently scolding voice. "You are frightening your guests! I'm sure you wouldn't want to drive them out into the snow on such a night as this."

A trickle of excited laughter from the people behind her let her know they'd heard and understood. This man was playing the role of the famous Ghost, and it was all part of the Medieval Weekend they had paid to be a part of.

Amy didn't know why she'd come to his rescue—he'd been quite frightening when he'd come bursting into the room. But she'd seen something in his eyes, in the tilt of his head, that made her think he needed her help. He'd helped her with Nicco; the least she could do was return the favor.

"Have you traveled far, my lord?" she went on. "From the Tower of London perhaps? Remind me, who *is* the king these days?"

She winked as she glanced up at him, inviting him to join in the game.

"King Edward," he answered promptly. "He bids

me keep my borders quiet, although it is not in his power to order me. I am king here in my own right."

He said it with such certainty, Amy almost believed it herself. There was a burst of delighted laughter.

"Ah," she nodded. "The Welsh are being troublesome again, eh?"

"Aye, they are always troublesome," he grumbled.

More good-natured laughter. Someone called out, "Especially when they beat us at rugby!" They all thought it was part of the reenactment, a little playacting for their benefit.

"Do you dance, my lord?" she asked.

"Dance?" he demanded arrogantly. "I have better things to do with my time, damsel."

That brought on shouts and hoots.

"Surely there's always time for a beautiful woman!" a voice replied.

Reynald frowned. "While I dance, my borders are breached."

They loved that.

"No, no," Amy held up her hand for silence. "Lord de Mortimer has no time to waste. Besides, it must be tricky dancing in a coat of armor. Imagine how long it takes to get it on and off. Do you ever take it off, my lord? It looks a bit rusty in places. Perhaps you bathe in it?"

The great hall erupted in laughter.

"You are making a jest of me, damsel," the Ghost said coldly, slamming his sword back into its scabbard.

Amy pretended to be contrite. "Only a little," she admitted. "You were frightening everyone. I didn't want you to get thrown out."

As if on cue, his gaze slid past her. He was reaching for his sword again. It was definitely a *real* sword, too. Whoever he was, he'd gone for authenticity over comfort. She should have been frightened, but she wasn't. It wasn't murder she saw in his eyes but a cool, intelligent wariness. This wasn't a man who panicked and struck out blindly; he was a man who watched and waited, then made his decisions.

"Ms. Fairweather?" a voice said at her shoulder.

Amy turned. It was Mr. Coster, the manager of the resort. He was eyeing the big man uneasily, and he looked twitchy, as if he might call in security. Amy couldn't blame him, but she certainly didn't want security, or worse the police, stomping all over the castle asking questions. She and Jez didn't need any investigation into who was who and why they were here—especially Jez, who was "a person of interest" according to the police.

"Mr. Coster." She smiled the charming smile that always got her out of trouble.

"This gentleman is upsetting my guests." Mr. Coster wasn't charmed. He reached into his jacket pocket, probably for his cell phone.

"Is anyone here upset?" Amy appealed to the crowd.

They were generous in their assurance that they weren't, but Coster appeared unconvinced. "I can't have any trouble," he said.

Amy knew it was time to take control. She was an expert at reading what type of person she was dealing with, and she'd already summed up the hotel manager. Coster was a stickler for the rules, the sort of man who would never belch without excusing himself even if he was alone. But he was also very aware of what others thought of him. He wouldn't want to appear foolish.

She grasped the big man's arm, and found it hard from sheer muscle. "I promise you, Mr. Coster, everything is perfectly fine. He's, eh, with me. If you want, I'll take *Lord de Mortimer*"—she winked—"back to his room. He's just flown in from Los Angeles, and he's tired."

"What's your name, sir?" Coster asked suspiciously. "Are you a registered guest?"

Amy widened her eyes, and then she laughed. "Oh, you're joking, aren't you? He's very good, isn't he, when he gets involved in a part? And he's taking this weekend very seriously. Aren't you, sweetheart? I shouldn't really tell, but he's just been offered a wonderful movie role."

In his helmet, Reynald looked down his nose at her, but there was something in his eyes she didn't expect to see. Amusement.

Coster's demeanor had changed, and he was staring at the big man, trying desperately to recognize in him someone famous he should know. Amy had read him perfectly; he was too worried about humiliating himself to ask again. "What movie role is that?" he asked tentatively.

"King Arthur, isn't it, sweetheart? Or are you playing Sir Lancelot. I keep mixing them up. I know that Spielberg is directing . . ."

Coster jumped in, relieved he knew *that* name. "Well, congratulations! I am very pleased for you, and for us, having you here amongst us for our Medieval Long Weekend."

Amy smiled. There were murmurs around them, and she heard a few well-known film stars mentioned, as everybody decided they knew who the man in armor really was.

"You were in that movie about the goblins?" Coster said with more certainty than showed in his eyes. "Not Harry Potter, the other one."

"The hobbits?" Amy corrected him.

"Yes!"

"No, not that one."

Coster looked crestfallen.

"Time for bed, darling." She began to lead Reynald away, not wanting to push her luck. She glimpsed Jez coming toward her, giving her a "What's-going-on?" look. "Coster wanted to call the police," she murmured urgently as he reached her.

Then she noticed Nicco was standing sulkily behind him. No doubt the prince had filled her brother in on the business on the battlements.

"I do not want—" Reynald began in an arrogant undertone.

"I don't care what you want," she cut him short. "Coster's right, you're frightening the guests. You'll get yourself arrested, and believe me, we don't want that. Come on now."

But it wasn't going to be that easy after all.

"I want you to stay for a drink, Amee."

Nicco moved to stand in front of her, his smile more sharklike than winning. Had Jez put him up to this?

"I'm sorry, Nicco, I need to go—"

"No, no, you do not need to go. I am asking you to stay with *me*." And he placed his hand on his chest in a theatrical gesture that made her wonder if he was quite sane.

"Nicco, really, I—"

"Amee."

"You shit-spitting toad," said a deep voice at her back. "She has said no. Be a man and accede to her wishes."

Nicco's eyes flashed pure fury. "What do you know of being a man, riffraff? I am a prince!"

"I have met princes before, and they had better manners." Reynald was unimpressed.

Amy held up her hands between them. "No, this

isn't going to happen here. Save it for later." She gave Nicco a forced smile. "I'm sorry, I am, but I have to go."

There was an expression in his eyes, something violent and dangerous that made her pause, just for a second, then she took Reynald's arm and tugged him after her, out of the room.

Back in the great hall, the music cranked up again, and there was a burst of excited chatter. Now that they were no longer being observed, the sugary act fell from Amy like a snake's skin, and she was all business. "You'd better tell me where your room is so that I can get you up there real quick. You might want to pack and leave, before Coster decides to throw you out after all."

He stared back at her, arms folded, eyes watchful.

"Where is your room?" she repeated, sounding out each word.

"The castle belongs to me. All the rooms are mine."

"A problem, Ms. Fairweather?"

Coster again. He'd followed them as far as the doorway, and now there was a burly security guard beside him, watching them suspiciously. As Amy had feared, he wasn't totally convinced after all. She resurrected her smile.

"This is a wonderful place, Mr. Coster. Do you hire out to film crews?"

He blinked. "Yes, of course."

"Mmm, you'll have to mention it to Steven," she murmured not-so-subtly to the man beside her. "Wasn't he looking for locations? Do you have any brochures?" she added, smiling again at Coster. "I could fax him details."

"I . . . yes, of course." The wariness in Coster's eyes was at war with his desperate need to believe in the possibility of what she was saying.

"I'll get some details in the morning." She yawned. "Well, good night!"

Amy grabbed Reynald's arm and began to lead him toward the elevator. "I don't know why I'm doing this," she said crossly, sotto voce. "Why do I get myself into these situations?"

"I am Lord de Mortimer," he began. "I own this castle and the land around it. I—"

"I've heard it," Amy said tiredly. "We all have. You're famous." She pointed her finger upward.

Four

Reynald looked up. And stared in utter amazement.

The ceiling was covered in pictures. Painted pictures. Men in battle. Men dining in the great hall. Men jousting. Men at their leisure. One of the men was tall with very fair hair, and he stood head and shoulders above the others.

It was meant to be *him.*

These colorful and vibrant pictures on the ceiling were meant to be the story of *his* life.

Reynald was astonished. Then there was a ringing sound, like a bell, and a whoosh, and before he could pull his thoughts away from what he was seeing, Amy had tugged him inside a metal box. The doors closed, locking them in.

He stood very still in the small space, afraid to move.

Amy was speaking, but he didn't hear what she was saying. Her chatter washed over him as he tried to come to terms with his current situation. Then the small space began to move. Upward. He knew his face drained of color because he felt his blood sink into his boots.

Amy didn't seem to find anything strange in what was happening. She continued to chatter away until the metal box came to a gliding stop, and the doors slid back again.

They were facing a wall painted dark red, and there was a soft tapestry or carpet upon the floor of a similar red. Her footsteps muted, Amy led the way down a corridor to a room with a solid door and a small brass shape of a woman fastened upon it.

"This is the Lady Suite. My room," she explained. "Now, you will behave, won't you?"

"I do not harm women," he said coldly.

"You wouldn't be here if I thought you did." And Amy opened the door by sliding a small piece of parchment into a metal slot.

Reynald followed her in. If he had ever known this room, he didn't now. The walls were pale yellow, and there were embroidered hangings of women standing in flower gardens, and a bed with curtains so flimsy they would be useless in keeping out cold drafts. An archway led to another room, where there was a table and chairs and a padded bench before a fireplace. Reynald took a step and cracked his shin on a trunk lying on the floor.

"Sorry about the suitcase." She dragged it out of his way, tucking in the colorful clothing spilling from it. There were shoes scattered about, too, and plenty of other odds and ends that must belong to Amy.

In fact the room was one of the most untidy he had ever seen. It made Reynald uncomfortable—because of his training as a soldier from an early age, he had never been able to look at mess without wanting to do something about it. A soldier who was careless with his belongings was careless with his life.

As he watched, bemused, Amy began picking some of the pieces up, holding them while looking about her, then tossing them into a corner, as if she didn't quite know what to do with them. After performing this action three times, she simply gave up.

"I'm not a person who has a place for everything and everything in its place," she said, with a shrug. But her eyes were sparkling, and there wasn't a shred of apology in them. "Now, I'm going to have a drink," she went on. "I think I deserve one after tonight. What about you? Bourbon and Coke? Whiskey? Scotch? Name your poison, my lord."

"My poison?" he repeated, suspicious. A friend of his father's had been poisoned and died a terrible death. Did they drink poison in this time for *fun*?

"It's a joke." She sighed.

Reynald shuffled about, edging around the furnishings and trying not to bump into anything. The room was not designed to accommodate a large man in armor, and the overwhelming feminine quality of it made it most uncomfortable. He'd felt exactly the same in his mother's solar— big and clumsy. As if he didn't belong. As if at any moment he might fall over, or break something, or do something to set her ladies giggling at his expense.

He did trip on something; a book. Awkward in his armor, he knelt to pick it up, his sword scabbard knocking on the bedpost. It was unlike any book he had ever seen before, with thin parchment for pages, and on the cover were a man and woman, boldly embracing.

"What is this?" he demanded, holding it out to her.

She looked at it with a puzzled frown. "Never seen it before." And then, when he just continued to stare at her, "All right, it's mine. I admit it. A girl has to have her dreams."

41

He inspected the erotic painting on the cover. The man appeared strong and tough, but his expression was strangely vulnerable, and the woman did not look as if she was being held in his arms against her will. In fact, she looked to be enjoying herself.

He smiled. Was this really Amy Fairweather's dream?

She snatched the book from his hands. "You'd better give me that," she murmured. "You might start getting ideas."

"Ideas?"

His mother had read the romances popular in the thirteenth century, and swooned over the poems and songs about undying, courtly love. It was all very innocent, really, and consisted of mannered speeches by men, who were too in awe of their beloveds to do more than stare longingly, and languishing damsels, who lapped up those stares, dreaming of love, but in reality were to be married to the choices their fathers made for them.

"Childish dreams, that is all," he stated. "Love is nothing but a distraction from the brutal realities of life."

"Is that right!" Amy slipped her book into a drawer, out of sight, and slammed it shut with more effort than was necessary. "Well, thank you for sharing that with me."

He'd upset her. He'd forgotten that women needed their dreams more than men. It was so long since he'd had to take account of a woman's feelings.

Slowly, Reynald straightened to his full height. "I beg pardon, damsel."

Amy was eyeing him curiously, as if trying to decide whether or not he meant it, then she smiled. "Accepted. Now, why don't you take some of that off?" she suggested, waving her hand at his armor. "It looks painful. How do you sit down in that stuff anyway?"

She was making a jest of him again. He could not remember a time in the whole of his life when he had been spoken to in the way this woman spoke to him. His people admired him, were in awe of him, hung upon his words, and strove to please him.

Amy Fairweather wasn't in awe of him, nor was she trying to please him. She smiled at him with her green eyes, while she teased him from her pink lips. She confused him, amazed him, amused him . . . *interested* him.

"Come on, Mr. de Mortimer," she said, "chill out."

Reynald considered striding angrily from her presence, but what was the point? Where would he go? He was a man out of his time—out of his depth—and it seemed that Amy Fairweather was his only friend.

Without a word, Reynald began unlacing his coat of armor.

Curiously Amy watched as the various components that made up his costume came off. He heaved the coat from him—it must have been at least eighty pounds—and it landed on the floor with a thud that shook the room. As she'd thought, he was heavily padded—beneath the armor he wore a long garment that afforded comfort and protection. When he stripped this off, he was still a big man. A very big man. But he was no longer a giant.

Now he was down to a pair of tight, fawn-colored trousers that hugged his legs, and boots that came to his ankles, and a whitish tunic or shirt that came to midthigh, with long sleeves and no buttons—it simply laced at his throat. Her eyes rose to the ugly scar on his neck, a puckered line that ran around it for about six inches, as if someone had tried to slice him.

She shuddered. She'd seen those sorts of scars before. They usually went with a lifestyle that was bloody and violent; not the kind of men she liked to spend her time with. That's why she'd left the Parkhill Estate, and sworn never to go back. Who was this guy anyway? She didn't know him from a bar of soap. It was time to send him off to whatever hole he'd crawled out of.

Amy looked up to do just that, but he'd taken off his helmet.

His face held her complete attention. The man

was handsome, with more than a hint of arrogance about the nose and mouth. He looked a serious kind of character, not the sort to crack a joke, but she'd already guessed that. His hair was cut very short, and it was pale blond—so pale as to be almost white.

Did he bleach it? It seemed to go with those colorless eyes. If she didn't know better—a shiver ran through her—she'd say he *was* the Ghost.

Those eyes were processing her just as she had him. His gaze slid over her face, and down the gauzy gown she was wearing, pausing at her breasts, then her legs. *Well, he is a typical man after all!* But there was more to it than that. Despite his scorn over her book, the stranger seemed as dazed by her appearance as she was by his.

In a moment they'd be in each other's arms, then . . . Amy smiled wryly, recognizing her feelings for what they were. Pangs of lust. She'd been here before. It was depressing, really, that no matter how she tried to be civilized and go for the snags, she was inevitably attracted to the macho types who were twice her size. Bulging muscles and bulging . . . well, it had been a while since she'd had a lover. The fact that her father was a small man, with a mean temper, was no excuse for her to go to the other extreme when it came to her ideal man.

Wearily, Amy sat down on the bed and kicked off her shoes, wriggling her toes back to life. If

Mr. de Mortimer was trouble then she'd better find out now, so that she and Jez could deal with it. Things were bad enough without him making it worse.

She fixed him with a no-nonsense look. "Okay then, tell me who you really are?"

Five

The Ghost was looking back at her, and she could see him summing her up. Deciding whether he would be frank with her, at last. Whatever he saw he must have liked, because he bowed his head in assent. He had a way with him, that was for sure. Maybe he really was an actor.

"My name," he began quietly, "is Lord Reynald de Mortimer. You know this, lady, for I have told you. I do not lie. I never lie. I *am* the Ghost."

Amy felt a sharp stab of disappointment. Irritably, she swirled the liquid in her glass. "I was hoping you'd trust me. That we could stop playing games now. I think you owe me something."

"Why should I owe you anything, lady?"

"I saved you from Coster. He was going to call the police. If you weren't on his guest list, you'd have been evicted. Arrested. Hauled up before a magistrate. At the very least you'd have been severely embarrassed. Because we both know you're not on his list, are you, *my lord*?" she added, with a sly glance.

"This is my home," he said doggedly. "He cannot evict me."

"Of course he can! He's probably checking through the names right now, trying to decide whether I'm having him on. It's lucky Jez told me a few of the guests haven't turned up yet. We'll just have to hope they don't, or he'll be knocking at my door with half a dozen constables behind him."

"Jez?" he demanded, with a haughty lift of his eyebrows.

"My brother. Short for Jeremy."

She could almost see his brain turning over what she'd said. It was as if she was speaking in a foreign language, one he had difficulty interpreting.

She sighed, swallowing her drink. "You can trust me, you know. I'm good with secrets. Are you undercover or something? MI5?"

"My name is Reynald de—"

"All right, all right. I'll call you Rey. Now, Rey, what am I going to do with you? I've got to go back to the party. Jez will be looking for me if I don't."

"Why does your brother bring you to a place such as this?"

Amy laughed wryly. "Believe me, Jez can be very persuasive."

Reynald puzzled over her words once more, wondering what it was she was not saying. In his experience women were often used as pawns in the games of men, and the higher born the lady, the higher the stakes. Was this what was happening to Amy? Was her brother, Jez, trying to use her to gain favor with the unpleasant man who had tried to stop Amy leaving the party?

She was beautiful, he thought dispassionately. Even if she were not wealthy, she would be a prize for any man. Many would be willing to do much to have such a lady for a night or two.

Inside him, he felt a stirring, a strange ache.

"So, *Rey*." Her voice startled him. She was gazing up at him, her short auburn hair curling like a fiery halo about her head. With her triangular face, pointed chin, and slanting green eyes, she looked like a creature from the forests. Some sort of sprite.

"Let's start again. Where do you come from? I can't quite place that accent."

"I am from Norman blood," he said slowly. "My father was a powerful man with many enemies. My mother was an heiress who lacked good sense."

A frown marred the perfection of her brow and drew her thin dark eyebrows together. "Well, we don't chose our parents, do we?"

"When I inherited, I became one of the most important men in England. My father conquered by force and fear, and still the Welsh defied him. I was determined to find another way to bring peace and prosperity to my lands and the people on them."

Melancholy fell over him. Despite the high standards he had striven for, he had tried and failed. And he had been so close . . .

"I died in 1299, and I was taken to the between-worlds."

"The what?"

"It is a place where the dead go to await their fate. I have slept there for seven hundred years, awaiting my second chance. To live again, to make right my wrong. And now I have that chance; I have returned to the mortal world."

Amy nodded slowly, as if she believed him, but there was a glitter in her green eyes that said otherwise. She set her empty glass down. "I've never heard of that one. Do many people come back to life like you? What's the point?"

"*The point* is that I was responsible for many deaths. The men of my garrison, the folk of my castle, and the surrounding villages, and the Welsh who lived on my borders and under my care. I wanted peace, but instead I brought destruction. That is *the point*, lady."

She met his pale eyes, refusing to be intimidated, and he admired her for it. "All right, let's say you really *are* the Ghost, returned to life. How are you going to right this wrong? You're seven hundred years too late."

He inclined his head very slightly. "I have already told the witch this—"

"Hang on . . . the witch?" Her eyes had widened.

"The witch who rules the between-worlds. She is the being who oversees time. She told me that the answers to my questions lie here, in this time. She said that *you* will help me find them."

"*I* will help you?" She stood up, clearly shaken. "Where is this witch? I want to tell her she's wrong."

He smiled. "I already have, but she will not be moved."

"Take me to her."

He laughed, and her eyes flashed. "I cannot do that. She will not obey me. She will come to us when she is ready. In the meantime, you are to be my companion in this adventure."

"Oh no I'm not," Amy retorted decidedly, and reached for her shoes. "Find someone else to be your companion, Rey. I'm here because of Jez, and after we're done, I'm going home."

"But—"

"I need to get back to the party." She stood up, the heels on her shoes narrow and impossibly high. He watched her cross to the door, the sway of her hips holding his attention. "Maybe you should think about going home, too." She turned at the door. For all her delicate, pretty looks, the expression in her eyes was strong and intelligent. This was no helpless woman to be dismissed lightly.

The door closed and he was alone. Reynald reached out and touched something lacy with one callused finger. It seemed to consist of straps or bindings, and cups in the shape of a woman's breasts. His hand shook.

Hot, vivid images filled his head. He brushed the lace again, and this time pretended he was touching the soft swell of Amy's breast. Her skin would be like the finest silk, with a smooth, bewitching sheen. And if he bent and licked her with his tongue, she'd taste like nectar and roses.

A powerful surge of desire gripped him. For all his pretty, poetic thoughts, he knew he wanted her as basically as any man wanted a woman. This was lust, pure and simple.

He shifted uncomfortably, his body reminding him it had been a long time. Reynald could have had a wife, but he'd never taken one. He'd never found the one he could trust. He wondered if he'd been overcautious to wait so long. Surely not all women were like Morwenna? Surely there were some who could be trusted? Loved, even . . . ?

Amy Fairweather.

He was smiling again, without knowing why.

The party was still going strong; if anything, it was rowdier than before. Champagne was flowing, and everyone was laughing, dancing, and having a good time. An actress she recognized was leaning against Jez, talking intently as only the very inebriated can, and Prince Nicco was busy dazzling a recently divorced brewery heiress.

As she made her way through the room, Mr. Coster gave her a nod, which made her think he'd believed her story after all. Several very nice men turned to look at her, and normally she would have returned that interest, but not tonight.

Tonight, she had never felt more alone in her life.

There had been other parties. Some where she had behaved in a way that was dangerously out of control, and some where she couldn't remember much after the first few drinks. Amy admitted that a few years ago she treated every day as if it were her last. She had certainly been less than scrupulous about the company she kept. She'd half thought this weekend would be like that, but now . . .

She'd changed. She'd become a different person, and she hadn't realized it until this weekend with Jez. She'd turned over a new leaf, but there was more to it than that. Since Rey had burst into her life, the change seemed to have accelerated.

The thing was . . . she couldn't get him out of her mind.

Impossible and ridiculous and irrational as it was, she wanted to believe him. He'd seemed so lucid and so sure. So believable. Was a man from the past coming to the present any more unlikely than flying through space? Or a cut-price sale at Cartier's? She *wanted* his story to be true.

Life on the Parkhill Estate had made Amy a down-to-earth and practical girl. She didn't try to glamorize the world around her. She might escape into romance but she didn't really believe anyone like those marvelous heroes would ever seek her out. But that didn't stop her from hoping.

Rey's story had a wonderful feel to it that caught her imagination, just like a romance. When she was with him she felt optimistic.

Maybe it was this place. The castle had an ambience, despite some areas being redecorated to within an inch of their life. But once you were away from the worst of that, in the stone passages and stairwells, you could almost hear the past calling to you around the next corner. Why shouldn't the Ghost live on?

Amy turned back through groups of happy people. Jez was now at the center of a large crowd, telling one of his stories. He used to do this when they were kids, hold everyone's attention with the ease of a seasoned performer. The stories and the suits had changed, but not her brother.

Jez caught sight of her, delivered the punch line, and smoothly made his exit while his audience was laughing hysterically. With his hand on her arm, he leaned in close to prevent their being overheard. The scent of his expensive aftershave tickled her nose, and the diamond stud in his ear winked in the light. If she didn't know better, she'd think he was a successful businessman or an entrepreneur. Maybe the owner of one of the more fashionable London clubs.

Jez fixed her with a look. "What do you think you're doing, sweetheart? Nicco came to me before in tears."

"I doubt that," she began to protest, but he was already steering her toward a quiet corner.

Amy sighed and let him have his way. There was a raised platform or dais, and behind that a wall covered in weaponry. Jez stopped in front of a dozen or so swords, somewhat incongruously arranged in a pretty circle around a shield.

"Have you forgotten why we're here?" He was bending his head, so that he could look directly into her eyes. "*Nicco*. Does that ring any bells?"

"You don't have to remind me why we're here, Jez—"

"I think I do. We have one chance. We have to take it."

You mean you *have to take it*, she thought, but didn't say it aloud. What was the point? Jez needed her, and she owed him in more ways than she could ever repay. Without him . . . well she wouldn't be here, and if she was, she wouldn't be the strong, well-adjusted woman she'd turned out to be.

"I get the message, Jez."

He relaxed. "Fine then. Let's have no more running off and doing a Greta Garbo. Go and find Nicco and win him back. He's smitten, sweetheart. Just needs a bit of stroking, and he'll spill everything. You'll see."

"Are you sure you're not underestimating Nicco? He's not a fool."

"He's a complete idiot," Jez retorted.

Amy laughed, then shook her head at him. "Don't you have any scruples, Jez?"

"Where Nicco is concerned? Not a single one," he assured her. "I've heard some things about our friend that would make your hair curl more than it already is."

"So you're not worried about leaving me alone with him?"

"Nuh. You can handle him. Now . . . go and do your stuff, beautiful." He turned her around and pointed her in the right direction.

Unlike Jez, Nicco was all alone. He was dressed in a sea blue suit, standing before the huge fireplace, where a couple of enormous logs were ablaze. It was a wonder he wasn't puce with the heat, but she'd already discovered that Nicco was a cold fish. As if to prove it, he gave a shiver as she approached.

"I would be warmer in Siberia," he said, his mouth turning down.

"No, you wouldn't."

He shrugged one shoulder, not bothering to argue with her. There was a sulkiness to him that some women might find attractive. Amy wanted to slap him.

"Have you finished with the riffraff?" he sneered.

"You mean the actor?" she said, ignoring his bad temper. "Didn't you recognize him?"

"Actor?" Nicco echoed suspiciously.

"Yes. He's doing a part in a movie set in medieval times, so he's using this weekend to immerse himself in the period. Didn't you realize that, Nicco? I thought everyone knew."

Nicco didn't like the idea that he might have missed out on something. "Of course I knew," he said irritably, "but I don't have to like him, do I? Come and we will have a drink, Amee. I am lonely here, a foreigner in a foreign country. You should be entertaining me and making me feel welcome."

Amy smiled as she took his arm, but inside she was anything but happy. She really didn't want to do this anymore. Why was she here with selfish, spoiled Nicco, when she could be upstairs with the mysterious and gorgeous Rey?

Far down in the earth, deep beneath the castle, an old chamber lay hidden and secret. Only a single tunnel led to this chamber, and it was narrow and half-choked with rubble, barely passable. No one had walked here for hundreds of years. And that was how it should be, for the creature within the chamber did not want visitors.

She was so old she remembered when the earth was a child. Enormous, her body covered with scales as hard as steel, her powerful wings tucked in, and her long tail curled around her. She breathed slow and soft. Sometimes she dreamed.

In her dreams she flew over green fields, tree-tops, valleys, and mountains. This was her domain, and once again a dragon was something to fear, not a myth in a musty book, or a tale told by those who no longer believed in it.

She stirred and gave a soft moan.

Far above, in the castle, she sensed an old and familiar danger.

Reynald de Mortimer.

This was all his fault. He deserved to die.

She had been hiding here for seven hundred years. Sleeping. She might have been sleeping still if it were not for the Sorceress's interference. Rage made her blood begin to boil. An anger that had waited seven hundred years to reach its zenith.

Revenge. She wanted revenge!

That witch of the between-worlds; it was she who had brought Reynald back. They would be sorry, they would all be sorry.

"I will fight him," the dragon hissed. "I will fight until there is only one of us remaining in the mortal world. And I will kill his woman, then he will know what it is to be bereft of the one he loves. Then he will finally understand."

The time had come.

Slowly, purposefully, the old dragon began to awake from her long sleep, ready to face her destiny.

Six

Reynald peered grimly through the arrow slit and saw that it was still snowing outside. Maybe it was the snow that made the air feel damp and cold, or maybe it was because he was in a part of the castle that hadn't been modernized. No one had painted these walls or added soft floor coverings. It was much as he remembered—a stark fortress with few comforts for the men who dwelt here. And why should it be anything else, when their every waking moment was spent keeping watch over the Ghost's borders?

He'd spent the last few hours making an inspection tour of his castle, as far as he was able. There had been additions since 1299, such as a new outer gate to the south, and new timber buildings in the bailey to replace the stables and kitchen and various workshops he remembered. In parts, the inside of the castle was almost unrecognizable, where rooms had been added or divided. Reynald felt angry when he thought of someone turning his home into a fairground for fools.

Were people no longer under attack from the Welsh or the Scots? Was the greed and treachery of their neighbors no longer an issue? Did no one take anything seriously anymore?

But there was satisfaction in finding that the secret passageways and stairways he'd built into the walls were still here, and untouched. By the thickness of the dust and the cobwebs inside them, it was likely no one had used them since 1299. He could move about the castle as he wished, without being observed. These people here now might believe they were safe and secure, but the Ghost had come from a time when nothing was certain, and he knew better.

"They say that the dragon will come and destroy us all."

Angharad's voice was like a distant echo as he remembered that day. She was translating for him in the great hall, he sitting in his ornate lord's chair and she standing before him in her simple gown, her long gray hair loose about her. A small group of Welshmen were gathered below the dais, proud, watchful, and suspicious.

They were right to be so. In his father's time they would have been thrown into the dungeon as a matter of course. It had taken Reynald years to gain their trust to this point. To make them realize he was not a man like his father.

"Dragon?" Reynald frowned. "Are they threatening me?"

Angharad smiled serenely. "I do not think so, my lord."

"Then they truly mean a dragon? A real dragon?"

"It would seem so. My lord."

"That is primitive nonsense, my lord." Julius spoke up. He was Reynald's chaplain and scribe, but although he wrote Reynald's letters and read those sent to him, he was more concerned with heaven and hell than day-to-day problems. And he didn't like Angharad; he didn't like the fact that Reynald paid so much attention to her. He took every opportunity to undermine her position. "These people are little more than pagan savages."

"Of course it is nonsense," Reynald said levelly. He met the old woman's eyes, trying to read the expression in them. Was it mockery he saw? Reynald knew she thought Julius a fool, despite his learning. "He is afraid of life, so he hides behind his God and his books," she'd scoffed often enough. As for her countrymen: "They squabble amongst themselves; they will never agree long enough to unite against their enemies."

Sometimes he wondered what she really thought of him, but she never said—not to his face, anyway.

It mattered not. She was a very wise woman, and to his mind she had proved herself. He found he was taking her advice more and more. She was his tongue, when it came to speaking to the Welsh, but she was also his eyes and his ears.

Even so, she had died that day with the others. He should have protected her, been able to save her. He should have kept his word.

Reynald shivered as frigid air blasted through the arrow slit in the wall. He was tired, and it was time to return to Amy's room. He took a step down the stairwell, almost stumbling, and it was then that he saw it.

A light.

Like a candle flame, it was flickering below him, moving down the twisting stairwell. As the light vanished around the corner he saw a shadowy shape that looked like a monk in a robe.

"Julius?"

It was madness to think that his chaplain might be here, but still his heart leapt. A familiar face would be welcome in this unfamiliar time. Had the witch given him a friend in his exile?

He began to follow.

When he reached the bottom of the stairs the shadowy figure was already well ahead of him, gliding across the floor. Was it Julius? He couldn't be sure. As it reached the door, it seemed to hesitate, half-turning toward him. As if it wanted him to come after it.

"Who are you?"

It paused a moment more, but it was only a black shape against the light. Then the door opened and closed, and it was gone. Reynald started after it, determined to discover who or what it was.

The door led into a corridor, and the figure was already moving away. After a while he realized that the light and its keeper were remaining just out of his reach, no matter how he quickened his steps. And the light wasn't like one of the lights he had seen in this new world; nor was it like one of those he had left behind. Rather, it was something from the between-worlds, ghostly and intriguing.

It had passed through another door now, into the bailey. By the time he ran outside, the figure was at the castle wall, already climbing upward.

Snow covered the ground, thick enough to sink beneath his boots. He shivered. He was wearing only his trousers and tunic; the bulk of his clothing was still in Amy's room. Ahead of him he could see the mysterious light on the top of the battlements, appearing and disappearing between the crenelations. Reynald considered himself a physically powerful and fit man, but whatever was ahead of him was far stronger and fitter.

If it *was* a mortal being! Perhaps it was an apparition? Did his chaplain really haunt the castle? He couldn't imagine anything less like Julius than wandering about with a light. If Julius was a spirit, then he would prefer the chapel, or a warm corner with some of his intellectual books on religion.

The wind was stronger up here, and the cold made his eyes sting. The light bobbed ahead of him, moving across the wall above the old gatehouse. He blinked. It seemed to be closer than before. He quickened his pace, thinking that at last he was catching up.

"Julius!" he called, and despite all his reasoning he was still hoping it was so. "Speak to me, old friend . . ."

He ducked through a low doorway, feeling his way along a passage in almost total darkness. Only the unearthly light ahead of him showed him the way. The men of his garrison had once slept here, when they guarded the wall day and night. Now the place was musty and empty, a desolate reminder of what had been. He turned a corner in pitch-blackness, and found himself momentarily blinded.

There, directly in front of him, was the light.

His quarry had proceeded through an archway and was now facing him head-on from the other side. He was sure that whoever it was was watching him.

"Julius, is it you?" Reynald's voice sounded very loud. He hadn't realized until now how alone he was—the music from the party was barely more than an annoying buzz.

The unmoving shadow said nothing, but the light was growing brighter, making it difficult to see. Reynald stretched out a hand to grasp one side of the archway, feeling the old stone crumble. Still the figure didn't move. He stepped out from the arch, through to the other side, and as he did so the light grew even more brilliant, dazzling him. Quickly, in an effort to escape being blinded, he looked down. And saw, fifty feet beneath him, the frozen ice of the moat.

Reynald grabbed desperately at the stones of the archway, his forward momentum already taking his body out into emptiness. One hand found a gap, where some of the mortar had fallen out. He dug his fingers into the crevice and, as he began to fall, swung himself around. His hip hit the wall, his feet dangling in space, and then he was scrambling back inside the arch. For endless moments he knelt, breathing hard and shaking. Knowing that he was fortunate to be alive.

Fury took hold of him, and Reynald came to his feet. "Who are you!" he roared. "Answer me!"

But the murderous shadow had begun to fade, and with it the light. In another moment it was gone, leaving him none the wiser.

Slowly, Reynald made his way back to Amy's room. He had much to think of, but he was cold and weary, and a dark depression had settled over him. He had been wary of locking Amy's door, in case he could not open it again, so he'd left it ajar. Now he closed it firmly behind him.

The small lamp on the table was still burning softly, and her bed looked very inviting. Maybe if he rested, he thought, yawning, he might feel better. Strange that after sleeping for seven hundred years he should crave more.

Whoever or whatever the figure with the light had been, it wanted him dead. But only someone from the past, someone with a personal grudge, would wish him mortal harm. Who could carry their hurt for seven hundred years? Who hated him that much?

Deep in his thoughts, Reynald did what he always did when he retired. He stripped off all his clothing and lay down. He never felt the cold, in fact he was often too hot. Yawning again, eyes closing, he stretched out.

He tried to remember all he could of the dark shadow, applying it to the people he had known. But it was an impossible task, and he was too weary to think straight.

In a moment, Reynald was asleep.

Amy opened her door and allowed it to click shut behind her, breathing a sigh of relief. It was very late, but she'd finally escaped from Nicco. With his usual arrogance he'd believed he could outlast her at the bar, but she'd proved him wrong. Still, it had been a near thing. The trouble was, she'd had to drink him *under* the bar to do it, and now her head was spinning, and all she wanted to do was to collapse into bed and sleep.

She kicked off one of her shoes, stumbled, and kicked off the other. Reaching out to steady herself on the bedpost, she glanced at her bed.

There was a naked man sprawled across it.

A very big naked man.

Amy swallowed and thought about screaming. But she was only human, and he was gorgeous. She swayed, peering down at the nearest part of him, his feet, and letting her gaze run slowly upward. It was a fabulous journey.

Big feet, long muscular legs, flat stomach, wide chest and shoulders, and well-defined upper arms. There wasn't an ounce of fat on him, he was trimmed down to sheer muscle. There were scars, too, as if he was a soldier who'd seen more than one posting into a battle zone. She reached out, her fingers hovering above what had been a long gash on his thigh that ran dangerously close to his groin. There was another serious-looking injury across his ribs, as well as plenty of smaller marks.

What sort of man was he?

Her gaze slid over the puckered scar on his neck. His face was unmarked, his skin tanned and smooth. There was dark stubble beginning to show on his jaw, which was odd for a man with hair so fair—perhaps it was bleached after all. The hair on his chest was dark, too, as was the line that ran down his stomach and clustered about his genitals. Her gaze lingered. Oh yes, he was impressive in every way.

She knew she'd had far too much to drink and her good-sense meter wasn't working, but this seemed special. There was something about Rey, something that made him very different from other men. Not just his appearance, but the way he spoke and behaved. The way he looked at her. She knew such a thing was impossible, and yet . . .

It was as if he really came from another time.

Maybe it was just that she wanted it to be true. It was so romantic, that some seven-hundred-year-old English lord could return to life. Amy wasn't such a cynic that she couldn't enjoy a little fantasy and romance—the fictional type—but this time fantasy and reality seemed to have fused.

Was Lord Reynald de Mortimer, aka the Ghost, really asleep on her bed?

She smiled and closed her eyes.

Bad idea. Amy's head began to spin. She plunked herself down on the end of the bed and took a deep breath, but when she opened her eyes the room kept spinning, and the naked man on her bed didn't stir. She lay back in her gauzy medieval gown and stared at the canopy above.

The room was warm and peaceful, and she could hear his breathing, deep and soft and steady. That was nice. Most men she knew snored.

Her head began to feel better. She supposed she should wake him up and throw him out, or at least cover him with the quilt, but she was too limp to move. Her eyelids began to close, then Amy, too, was sleeping.

Seven

Reynald woke to the sound of a bell. *Deep,* somber notes echoing through his castle. He sat up, heart beating hard, wondering what catastrophe was taking place that it was necessary to sound the warning. Were they being attacked? Had the kitchen caught fire? Was there sickness abroad? And then he realized where he was—*when* he was—and fell back with a sigh.

His gaze drifted lazily about the room, then sharpened.

Amy was at the bottom of his bed. She was still dressed in her semitransparent gown from last night, and she was lying on her side, one hand curled under her cheek, her lashes dark against her pale skin, and her lips slightly parted.

He peered closer. There was a sprinkling of

freckles on her face. He hadn't noticed them last night, but now in the morning light they were clearly visible. For some reason they made him smile.

As if she felt his gaze, Amy began to stir. That was when Reynald remembered that he was naked and hastily pulled the quilt up over his hips. To have a woman here in the morning was not something he was used to. There were many serving wenches in his castle, and some of them would be more than willing to share his nights, but Reynald had his reasons for being cautious where the act of sex was concerned.

Amy yawned, gave a big stretch, then froze. Her yawn turned into a groan of agony, and she reached up to clutch her head. *"Oh my God,"* she gasped.

Fear laced through him. "Damsel, are you injured?" He searched with his eyes, but could not see any wounds upon her. Should he feel with his hands? He became distracted at the thought, and also that, because of her transparent clothing, he could see the lines of her body and the pale color of her flesh. Touching her was a temptation he was having difficulty resisting.

As if she'd heard his thoughts, she opened one eye and rolled it toward him. It was bloodshot and dulled with pain, and she closed it again quickly.

"You're not here," she croaked. "Please, say you're not here."

The deep bell sounded again, echoing through the castle.

"Why is the warning being sounded?"

"I thought that was in my head."

"No, it has been ringing out for some time."

Amy opened both eyes wide. "Oh no! It's the gong to let us know about the sword-fighting tournament."

"Sword-fighting tournament?" he echoed. "What madness is this?"

"It's a contest kind of madness. I put you down for it last night. Nicco was needling me. He says he's an expert at fencing, and I thought it would be . . . fun?" She grimaced. "I think I put myself down, too. What was I thinking?"

"Put me down for it?" he quizzed. "What do you mean, damsel?"

Instead of answering him, Amy moaned and rolled off the bed and onto the floor with a soft bump. Concerned when she didn't reappear, Reynald moved down toward the end of the bed to see if she was all right. Just as he went to peer over, her head bobbed up, and they nearly cracked skulls.

"We have to get down there," she whispered, staring woefully at him from her green eyes, while her red curls stood up in disarray all over her head.

She was serious. She wanted him to go downstairs and play at swords. Did she know this was no game, and he was no child?

"If we don't turn up, then Nicco will come and find us. I can't let him see you here."

"Never fear, I will protect you."

Amy blinked. "Do people still say that? 'Never fear'? Anyway, I didn't mean that. I don't need protecting. It's *you* that needs protecting, Rey. Despite the pretty suits and the prettier smile, Nicco isn't a very nice person. He'll probably try and kill you."

"He cannot kill me," he said evenly. "And wenches always need protecting."

"Not this wench. Come on, get dressed. Hurry up and get your, eh, armor on. At least he can't hurt you if you're covered with that."

He found her concern for him pleasing, if ill conceived. It was a very long time since anyone had worried like this for the Ghost; usually *they* came to *him*, and expected him to take on their burden. He found himself obeying her without argument because of the sheer novelty of the situation. Besides, he'd nothing else to do, and he would enjoy putting the execrable Nicco in his place.

Amy crept into the shower, and stood under the hot water. Gradually her head cleared, and she began to feel more human. Quickly she dressed in black jeans and a green sweater and black boots, and brushed her hair before venturing back into the room. Reynald was dressed, too, thank God. She didn't need any more distractions.

Why had she thought it would be amusing to

see Nicco and Rey fight each other? Some sort of warped vision of knights of old battling over the lady of their choice—that lady being her? Or had she just been hoping that Rey would bring Nicco down a peg or two? She glanced at the sword and scabbard strapped to Rey's side. "Can you even use that thing?"

His mouth twitched as he pulled on his helmet. "I think I can manage."

The helmet made him seem far more intimidating. A stranger. As she snagged her jacket, and led the way out, Amy had to remind herself he was on her side.

Downstairs there were guests milling about, some in medieval costume, some in their holiday clothes. The sword tournament was to take place in a purpose-built pavilion in the castle grounds, and a buffet breakfast had been laid out for those who needed refueling before they made the trek through the snow. Amy couldn't face more than a cup of coffee, and Rey looked askance at the selection of muffins.

"Is there no beef and ale?" he demanded.

"I take it you're no vegan?"

"I am of Norman stock, I told you. I do not know this place called vegan."

"A vegan is someone who doesn't eat meat or dairy and . . ." Amy stopped, turned, and studied him. "Oh, you're good," she complimented him. "I particularly like that slightly bewildered look.

'Place called vegan,' huh? You even had me fooled then."

"I do not—"

"Come on, we'll be late!" She grabbed his hand and pulled him toward the outside doors.

They dashed through the snow to the pavilion. Amy caught sight of Jez, looking sharp, and Nicco huddled in an ankle-length fur coat, as if he'd never seen snow before. He looked hungover, too, which pleased her. She hoped his headache was as rampant as hers, because she blamed him for making it necessary for her to have to drink him unconscious. The alternative had been to sleep with him. He was attractive, in a bad-boy kind of way, and maybe a few years ago she might have returned his interest, but not now.

He repelled her.

The realization made her shiver. She was trapped, and there was no way out, not without someone getting hurt.

It was a relief when Mr. Coster started clapping his hands, calling for attention, and she didn't have to think about it anymore.

The instructions for the sword tournament were simple. The first person to touch the other with the tip of his sword over the heart was the winner. "The swords are replicas, of course, but I would still remind you to be careful. No rough play, please."

Amy was quickly demolished by her opponent,

but she knew she wasn't concentrating. She was too busy watching Rey, and worrying. But after the first two bouts, she was relieved to realize he wasn't going to get hurt. He wasn't going to get beaten either, not easily. For such a big, strong man he was nimble on his feet. Nicco was also working his way through his opponents, and as the names were crossed off the board and the winners of each bout paired together, the two men came ever closer to fighting it out in the finals of the tournament.

It won't happen, she told herself. *You're worrying about nothing.*

But it seemed that both men were determined to make it happen.

Rey swept through his last two bouts, and after a nasty tussle with Robin Hood, Nicco also landed in the final. Tense and worried, Amy watched on as "Lord Reynald de Mortimer" and "Prince Nicco" faced each other in the final bout. Whoever won, it would be a disaster, but as much as she wanted to cover her eyes, she couldn't. She had to watch.

Nicco was giving his replica a scornful look. "This is no longer a game, it is the final. I will use my own weapon," he said haughtily.

"You can't possibly—" Coster blustered.

"I will use mine, too," Rey cut in.

"You must take off your fancy dress," Nicco said, with a smirk. "I want to see who I am beating."

Rey shrugged and swiftly stripped down to his trousers and tunic. He'd hardly broken a sweat,

Amy noticed, as the two men eyed each other like bristling dogs. Her heart sank. This wasn't going to be a gentlemanly contest.

As if to confirm it, Nicco said, "You will take back what you said to me. You will apologize for calling me a toad."

"I believe it was a *shit-spitting* toad."

"You will pay for that," Nicco said between his teeth.

"I can't take responsibility—" Coster began again.

"No one is asking you to," Nicco interrupted coldly. "We are grown men, are we not? This is a personal matter. We can take responsibility for any injuries."

Amy didn't like the way Nicco dwelt on the last word. The sword he'd produced from a leather case was slim and wicked, and as he made a few practice swipes through the air, no one could mistake him for anything but an expert. In contrast, Reynald slowly withdrew his sword from its scabbard and stood with both hands resting on the hilt, the tip on the floor. He looked big and slow, compared to Nicco's darting swiftness.

Quietly, Rey bowed his head, as if he were performing some kind of ritual.

"Say your prayers, riffraff," the Russian mocked, as if he had already won.

Amy groaned softly.

Coster, looking as edgy as Amy felt, called to silence the noisy crowd that the final bout in the tournament had attracted, and began the match.

Nicco circled his opponent, like a snake looking to strike, while Rey turned slowly, following his movements. Nicco smiled. "I will try not to hurt you too much," he said. "But you must learn to respect your betters."

"You will not hurt me, little toad," Rey said.

With a growl, Nicco pranced in, pricking at Rey with his sword. But effortlessly Rey knocked Nicco's weapon away—or maybe it was just luck.

Nicco favored the latter. "You were lucky then," he said. "It will not happen again."

But it did happen again. And again.

Despite her feelings of guilt and dread, Amy was riveted by the contest between the two men. She didn't want anyone to be hurt, but she didn't want Nicco to win, either. She wanted Rey to win. Absolutely, no doubt about it.

As the bout went on, Amy could see Nicco becoming more and more frustrated and angry, as he wasn't able to claim victory as quickly as he'd believed he would. Maybe he'd never been beaten before. Then Nicco came in again and was knocked away again, but while Rey's weapon was still lifted, Nicco struck like lightning, ducking under Rey's guard. Amy thought then it was all over, but the next moment Nicco was flat on his back on the ground, with Rey standing over him, the point of his heavy sword resting lightly in the middle of Nicco's heaving chest.

There was a collective gasp from the audience, as if everyone had been holding their breaths until now. It had happened so fast. Rey looked up, his eyes searching the faces around him, and found hers.

He stared at her for a moment, so that there was no mistaking it was she he was seeking.

And then, like those knights of old she loved to read about, he inclined his head to her in homage.

Eight

Amy couldn't think straight. Did he mean to dedicate the victory to her, as in the days of old? She could see now that he'd anticipated Nicco's every move and countered it with deceptive ease. If this had been a fight to the death, rather than a game, Rey would have decided the outcome much sooner.

Everyone else was applauding, and belatedly, a little dazed, she put her own hands together. Rey, looking more like the Ghost than ever, acknowledged the crowd. Nicco was cursing, pushing Rey's sword away, but Rey stepped back and offered his hand. Nicco ignored it, climbing angrily to his feet.

By the time Amy reached them, Rey already had a gathering of well-wishers around him, but Nicco was alone. She felt as if she really should do something to make it up to him. In a way his public humiliation was her fault—if she hadn't egged him on last night, when he had too much to drink . . .

"Nicco, are you all right?"

Wrong choice. He gave her an icy look, his eyes glittering like the jewels he loved so much. "The man is a cheat. He did not fight like a gentleman."

Her sympathy evaporated, but she didn't show it. After all, her cynical side reminded her, here was a chance to inveigle her way into his good graces and get the information Jez wanted. "I'm sure you're too much of a gentleman yourself, Nicco, to make a fuss. The poor man obviously hasn't had your advantages."

He hesitated. The narrow look he gave her told her he suspected she was manipulating him, but maybe he decided she was right anyway, because he gave a magnanimous shrug. "Of course."

"There will be other opportunities this weekend. Perhaps you can have another go? Take him on at chess or something."

Nicco's eyes were still fixed on hers and she could see his mind ticking. He smiled like a shark. "Yes," he said softly, "before it is over I will teach him a lesson he won't forget."

No you won't, not if I have anything to do with it.

Amy murmured some more words of commiseration, before the resident hotel nurse arrived to check whether Nicco was harmed. "I'm sorry, Mr. Coster's orders," she said, over his complaints.

"You'd better let her do her stuff, Nicco." Amy caught the other woman's grateful glance.

"It won't take a moment. My name is Gretel, by the way," she added, in a lilting Welsh accent.

Nicco took a second glance. Gretel was a pretty blonde, and now she gave him a smile. Nicco smiled back and theatrically began to unbutton his shirt. Amy laughed and left them to it. She was making her way to the door, thinking she might have time to nip back to her suite for a nap, when Jez came up behind her and followed her outside.

It was bleak and bitterly cold, and although it had stopped snowing for the moment, the sky gave warning of further bad weather. "At this rate the London road will be impassable," Jez complained. "We could be trapped here."

Amy knew she should be upset about that. Strange that she wasn't.

Jez didn't give her time to ponder over the reason. "I don't know what you think you're doing, sweetheart, but you aren't helping me."

Amy shot him a knowing look. "You're just saying that because you bet on the wrong man. I'm right, aren't I?"

Jez shrugged, but his eyes shifted.

"Amy, I need you to come through for me. How am I supposed to know where Nicco's hidden the Star of Russia if he bursts into tears and goes home?"

"It's not my fault."

"It *is* your fault. What was last night about? And just now, cheering on the opposition?"

"I wasn't! I didn't say a word! And I sympathized with Nicco afterwards. You saw me."

"Nicco isn't a fool. He likes you, but he's not looking for your sympathy. He wants your full, uninterrupted attention."

"Jez—"

The door opened behind her, and Jez looked up, his expression turning hard. "Your champion is here, my lady," he said, giving her a final warning glance before he walked away.

Rey was watching her solemnly. Had he overheard them? For the first time, Amy felt awkward around Rey, and as usual when she was nervous she tried to shrug it off with a joke.

"Sorry about that," she said. "My brother had his money on Nicco. It's a wonder he didn't get you to throw the fight." And she laughed.

Reynald stiffened. "Throw the fight? I do not understand."

"Lose it on purpose. So that Jez could win his bet."

She could actually see the cold anger icing over his gray eyes. It was just like water freezing. His voice was equally chilly.

"I do not lie or cheat, lady. I am a man of honor. A man of my word."

Amy's smile faded as she looked into his eyes. She believed him. He *was* a man of honor, old-fashioned as that seemed these days, and she admired him for it. Rey was unlike any man she'd ever known, and she'd known a few. Maybe that was the attraction for her. He was beyond her reach.

Because if Rey was honorable, then he certainly wouldn't want anything to do with her.

If he knew her, knew her family, knew her reasons for being here, he'd run a mile. He might not lie and cheat, but she did. Nicco might be deficient when it came to kindness and charity, and his business dealings were questionable, but that didn't give her the right to try to take something from him that didn't belong to her. That didn't make what she and Jez were doing right.

"Amy?"

Rey was watching her with concern, as if he sensed her inner turmoil. Sweat had dampened his short-cropped hair; in spite of the cold he was hot. She wondered how his skin felt. How it *tasted*.

"It . . . it's nothing," she stammered, and forced a smile. Suddenly she couldn't bear to be in the same space as him in case he guessed what sort of person she really was. It was shocking to know just how much she wanted Rey to think well of her.

"I have to go," she added, and walked away.

As she plodded through the snow, her feet slowly freezing solid in her thin but very fashionable boots, Amy was suddenly flooded with memories of the past. Her childhood hadn't been happy, far from it, but she wasn't ashamed, it wasn't that. It was just that sometimes she wished things could have been different.

Even now, so many years later, Amy remembered sitting on the swing in the playground. It had started to rain, and she kept her feet up because she knew the muddy ground would ruin her new white shoes with the strap across the instep. She'd only had them three days, and she'd been trying her best to keep them clean.

Her father had given them to her, with a warning about making sure she looked after them. "Shoes like that don't grow on trees," he'd said. "No, they fall off the backs of lorries," her mother had retorted, which meant her father'd stolen them.

He'd been in and out of prison all of Amy's short life. For petty crime mostly, he couldn't seem to help himself. There was a perpetual bitterness inside him, as if he believed he deserved better and the only way he could have it was to take it.

"Amy!" Suddenly Jez came running up to the swing, grabbing her hand, and pulling her after him through the puddle. She squealed as muddy water splashed up her legs and soaked her shoes, but he only laughed and wouldn't let go.

"Stop it," she wailed, tripping and almost falling, close to tears. Jez drew her into the shelter of a gray cinder-block wall. His hair, dark rather than Amy's fiery red, was wet and dripping, and he was shivering. His face, at ten years old already showing the beginnings of his reckless good looks, grew pinched and serious, like an old man's.

Amy watched him in silence. She knew what that look meant.

"We need to get away from the flat for a bit," Jez said. "Mom gave me enough money for fish and chips."

"Is Dad—"

"I'm starving."

Jez was always starving. She didn't argue, trotting after him down the hill in the direction of the greasy shop. She knew without asking that their father had come home from the pub, drunk and dangerous. It wasn't safe to be in the flat when he was like that. One wrong look, one clumsy move, and he'd focus in on you with a stare like he hated you. Really, truly hated you. Even when you hadn't done anything, you found yourself searching your memory, thinking there must be something you'd forgotten.

Jez said it was the drink that did it, but Amy thought whatever made their father change was already inside him, and the drink just set it free. Her father terrified her more than she could say, but she didn't have to tell Jez that. He frightened Jez, too. Her brother pretended to be brave, but Amy knew he was more than happy to escape with his little sister for a few hours, until things calmed down.

Afterwards, they'd come back and find their father snoring in his chair in front of the telly and their mother quiet, moving a little stiffly probably, and maybe with a bruise or two on her face. It was the bruises you couldn't see, Jez said knowledgeably, that were the worst. Sometimes he seemed far older than ten.

That day when they came home, she was terrified, she with her muddy shoes, but for once it was fine. Their father was awake, and cracked silly jokes and laughed loudly. He didn't notice her shoes, he was too busy boasting about his latest venture. Her dad was a great one for swindling people out of their property—he liked to think of it as an art—and yet he despised his victims. If someone was stupid enough to trust him, he said, then they deserved all they got.

The next morning, Amy woke to the bedclothes being dragged off her and her father's red, furious face as he held up her shoes and shook them at her. She'd carried the stripes from his belt for weeks.

A year or two after that incident—one of many—Jez started stealing cars, and joyriding around the streets with his friends, and sometimes Amy. The fear of being caught and the excitement of riding in someone else's car was thrilling at the time. Before long Jez moved on to bigger and better things. He'd been lucky to stay out of prison, and after a close call and a sympathetic magistrate, he'd sworn to Amy that he'd never do anything so foolish again. "So foolish as to be *caught*," he'd laughed.

And so far he hadn't. Not that the police weren't keeping an eye on him. They'd known about him for years; they just couldn't get the evidence to put him away. Detective Inspector O'Neill, he was the one. He seemed to have made Jez his personal crusade, but so far Jez hadn't slipped up. He'd learned from their father's mistakes, and he didn't drink and never boasted.

For a while, he and Amy had teamed up. She'd been as wild as he was, and there were times when the buzz of it kept her on a permanent high. And then she turned twenty-two and suddenly everything changed. She woke up at 6:00 A.M. with a man she hardly knew in her bed and the police banging on her door. They were looking for Jez, but they were happy to arrest her if they could find the evidence. She sat in a cell for a couple of hours, was interviewed, then released.

It was horrible. She felt horrible. Later, Jez apologized for getting her into trouble.

"It's that Detective Inspector O'Neill," he'd said, as if he'd swallowed something nasty. "He'll use anyone to get at me."

"It was him who interviewed me!"

"I'm sorry, Amy, but he's made catching me his New Year's resolution."

Amy remembered the cold glint in his eyes. She shivered. "I don't like it, Jez. He's not mucking around."

Jez laughed, said something about it taking more than O'Neill to trip him up. But as the nightmare birthday wore on, Amy began to come to an understanding about her life—perhaps she'd known it, deep down, for a while.

The life she was living wasn't the life she wanted.

She got a job, a proper job, in a bakery. The woman in the flat next door worked there, and she and Amy had become friends. Over the past months, listening to her talk about her ordinary life, Amy had begun to crave such a life for herself. She wanted to go to work somewhere she didn't have to lie about, she wanted her wages to pay the bills and to save up for special occasions. She wanted a boyfriend who didn't forget her name in the morning.

So, in hindsight, maybe the change in her hadn't been as sudden as it seemed.

Jez didn't understand. She'd tried to explain to him, but had given up when it threatened to cause a major argument. Amy owed Jez so much, and she loved him, but she knew with a bleak certainty that, if she was going to survive, then the time had come to break away from him.

They'd drifted apart. A couple of times over the past three years, Jez had come looking for her and persuaded her to help him with a job—which she'd later regretted. He hadn't been around for a while, and recently she'd been getting along on her own perfectly well. But now Jez was back again.

He was in trouble. She'd known it the moment she'd looked into his eyes. He admitted that he was in debt, but joked about it. Amy knew the names of the men he owed money to—they were dangerous. Jez said he had a scheme, though, and if it came off, he'd be able to pay his debts and have some left over. The only thing was he needed her to help pull it off.

"It'll be just like old times." He'd grinned, as if he was looking forward to it. As if she should be, too.

He really did need her. Despite his smiles and games, he was in trouble. What could she say but yes?

And now she'd met a man who was the direct

opposite of everything Jez and her father stood for. And she hated what he made her feel about her family.

She hated what he made her feel about herself.

Nine

The dragon stretched, stiffly testing each muscle and sinew. She was slowly regaining her strength, but the secret chamber was cramped and uncomfortable. She had pressed her back and flanks against the stone perimeters, and chips and dust scattered about her like rain. She twitched. It had been a long time since she'd felt the sweet touch of rain.

Or sunshine.

Very soon now, the dragon would be ready to begin moving out of this place, where she had spent so long sleeping and waiting. And grieving for her beloved.

She opened her mouth and released a hiss of steam, filling the chamber with its damp warmth. *Better.* She stretched out her front legs, spreading her sharp talons and raking the ground. Her long tail whipped, striking the walls. Satisfied, she knew she had lost nothing of her great power. Soon Reynald would understand how puny he was, and all those mortals who walked upon her land would know how insignificant and unworthy they were.

They would bow down before her majesty!

The dragon lifted her head as far back as she could and gave a deep and terrible roar. The castle above her shifted on its footings. A tremor ran up through the thick stone and mortar walls, causing doors and windows to shake and floors to rock. A shelf of glasses in the kitchen crashed down.

I am here.

The dragon opened her eyes. They were soulless, black, and ancient. Reynald had shown no pity for her beloved; he could not expect it from her, when it came to the final battle.

Ye Olde Medieval Feast was due to begin at two o'clock in the afternoon. That gave her long enough, Amy decided, for a well-deserved nap. But it didn't turn out that way. Just as she closed the door to her room and kicked off her boots, the castle gave a shake, like a brief earth tremor, and the telephone rang. On the other end was a flustered voice, calling on Mr. Coster's behalf. Could Amy come at once to the manager's office on the ground floor?

"Why?" Amy demanded, not in the mood to be accommodating.

"Mr. Coster says that your, eh, actor friend is causing problems."

Wearily, Amy pulled on her boots—still wet from the snow—and went downstairs. It took her half an hour to settle things, promising Mr. Coster that Rey hadn't meant to draw and quarter the Singing Santa, whose body had been found this morning behind a Christmas tree.

"The creature swung its hips at me," Rey said, in explanation.

"Well you've put a stop to that, haven't you?" Coster replied angrily. "That was top-of-the-line, that Santa. Not only was it voice-activated, it was able to move toward the sound on its motorized sleigh."

"I'm sure it was an accident," Amy persisted, overcome with a terrible urge to laugh.

In the end she persuaded Coster that Rey was just getting overenthusiastic about his upcoming role in Hollywood, and she would make certain he behaved from now on. "Add Singing Santa to my bill," she said, hoping "top-of-the-line" didn't mean it was imported by reindeer from the North Pole.

"I won't be able to get another one now before next year," Coster complained, although he was less animated.

"Another one!" Rey roared.

Coster's eyes narrowed, and his secretary cowered.

Amy threw up her hands. "Why do I bother?"

Cross and tired, Amy trudged back to her room, the journey made longer because Rey refused to use the elevator, and she dared not leave him alone in case he caused more mischief.

"Why did you murder 'Jingle Bells' Santa, Rey?"

"It crept up behind me. I thought it was an assassin," he said, as if his explanation was perfectly logical.

"I'll have to remember never to creep up behind you then. Why did you tell Coster it was you who'd done it? You could have kept quiet about it."

"When I came back after the sword tournament, he was shouting, holding that creature in his arms. I thought it must be precious to him. When he asked who could have done such a thing, there were tears in his eyes."

"So you told him the truth? Of course you did!"

"I could not lie, damsel."

"No, you leave the lying to me," she muttered.

Amy wondered when he had become her responsibility? She wasn't his jailer, or his nurse, and yet she seemed to have ended up as both.

"I am offended."

"*You're* offended!" Amy burst out, as she unlocked the door.

"Aye. I am offended that my castle is being used for these mindless frivolities. That they are making fun of matters that should not be made fun of. This was not something to be mocked in my time."

"Rey, they're not mocking you. They're celebrating your life. There's a big difference."

"They mock me!"

Amy slammed the door behind them and pulled off her boots, aiming them at the corner of the room. "Insulting Mr. Coster won't help. I had to use all my feminine wiles to stop him throwing you out. Again."

"You mean batting your eyelashes and simpering like a lackwit," he rumbled.

Amy sat down on the bed, feeling flushed and angry. "I saved your skin, your lordship. You should be thanking me, not insulting me." The room felt hot, and she stripped off her sweater and threw it after the boots. She wasn't the sort to lose her temper, but Rey was seriously testing it. Didn't he realize that all those lies she was telling on his behalf could get her into trouble? Instead of complaining and looking down his nose, he *could* try and help. Maybe his inflexibility was one of the reasons he died in the first place? Maybe that was the lesson he'd come back to learn?

"And I must be going crazy," Amy groaned, "for believing he really is *the Ghost*."

Reynald knew Amy was right about his causing her trouble, but he couldn't seem to help it. He hated the way his castle was being used as a fairground, and he hated the people who had come here to play at the life that had been deadly serious for him. His battles had been brutal, frightening affairs, not something at which to giggle. To them it was nothing more than a game, an amusement they would forget as soon as they left this place. To him, and all the souls he protected, it had been life or death.

He felt belittled.

Amy had laid her head down as if she had gone to sleep, but he could tell by the little crease between her dark brows that she was pretending. He remembered her in Coster's office, and the lies that rolled off her tongue so glibly. At first he'd been shocked at her attitude to the truth, but he was growing used to her ways. It was a good thing, he thought, she was not born in his time. If she had appeared before him at the manor court for her lying, he might have had difficulty doing his duty in punishing her.

Reynald noted the crease had deepened, as if she had an aching head. She was trying to help him, it was true. He could accept that she meant well. She had soothed Coster, and last night in the great hall she had helped him escape the embarrassment of the situation, when he had been about to do battle with his own reflection. Perhaps, Reynald admitted grudgingly, she was right. He should be more grateful and judge her less harshly.

"You have my thanks, damsel," he said quietly.

One green eye opened.

"I am very sorry if I have upset you by implying otherwise."

The other green eye opened, and she gave him the benefit of her limpid gaze.

"As you know, I am here to discover what I did wrong in my time, but . . . I don't know where to look. I don't know where to start. I cannot even leave the castle. I have tried, but there is some . . . some shield around it that prevents me from taking a step beyond the gatehouse."

"So in fact you're trapped here?" she said, taking his words at face value.

"Yes."

"Well, I suppose that means the answer must be within the castle."

"The witch said that."

"Ah, yes, the mysterious witch who controls time. I'd like to meet her."

"Believe me, you would not," he said with feeling.

"Let's go back then, in your mind, to 1299 and the day it happened . . ."

He folded his arms, looking haughtily down at her.

But Amy ignored him; she was too busy trying to help. "What decision could you have made to change what happened that day? How could you have saved lives?"

He sighed. "I wanted peace. I wanted to show that with peace we could *all* prosper."

"So why didn't they listen?"

"They did. That was why we were there that day—to celebrate the signing of the peace. I arranged feasting and games and mock-battles. My guests included a bishop and four lords, and their retinues. If I had known, I would never have invited them, but there was no reason to believe anyone would die that day."

"You didn't suspect, eh, treachery?"

"No! Angharad told me that the Welsh were well pleased, that they wanted peace as much as I. We had already signed the papers before the feasting began. All witnessed the moment. The deal was done. And then . . ."

"This Angharad, you trusted her?"

"With my life," he said solemnly, for it was true.

Amy wasn't so easily convinced. "Well you did, didn't you? Gave up your life on her say-so? Did she die, too?"

"I did not see her die. I have prayed that she escaped. She deserved better."

"I don't know if anyone deserves to die, Rey. What made this Angharad any better than the rest?"

He wanted to argue, but one glance at her green eyes, and he bit his tongue. For some reason Amy Fairweather had taken against Angharad, and his championing of her only seemed to make it worse.

Amy yawned. "Did she help polish your armor, was that it?" She yawned again. "I'm sorry. I really want to help, but I need to sleep for an hour before the feast. Do you think you can stay out of trouble for an hour, Rey?"

This time his tongue broke free. "I resent your implications, damsel. I was a Marcher Lord, a king in my own lands. When I rode by, people hid their eyes for fear of me. And yet you speak to me as if I am a foolish child!"

She had gone very still.

He took a deep breath, then another, trying to calm himself, realizing he might have frightened her badly with his display of anger. "I am no child, I am a man," he went on, in a more measured voice. "You should remember it, damsel, and pay me the respect I have earned."

Still she did not reply.

"Amy?" And then he saw the slow rise and fall of her chest, the gentle parting of her lips on a snore.

She was asleep!

Reynald groaned. What was to be done with such a woman?

With a smile and a shake of his head, the Ghost strode to the door. *He* had no time to sleep. If he didn't get the answers to his problems by the end of this weekend, then he would have to return to the between-worlds. This was his one and only chance, and he would do all in his power to claim it and save the world he had tried so hard to create.

* * *

The Sorceress strode down the tunnels of the between-worlds, her wolfskin cloak heavy about her shoulders, her auburn hair loose and wild. The primitive power of the hunt surged through her. Dragons were dangerous creatures, the most dangerous of all those she faced. Not that she intended to fight the Ghost's battles for him, but whether he won or lost, it would be necessary for the Sorceress to complete the task.

She must capture the dragon.

All around her the heat began to intensify, making it hard to breathe. The Sorceress felt no discomfort, but a mortal would already be struggling to survive in such an atmosphere. For the dragons, though, it was perfect.

She entered the huge chamber. It was a fiery world, where a liquid red ocean bubbled, and geysers sprayed out steam, and hot mud spat. To one side was a lush, green jungle that throve in these conditions, and honeycombed cliffs with caves to offer shelter. The Sorceress could never understand why the dragons complained so much about their prison. Surely this was paradise?

"Ah, 'tis the witch!" cried a lilting voice.

A big gray dragon sat watching her from a rock, tail lashing, black obsidian eyes fixed upon her. There was something about dragons' eyes that unnerved even the Sorceress, upon occasion.

"What is it you want, *cariad*?" the dragon sneered, playing at an affection she knew it didn't feel.

Another one, smaller, darker, stuck its head up over the same rock and peered at her wickedly. "What do you want, witch?" it hissed. "This is our place, and you are not invited."

"I've come to tell you that soon another will be joining you. An old friend of yours. Aren't you pleased?"

There was silence, then a keening sound, as the dragons began speaking to each other in their own language.

"Stop that!" she ordered irritably. "You know I cannot abide that noise."

The gray dragon lifted her massive head and blew flames high into the air. The stink of sulfur filled the cavern, but the Sorceress watched on, not moving an inch.

"You lie!" the dark dragon hissed. "You will never capture *her*. She is the old one, the queen of our kind. She would die rather than be caged in this zoo."

The Sorceress looked about her in mock-surprise. "Zoo? I think it's quite nice myself. You can't expect to roam free forever. Everything has its day, and yours is finished and forgotten."

"Forgotten?" another voice piped up, as a smaller dragon crawled toward her, sharp claws digging into the soft mud for purchase. It flapped its wings, fanning the ovenlike heat. "We will never be forgotten! She has promised to win the mortal world back for us!"

"She has promised!" More of them took up the chant.

"She is too wily for you, witch." Another dragon, thin and serpentlike, whipped out of the forest. "And when she takes back the mortal world, she will come and free us all. She will lead us into a new era. Soon dragons will be the new masters."

"Soon, soon!" they chanted.

"*Stop it.*" The Sorceress had grown impatient. "The mortal world doesn't want you—you cannot exist there, no matter how much you might want to. You have become dangerous anachronisms. Your time is over. You have no choice but to make the best of your 'zoo' here, in the between-worlds. Be grateful for what you have."

But they wouldn't listen to her.

"No, no, our time will come again! She has promised!"

The keening rose again, so high-pitched that it hurt her ears. She whirled about, spinning in a circle, her cloak billowing around her, her hair flying. Magic crackled, sparking from her skin, her chanting voice boomed like thunder. The dragons screamed and lifted from the ground, their wings slapping like wet sails in a storm.

By the time she was still again, the cavern was quiet and the dragons had taken themselves off to the far end. They would be complaining and plotting, or arguing amongst themselves.

Maybe their time would come again. But for now the mortal world was for the humans who lived in it, and they must be kept safe. If the last dragon, the queen of all the dragons, did not know that already, then she must be taught.

Ten

While Amy slept, the Ghost made his way down the stairs to the antechamber outside the great hall. He'd been thinking about the ceiling painting and wanted to see it again, and he found the room mercifully empty. Everyone was probably resting before the feast, like Amy. He could smell food cooking, and it made his stomach ache. With seven hundred years to make up for, he seemed to be constantly hungry.

He looked up.

The dazzling colors and the realistic depiction of the figures was just as astounding as he remembered. Still looking up, he turned, slowly, taking in the story of his life and its many parts. The artist had done a fine job, and Reynald easily recognized himself in the tall, fair man who was at the center of each scene.

There was his mother, her long, blond hair combed over her back and shoulders, as she held her newborn child. Julius would say it was too much like the Madonna and child to be anything but sacrilegious, but it made Reynald smile. Then his father, brutal in his treatment of everyone in his world, at the head of his troops as they rampaged through Wales, burning the land and subduing the people. Victory by force. Except he hadn't really won. The Welsh were just pretending to be subdued; they rose again as soon as the danger was past.

Now here he was as a boy, learning to fight and to rule his future kingdom. There was a scene with him practicing his longbow, the arrow ready to fly. Shocked, he realized they'd even painted someone who was supposed to be Morwenna, and the almost tragedy she had wrought. And then—he shuddered—the young woman falling through the blue sky, birds circling her, to her death. The artist had made it look almost pleasant, as if she were floating rather than falling, but Reynald knew differently.

Now he was a grown man. There were scenes where he was meeting with his enemies, of him standing upon his castle walls, of him doing the things he had been bred to do. He was a strange mixture of his tough, arrogant, warmongering father, and his gentle, melancholy, romance-reading mother, although few realized it. He took care that not many saw his softer side.

The artist had reached the crucial day. With a bit of imagination he recognized Julius and the captain of his garrison. And there were the Welsh princes reaching to take the hands of the bishop and other important English guests. Peace at last on the border. Just for a moment. If he were a sentimental man, the memory might have brought tears to his eyes. But the Ghost hadn't cried in a very long time. And if he'd been tempted, then the final scenes of the artist's portrayal of his life would have dried up any tears in an instant.

There appeared to be a battle going on. With his head tipped right back, he turned on his feet, trying to make sense of it. His men and the Welsh were at war! But . . . that was wrong . . . Where was the monster whose terrifying image was burned forever into his brain? Where were the people, Welsh and English alike, running for their lives? Why hadn't the artist shown what *really* happened?

"A fine piece of work, is it not?"

Bewildered, still stunned by what he hadn't seen, the Ghost found himself confronted by a small, rotund woman wearing a bright orange gown tied with a tasseled cord, and long, blond tresses framing a face of middle age.

"I said, it's a fine piece of work," she repeated, raising her voice as if he was hard of hearing.

"It has its merits," he said, still distracted.

"I do think the artist has captured the urgency and barbarity of the thirteenth century. As well as the pomp and cruel beauty of life in that time. What do *you* think?" She had a way of rolling each word around in her mouth before letting it go.

"I think the artist got it wrong," Reynald said, fascinated by her hair.

"Got it wrong!" the woman boomed. "What on earth do you mean, 'Got it wrong'?"

"I mean wrong. Incorrect. Mistaken."

Her eyes flashed, and she tossed a few blond tresses over her shoulder. "Well, I happen to know it is correct in every detail, because it was *I* who advised them on those details, and although I do not normally like to blow my own trumpet, I will make an exception in this case. My name is Miriam Ure, and I am the country's leading authority on Reynald de Mortimer. Perhaps you've heard of me, Mr. . . . ?"

Reynald struggled to understand. Did she say she was a trumpet-blowing authority on him? Did that mean she thought she knew more about Reynald than Reynald knew about himself? He found such an idea very disturbing, not to say bizarre. He wished she'd go away and leave him alone.

"Will you answer me, sir!"

She wasn't going away.

"It is still wrong," he said, flatly. He pointed at the part of the ceiling he objected to most. "Why is everyone fighting each other?"

"*Why?*" Miriam Ure's voice rose. "Because there was a battle. That was how everyone died that day. Reynald lured the Welsh here with promises of peace, but he didn't mean it—he was his father's son after all—and when he had them, he struck! But the Welsh were prepared—they'd never trusted him—and they refused to surrender. To be put it simply, they all fought *to the death*. No half measures in the thirteenth century."

"*Lured them?*" Reynald echoed, filled with anger and disbelief. "Everyone came to make peace, no one wanted to fight. Why would they? They had seen war enough, and it was in all their interests to live without war. They wanted to grow their crops and farm their animals and have their children without always fearing one or all of them might be killed. You are wrong, woman!"

Her dark eyes narrowed; she tightened her tasseled belt. "Listen to me, *man*. Reynald inherited land that the Welsh tribes considered was their own. They wanted it back, and he wouldn't give it back. It was like a constantly festering sore between them."

"He inherited the land from his father. His father who was always at war, up and down the border. There had been enough war—everyone agreed. Reynald wanted peace, and the prosperity that it would bring. It took years, but eventually he persuaded them he was in earnest. They all came together in agreement. There-was-no-fight-to-the-death!"

She sniffed. "You don't know what you're talking about. I can only think you're drunk, or mad."

"Lady, you are a yammering shrew."

"Well, really! Being rude doesn't make you right, sir."

"You are accusing me . . . Reynald of lying and plotting murder, woman. That is why I am being rude."

"I'm not saying that he did lie and plot, only that it is in keeping with his character—"

"No!"

She sniffed. "Yes."

He could see that the "authority" was convinced of the rightness of her argument. She truly believed that a battle was how they had all died that dreadful day and that somehow he had planned it. But the Ghost knew the truth, and it was time he spoke it.

"The dragon came," Reynald said quietly.

Her eyes seemed to pop, and she made a choking sound. "The dragon?" she repeated. "The Welsh dragon is a metaphor for the Welsh people. It is a symbol. When Julius writes in his chronicle that the 'dragon' fought, he means that the Welsh fought. Surely you don't believe he meant a-a real—"

"Julius wrote a chronicle?" Reynald interrupted. "But Julius died that day."

"No, he didn't die," she answered, with exaggerated patience. "He survived, but with terrible injuries." The woman stared hard at him. "I really would advise you to get your facts right if you're going to go about disputing the experts."

Reynald stared back just as hard. "There *was* a dragon. A great red dragon, with enormous wings and a long tail and claws like daggers. It came from the west, across the ravine and over the treetops. At first we . . . they could only hear the sound of its wings, a slapping and hissing in the still air, then a moaning, keening sound, like a banshee. Everyone was staring. And then the dragon came over them, filling the sky. Reynald looked up and saw its eyes. I tell you, woman, there was more than animal cunning in them. That dragon hated. It was intent on harming everyone it could.

"There had been talk of its coming, but . . . it wasn't believed." I *didn't believe it.* "So there was no preparation for battle. And, anyway, how could such a creature be fought? They were not magicians, just ordinary men and women. Reynald tried, but . . . he failed. The carnage was beyond description."

Miriam Ure was staring up at him and shaking her head slowly, pityingly. "My poor chap, there was no dragon. Dragons are the stuff of myth and legend, they only exist in fiction. You must see that, in reality, such a thing would be impossible. The truth is Reynald de Mortimer and the Welsh thrashed it out, and because neither side would give in, neither side won."

"The dragon won."

She shook her head again, and now scorn curled her mouth. In other circumstances Reynald would have understood the woman's feelings—he was no superstitious fool, and had never accepted talk of the giant flying serpent until he saw it for himself. But he had been there, he knew the truth, and she didn't. It made him both frustrated and angry.

"I believe there's a very good psychiatric hospital a few miles down the road," she said.

Reynald wasn't exactly sure what she meant, but he knew a hospital was for the sick.

He took a step forward, meaning to remonstrate with her again. Her eyes widened, and she stumbled back. Then it was as if he heard Amy's voice in his head:

Rey, don't you dare make another scene!

At once he stopped, all the anger going out of

him. What did he think he was doing? The woman didn't believe him, but that was no reason to frighten her. He should be looking for whatever it was the witch wanted him to find out. The truth that would right the wrong. Only then could he complete his task and return to his own time.

Deliberately, he moderated his tone. "What you have said, about the fighting between the Welsh and my . . . and Reynald's men . . . this is what everyone believes?"

"Of course."

The dragon had been forgotten. Or dismissed. But Julius must have written down the truth, and Julius was the least likely of any man to indulge in flights of fancy, so why did not one believe him? Somehow the story had been changed in the telling.

Perhaps Amy could explain it to him . . .

And then it occurred to him that Amy probably didn't know the truth either. Did she believe he was the kind of man who would lure the Welsh to their deaths? A man without honesty or honor? He had to tell her about the dragon. He had to explain it to her right now.

Reynald made for the stairs, leaving the woman in the wig staring after him, but just as he started up them, Mr. Coster called out to him. Against his better judgment, Reynald stopped and looked back.

Coster was walking toward him, and he seemed

to have gotten over his grief at the death of the Singing Santa. In fact, he was smiling. "Ah, good, good. I was hoping to catch you. I wonder if I might have a word . . ."

Eleven

*Amy woke suddenly and glared at the illumi-*nated numbers on the clock. It was late. She should have been downstairs at the feast by now. Why hadn't Rey got her up? She sat up, calling his name and looking around at the empty room with a growing sense of unease.

"Rey? Where are you?"

Well, he wasn't in here, and there really wasn't time to go looking for him. Amy barely had enough minutes to shower and dress in the costume she'd chosen for the feast. It was a dress with a tight-fitting dark green bodice and an uneven, zigzag hem. The skirt was constructed of different colors, sewn in strips, and when she twirled they billowed out like a carnival pinwheel. She thought of it as a female version of a harlequin or a jester, and had teamed it with flat, velvet green shoes with bells on the toes. Satisfied with her appearance, Amy brushed her curls, tied some colored ribbons in amongst them, dabbed on makeup, and was out the door.

She could hear the noise long before she reached the great hall; medieval musical instruments competing with the chatter of modern voices. As she passed through the outer room, she instinctively gazed up at the paintings that tracked the life and exploits of Reynald de Mortimer in the thirteenth century.

There he was, standing on his castle walls, gazing upon his subjects as they crowded below, awaiting his words of wisdom. She could imagine Rey looking just like that down his nose—arrogant. As if he was scornful of the weaknesses of lesser mortals.

Like her.

For reasons she preferred not to go into, Amy shivered.

"Amy." It was Jez, in one of his expensive dark suits.

Amy shot him a narrowed glance. "That's not medieval."

"No, but it's Saville Row," he said, flicking an imaginary speck off the cuff. "Where's your big friend?"

"I don't know."

"Perhaps he's gone home," Jez said hopefully.

"I don't understand why you waste your time with him."

"You know why, Jez. Coster was going to call the police. Did you want that?"

"I'm not a fool, Amy. I know when you're playing with the truth to suit yourself."

She said nothing. How was she going to explain to her brother about Rey? Where did she begin? Even if she left out the seven-hundred-year thing, he'd have her committed.

Jez wasn't waiting for a reply. "Nicco's around here somewhere. He was looking for you."

"Oh good."

"Amy, you're trying my patience—"

A tremendous whining, hooting sound blasted out behind them, as two medieval trumpets gave it their all. Amy covered her ears, and Jez gave her a brotherly dig in the ribs.

"Make way! Make way!" boomed a voice.

Amy turned, just in time to see Rey entering at the head of a small procession of people dressed in colorful medieval costume. One of the local theatrical companies had supplied clothing and players. Coster, a crown on his head and a purple cloak about his shoulders, was prominent, with several women gowned in long dresses and pointed hats with veils.

"Make way for King Edward and Lord de Mortimer!"

"Oh my God," Amy breathed.

Rey was wearing tight dark trousers and a deep red tunic over a white shirt. He looked very handsome, and very imperious, as if he was perfectly at home in the situation. But then, if he really was who he said he was, he would be, wouldn't he?

As he passed by, he met her gaze, and there was a gleam in his eyes. His lips twitched. He was enjoying himself, and he certainly fit the part. Her gaze sharpened. "Who's that woman beside him in the Lady of Shallot getup?"

"Terri Kirkby," Jez said, finally showing some interest. "I'd heard she was coming. They say she's the next Keira Knightley."

Amy pretended to yawn. "A blond teenager as thin as a stick. Why am I not surprised?"

"Your claws are showing, little sister."

They found a place to sit, close enough to the fire to feel its warmth but not be roasted. The meal was a triumph of simple food cooked well: salmon and turkey and beef, and bowls of winter vegetables, as well as chestnut soup, sweet and savory tarts, and, to top it off, a huge Christmas pudding, which was ceremoniously flamed.

"Christmas pudding, as we know it, isn't medieval, of course," said a plump woman across the table, who had introduced herself as Miriam Ure, "but it's so delicious, perhaps we can forgive them for that."

"I don't know if *I* can forgive them," Amy

whimpered, feeling her stomach expanding. "I haven't eaten this much in years."

"Of course, Yuletide was a time of the year when there was little fresh fare," the woman went on expansively, tossing back a lock of her blond wig—she'd explained she was here as Lady Godiva, with clothes. "They would have used wild herbs, mushrooms, anything growing in the woods, and foods already in storage, like apples, from the previous growing season. With the weather likely to be cold and bleak outside, everyone wanted the opportunity to eat and be merry."

"They certainly look merry," Jez said, nodding to the table on the raised dais, where Coster and Rey were seated with pretty Terri Kirkby. "Don't you think, Amy?"

She ignored him.

He leaned closer, so as not to be overheard. "Here's your chance to get rid of him. I know that having saved him, you feel obligated to keep him, but now he's made new friends . . . ?"

Miriam Ure broke in loudly. "Do you know that Reynald de Mortimer, the real one, that is, was very fair of coloring—both hair and eyes? That was why they called him the Ghost. And also, I think, because he had been in many situations where he might have died but somehow survived. When he was a youngster his father's enemies planted a serving girl in the de Mortimer stronghold to kill the boy. She seduced him, or tried to, then produced a dagger. He survived, but it had its effect. He never allowed a woman to get that close to him again."

That horrible scar! Amy stared at her with wide eyes. "She tried to . . . to cut his throat?"

"Yes," Miriam smiled. "You've heard the story, then? It was a close thing, evidently. One can't blame him for not wanting anything to do with women afterwards, although he'd have to marry, eventually. Every great man needs an heir, and Reynald was a very great man, with a vast amount of wealth."

"Good lord," Amy murmured feebly. The scar, she'd seen it, and it looked real. It *was* real.

One of the traditional buxom serving wenches arrived to pour more mead and ale, but she declined, and asked instead for coffee. She was then treated to a ten-minute lecture by Miriam on the origins of coffee and its introduction into England.

In the middle of it, she felt a wave of depression coming on. It seemed a strange moment to feel depressed, during a medieval feast with plenty of food and merriment, and with Jez at her side. She should be making the most of it, reminding herself that after Monday she'd be returning to her real life and leaving all of this behind her forever.

Laughter erupted from the main table. *Well, Reynald was obviously enjoying himself enough for both of them.* So much for his desperate search for the truth and Amy being his chosen companion. It seemed he had plenty of time after all, or maybe that was because he was sitting next to Terri Kirkby.

Abruptly, Amy stood up. "You know, I'm not very good company," she said to Jez. "If Nicco comes looking for me, tell him I'll definitely see him later."

Jez eyed her quizzically. "What's wrong, sweetheart?"

"What could be wrong?" she retorted, and leaned down to kiss the top of his head. "Be good."

She skirted through the tables and chairs, feeling like the only one on the Welsh borders who wasn't having a good time. A black cloud on a sunny day, that was her. She'd reached the door when a hand closed on her arm and stopped her dead. *Nicco?* But her prickle of awareness told her it wasn't. With a sense of the inevitable, Amy turned to face her captor.

"Hey, Rey," she said, as if she wasn't in the least disturbed by his sudden appearance. "Bored already?"

There was a gleam in his eyes. Sitting beside Terri Kirkby for a couple of hours probably did that to a man.

"I need to speak with you."

"I really don't feel like talking. Can we do it later?"

"I want to tell you about—"

"Why don't you tell Terri? She's probably dying to hear all about whatever it is."

Oh God, why had she said that? She could have bitten her tongue off. It made it so obvious. Nervously, she watched his puzzled frown, as he tried to read her. And then his gaze sharpened. He glanced back at Terri, and he smiled at Amy. Color ran into her cheeks.

"You are jealous," he said.

"Why on earth should I be?" She turned and walked away.

He followed. "You did not like me sitting with Terri. It made you jealous." He seemed so pleased about it, and she felt so embarrassed, that she just couldn't bear it.

Amy put on her most world-weary tone. "Rey, I agree that you're a good-looking bloke, but I'm not looking for a relationship just now. I'm more interested in sorting out my own life than ironing some guy's shirts."

He wasn't fooled. He laughed softly, deep in his throat. It made her stomach drop away.

"Amy, *you* are my companion. I need you to help me right my wrong, to redeem myself. You and no one else. Already, you have done much, and I am grateful to you. You must believe that. I am not looking for a bedmate, and if I was, I would not offer you insult by asking such a thing of you."

"Rey, flattered as I am by your sweet talk, there's something you should know." She hesitated. He was looking down at her as if she was the angel of goodness. Suddenly she couldn't bear to spoil it, not just yet. "I'm not what you think," she ended lamely.

He smiled as if he didn't believe her, but didn't press the matter. "I wanted to tell you about the painting," he said. "The battle between my people and the Welsh. It is wrong."

Amy was confused. "Why is it wrong?"

"Look." He tugged her by the arm he still held, until she was underneath the section of the painting he seemed interested in. He pointed excitedly up at the ceiling, and because he was so agitated, Amy let him say what was on his mind. "You can see fighting, a great battle."

"Yes, I can see fighting. Oops, there's an arm . . . and a head."

He frowned at her levity. "What you are seeing is something that didn't really happen, damsel."

"There was no battle?"

"No. The dragon came. It was the dragon, Amy!"

Amy stared at him, amazement warring with skepticism. She couldn't help it. What he was saying was completely ridiculous. Or maybe she'd reached her gullibility limit.

"So you're telling me that there was a real-live dragon there that day? Is that what you're telling me, Rey?"

"Yes!" he cried. "A dragon. It flew over us, and its breath was fire and steam and ash. People were running and screaming, thinking only of getting away. I had my longbow, but I did not strike true.

I . . . did not trust myself to strike true. And then the dragon was upon me, and there was nothing."

He stopped, breathing hard. His chest was rising and falling beneath his red tunic. Amy wanted to put her hand on him. She felt goose bumps on her arms. He was so sincere, so earnest, and she knew him to be an honest man. But how could she believe him? How could any sane person believe that dragons existed, never mind seven-hundred-year-old warriors?

She was well out of her depth.

She looked away, gained some time by smoothing her multicolored skirt and tinkling the bells on her shoes. "I don't know what to say. You're telling me that you were killed by a dragon in 1299?"

"Yes."

"Rey . . . where did you get that scar on your neck?"

He didn't answer. When she looked at him, she saw the shocked expression in his eyes. *It was true, it was all true!*

Whatever the facts, right now it was too much for her. Amy shook her head and walked away.

Twelve

Reynald watched her walk off. He was disppointed that she didn't accept the truth instantly, but he couldn't blame her for her confusion and lack of faith. He was confused, as well, about why he was here in this time and what he was supposed to do. To learn.

Her question about his scar had really thrown him. Looking into Amy's beautiful green eyes, and at the same time remembering how he'd come by the shocking wound on his neck, had felt like a kind of blasphemy.

Morwenna had been the last woman he'd wanted to hold in his arms, to join with his body, but now . . . He realized the feelings he had had for Morwenna were nothing compared to the raging lust he had for Amy.

And Amy was jealous of Terri. Did that mean she reciprocated his feelings? That she wanted him as much as he wanted her?

He wanted to smile. Julius would preach that jealousy was an evil, destructive emotion, and was not to be tolerated. But Reynald welcomed it. If Amy was jealous, she cared about him. She thought about him in the same way he thought about her, with the need to know and possess.

There was more to his feelings for her, but no doubt Julius would have something instructive to say about carnal imaginings, too.

"You and my sister seem very cozy."

He hadn't heard anyone come up beside him, but he recognized Amy's brother's voice. He found Jez's expression less than friendly, but Reynald didn't blame him for that—a man must protect the women in his family—but he did wonder if Jez's coolness was more to do with his desire for Amy to spend her time with Nicco rather than him.

"I'm Jez, by the way." He held out his hand.

"Amy calls me Rey," Reynald said, and took the hand.

"Look, mate, I don't know you, so I'm giving you the benefit of the doubt, but . . . Amy has a good heart, and I don't like people taking advantage of her."

"Other than you?"

Jez's eyes narrowed. "See, you're treading on dangerous ground now, Rey."

"You are aware, Jez, that this is the Ghost's castle?"

Jez raised an eyebrow.

"In the time of the Ghost, the men would use the women of their family to gain favor. If a brother could sell his sister in marriage to a man of wealth and prestige, then he would. It did not matter whether or not the woman was willing or happy. Women were only there to serve their menfolk, to be used . . ."

Jez snorted. "I don't need a lecture on social history—"

"No, but perhaps you need to remember that what benefits you may not benefit your sister."

"I'm not selling Amy to Prince Nicco!"

"No?"

"I would never ask Amy to do anything she didn't want to."

Reynald said nothing.

Jez's anger waned, and concern flickered across his face. "I promise you, you're wrong," he said, and there was a sincerity in his voice that hadn't been there before. "I watch out for my sister. I always have."

"I, too, watch out for your sister," Reynald said quietly. "I will not hurt her. You have my word."

There was an uncomfortable silence, as if neither man quite knew what to say next, then Jez nodded brusquely, and said, "I might hold you to that," and walked away.

Reynald watched him go. Of all the emotions he might have felt, he was surprised by what stirred within him. Envy. Reynald had no brothers or sisters—he was an only child. His mother had been an unhappy woman, an heiress forced into exactly the sort of situation he had been explaining to Jez. His father was often away fighting or traveling his lands; with so much to hold on to, he was always worried he might lose some part of it. Reynald's upbringing had been left to the castle retinue, under his father's instruction. He had longed for a sibling playmate, someone with whom to share his thoughts and feelings, but it was not to be. After he was sired there was no need for his parents to resume a union that made them both unhappy.

And as for friends among the castle children . . . it was discouraged. His father thought that his heir needed to stand apart from others, to be a man alone. He didn't realize how much Reynald craved company, and the reassurance and love of others. Not to make him weaker but to strengthen him.

That was why he envied Jez and Amy their ties, and their love for each other. He was alone, and he had never felt it more than he did now.

Amy was walking aimlessly, her mind in a whirl. She felt as if there was a terrible conflict going on inside her between her need to believe Rey and her serious doubts about him. Her steps slowed. It was bad enough that he said that he was a man who had come back to life after seven hundred years, but now he was talking about real-live dragons. Ridiculous! Fairy book stuff.

She ran a distracted hand through her curls. What was she going to do with him? She'd have to send him away. But even as she made the decision, Amy knew she didn't want to do that. She was attracted to him in a way she'd never felt before—not just physically, although there was that, but emotionally and intellectually. Besides, she trusted him, and Amy's inner feelings were inevitably right.

Something small and gray scampered across the floor in front of her. A mouse? Startled, Amy looked about her, and realized she'd wandered deep into an unfamiliar part of the castle. This wasn't the nicely carpeted section, where her room was situated. This floor was dusty, bare timber, and there were narrow window slits in the stone walls—or were they for arrows? Cautiously, she put an eye to one of them and peered down into a dim courtyard.

The snow was thicker than before. When she looked out into the distance, she could see the white-topped hills of Wales staring back at her. They looked ominous and foreign, or could that be because she was so used to the London skyline? She tried to imagine what it must have been like in the thirteenth century, living in what amounted to an Anglo-Norman outpost on the fringe of enemy territory. No wonder the people here were tough and serious, like Rey, and no wonder they made the most of their limited pleasures.

Amy stared at the horizon, trying to picture a dragon flying right at her. Big and angry, with its wings beating, and flames spewing from a mouth like an open furnace. Its face would be long, almost reptilian, with prominent nostrils and big eyes . . .

Black eyes, without any soul, without any feeling apart from a deep, abiding hatred. Now those eyes were fixed on hers. The lilting Welsh tones were unlike any voice she had ever heard before: "Ah, there you are, cariad. I see you now, pretty one. I see you now."

Amy jumped back, heart thumping. She forced a laugh and shook her head, thinking that soon she'd be wishing upon stars and watching for Santa's reindeers . . . But the frightening moment was slow to fade. It had seemed so horribly real.

There was a shuffle to her left. She turned sharply, and for the first time realized she was not alone. There was someone at the end of the corridor—a silhouette against a halo of light. *Light?* There wasn't a window large enough to cause so much light. But then the figure shifted slightly, and she realized that whoever it was held the handle of an old-fashioned, swinging lantern.

"Excuse me?" she called out. "I think I'm lost. Can you tell me how to get back to—"

The figure turned and moved away. She noted

that it was wearing a long, dark garment, a bit like a cloak, that seemed to cover it from head to foot. A monk's habit, maybe? Although what a monk would be doing wandering around the castle was a puzzle, unless it was someone in fancy dress? One of the guests, or a member of staff, practicing their part? Whoever it was, Amy didn't intend to let them get away.

"Is that the way out of here?" she said, quickly following. This corridor was gloomy and unfriendly, and she wasn't going to be left behind.

But the figure was moving swiftly, as if he didn't want her to catch him. Ahead was a bare, stone stairwell that appeared to be even more abandoned and desolate, if that were possible.

"Where are we?"

The figure was descending the stairs, and the light was fading. Obviously this must be the way back to the more familiar part of the castle—What else could it be?—but Amy hesitated. It felt wrong. She glanced behind her, and the darkness seemed to be closing in.

"Any other ideas?" she murmured to herself. But she hadn't, so she started to follow the mystery monk down the stairs, the bells on her shoes tinkling forlornly.

The stone wall felt chill and damp to the touch, and the air was undisturbed, as if no one had walked here for centuries. Amy felt as if she'd taken a step through time.

At any moment, I'll turn a corner, and there will be the Ghost, the real one, looking down his nose at me.

Except that now, when she thought of the Ghost, she saw Rey. Her Rey.

Amy stumbled. When did he become *her* Rey? A moment before she'd been promising herself she'd tell him to go, now he was *her Rey*. She shook her head; better not to think of that now. She needed to get out of here first, then she'd worry about what she was going to do with her pet thirteenth-century warrior.

The possessor of the lantern had reached a landing and started along another of those dank, dark corridors. Amy hesitated again. This section of the castle looked as if it was in the throes of a massive renovation. The floor was nothing more than planks laid over the original timber, with metal safety railings either side. There were also heavy wooden poles propping up the ceiling. The smell of sawdust and rotten wood was everywhere. Amy looked around, expecting to see KEEP OUT—DANGER signs, but there were none.

"Hello!" Her voice echoed mournfully. It was very atmospheric, and claustrophobic. It reminded her unpleasantly of the décor on the Parkhill housing estate—grim gray with a touch of menace.

She started down the corridor. The walkway felt stable, but just in case, she kept her hands on the railing. She was concentrating on where she was walking, and it wasn't until she looked up that she saw that the lantern was getting brighter, and that at last she was catching up. Knowing that should have made her feel better, but instead it made her even edgier.

Was she doing the right thing? Instead of finding her way out, she was getting more and more lost, and whoever it was she was following didn't seem to care. If it *was* a real person.

The figure in front of her stopped.

"Hello?"

Was he waiting? Amy, peering down the gloomy passageway, wondered whether she really wanted to get close to him after all. And then she saw him raise an arm, in a beckoning motion.

Uh-uh. This didn't seem right.

As she dithered, the lantern suddenly grew so bright that it hurt her eyes.

"Hello?" she called again, taking a step, then another. "Can you turn that thing down for a minute? I can't see where I'm going."

Monkman said nothing, just stood there, waiting. And, suddenly, Amy knew that this really wasn't a good idea at all.

She stopped and squinted her eyes, trying to see through the dazzling light, to the face of . . . whoever. "Who are you?" she demanded, sounding angry. She *was* angry. "I'm not coming any closer until you answer me."

Nothing. Silence. In fact, it was an unnatural silence. The moment stretched out, and Amy had just decided to get out of here, when the monk began to shimmer, like dark water, against the light. Then, before Amy's startled gaze, he began to fade to sepia, like an old photo. In another moment, the monk was gone, and, although the light remained, briefly, it, too, began to disappear. Soon it was nothing more than a pinpoint that hovered briefly in the air before it was snuffed out.

She was alone, with only the sound of her breathing to keep her company.

Amy didn't turn and run. She would have liked to, but she knew she'd never forgive herself if she didn't investigate. Was it a trick? Maybe one of the staff got his kicks by terrorizing the guests?

She took a step forward, looking down at the floor to see if there was a trapdoor. And that was when she saw the gaping hole.

For a heartbeat she was too shocked to do anything but stare into the murky darkness below. The drop looked to be about ten feet, at least, and there were broken beams and jagged slivers of wood at the bottom. If she'd kept walking toward the figure with the lantern, she'd have fallen into that hole. She might have been killed.

All the time she'd believed she was being led to safety, the monk was planning to hurt her. To kill her.

From somewhere in the darkness there was a rustle. Amy stumbled backward. She was very isolated. She needed to find her way back to safety and civilization, then she'd think about all that had happened.

She turned, her legs wobbly, and picked her way with extra care back along the walkway. The stairwell looked safe enough, and she began the descent. After a few turns, she found herself standing before a set of arches, rather like a cloister, that led into the grounds. Relieved, she recognized the pavilion where the sword tournament had taken place, and knew then that the main entrance to the hotel was just around the corner.

She was safe.

Why would anyone want to hurt her? Jez, well, she could understand people coming after him, especially at the moment, but not Amy. Whatever she had been following was something else. Something supernatural and beyond her understanding.

Amy stood in the growing cold darkness and tried to steady her nerves. She was a practical girl, not prone to letting her imagination go wild. What had just happened to her was impossible, she knew it, but she also knew what she'd seen. There seemed to be a lot of impossible things happening to her recently.

Thirteen

Amy had barely taken a step into the reception area when Rey was there, right in her face, his cool eyes lit with excitement.

"Damsel, I need to speak."

"Not now, Rey." She kept walking. The trauma of the experience with the shadow with the lantern was still strong, and she needed to think.

But he reached out and clasped her arm with enough force to stop her, while not hurting her.

"Rey," she whispered, "not *now*."

To her horror, tears sprang to her eyes. Quickly she looked down, but not soon enough.

"Amy," he whispered, cupping her face with his hand. "You are upset. Tell me what is wrong that I may make it right again."

She smiled; she couldn't help it. "You can't fix

everything, Rey." Her smile faded. "You can't fix *me*."

"I can try," he said.

His breath was warm on her lips, and for a moment she thought he intended to kiss her.

"You should be looked after, Amy," he spoke firmly.

"Hmm, as a feminist, I probably should take exception to that," she replied. But she didn't. He made her feel special in a way she'd never felt before.

Amy lifted her chin, their lips so close now that she was sure he'd have to kiss her. She wanted him to. But instead he brushed her lower lip with his thumb and smiled.

"I respect you, damsel," he murmured.

Amy nodded, wondering where the hell he was coming from. No man had ever said that to her before, not when she was all but offering her mouth to him. Suddenly it occurred to her that they were standing in a crowded lobby amongst plenty of interested spectators. She began to back away.

"Right, eh . . . I'll see you later . . ." And Amy turned and fled.

But she wasn't to get the peace she craved.

Jez was waiting in her room.

Amy stopped and stared at her brother from the doorway, then shook her head and went to the minifridge to pour herself a drink.

Amused, he watched her. "That bad, was it?"

"And more."

"Where were you? I've been waiting for ages."

For a moment she considered telling him the truth, but only for a moment. Jez was like her, he considered himself to be a practical and no-nonsense kind of person, and he'd laugh himself sick if she told him she'd been off following a ghostly monk with a lantern. Then he'd rationalize it. Amy didn't need him to do that; she could rationalize well enough for herself.

"I was sightseeing," she said. "How did you get in here without a key?"

"You don't want to know."

Amy couldn't help but smile even though she knew she shouldn't encourage him. She took a deep swallow of bottled vodka and lime before she sank down onto her bed. "What did you want, Jez?"

"I don't have to want something to come and see you."

"It usually follows. Anyway, you saw me at the feast."

Jez seemed annoyed. "You make me sound like a selfish bastard. Am I really that mercenary?"

If he wanted home truths, then she'd give him home truths. "I'd call you single-minded, but yes, you can be, Jez. That's not to say I don't love you for it." She smiled, and after a moment he gave her a smile back.

"Jez," Amy began, more seriously, "I said I'd do

this job for you, and I will. You should trust me. You don't have to check up on me every other minute. Where is His Royal Highness, by the way?"

"I went to see him just now. He's tucked up in bed. Seems he strained some muscle or other in his back during the sword business. He's been resting. Personally, I think it has more to do with the nurse than any injury."

"I'm jealous."

Jez raised an eyebrow. "Of course you are, sweetheart. But never fear, Nicco promised me you weren't forgotten. He'll be at the cocktail party later tonight."

"*Medieval* cocktail party. How do you mix a medieval cocktail, by the way?"

"Hmm. Carefully?"

Amy chuckled and took another swallow of her drink. "Will you be there tonight? Just in case I need your expertise."

"Without fail." He fiddled a moment with a pair of earrings she'd left on the table beside his chair. It was a nervous gesture, unlike Jez. "I spoke with your big friend after you left," he said.

"Oh?" Amy felt herself stiffen with anxiety, and forced her body to relax. Jez was always hyperalert when it came to other people's body language. It was embarrassing enough, being so attracted to Rey, without her brother knowing about it. "I wouldn't have thought you and Rey had much in common."

"Well, it seems we do. He was very protective. Of you."

"Of me? You were talking about me!"

"Amy—"

"No, Jez. Don't question me, and don't talk to Rey about me."

He gave her a look like he was trying to read her mind, but she showed him a stony face. In the end, he shrugged and stood up. "Okay, you win, I won't interfere. Just be careful, all right?"

"Aren't I always?"

He shook his head, and for a moment seemed about to say more, but then he changed his mind. He went to the door, and, with a wave of his fingers, left.

Amy stared down into her glass. *I should have told him I don't want to do this thing with Nicco. Why didn't I tell him?* Because she owed him too much to let him down, and it was the last time. The very last. It shouldn't be worrying her—it wouldn't be worrying her—except for Rey.

He was so straight, so honest. She'd never met a man before who impressed her so much. He was truly honorable in the old-fashioned sense of the word. Her father had been the exact opposite, and Jez, although she loved him dearly, wasn't honest or straight. Perhaps, in his own way, he had a certain integrity, but he was no Rey.

And the depressing thing was, if he knew why she was really here at the castle, he'd despise her.

He'd turn away in disgust. She didn't want that. She was enjoying the way he was treating her. As if she were gold-plated. Special. No one had ever treated her like that before.

But she knew she wasn't the woman he thought she was, and sooner or later he was going to find out.

You're an idiot. You'll probably never see him again after Monday. Why should it matter what he thinks of you? This is exactly the sort of situation you don't want to get yourself into, Amy Fairweather.

I just hope it isn't already too late.

Mr. Coster had proved a good source of information when it came to the history of the castle. He knew the stories and had done some research of his own. Reynald was able to confirm that Julius had survived the dragon's attack, just as Miriam Ure said he did. Reynald was very glad to hear it, but he was also curious about the chronicle his chaplain had written afterwards.

"The original is kept in the British Museum," said Coster, "but we do have some copies here. Would you like to borrow one? They're just rough copies, black-and-white, nothing like as glorious as the original. Julius was certainly a talent."

Reynald took the book from Coster. The cover was stiffened white parchment of some kind, and the pages within were thinner, covered in close black writing that was to Reynald unreadable.

Coster noticed his puzzled look, but misinterpreted it. "Yes, I'm afraid it's in medieval Latin, but we have a translation at the back. The historian, Miriam Ure, did the work on the chronicle. In fact she's here this weekend. Perhaps you've seen her about? She's Lady Godiva."

"I have met her."

"Ah. She's a great authority on the Ghost and his period in history, as well as Reynald's castle."

Reynald said nothing, fidgeting with the book and wanting to escape so that he could persuade Amy to read it to him.

"You'll be at the cocktail party? Terri Kirkby will be here. She seems to be a fan of yours."

Reynald smiled, but not for the reason Coster thought. "I will be at the cocktail party," he promised.

Amy was jealous, he chanted to himself, as he walked away. She cared about him, and she did not like him to be with other women. Knowing it brought a spring to his step and a beat to his blood. Amy was everything he had been searching for— good and kind and true—although he hadn't even known he'd been searching until he met her. But he understood at last how empty his life had been, how he had filled it with the business of his position and his lands so that he would not notice. But he knew now, he understood now what a difference Amy would make to him, if only it were possible.

If only they weren't from different worlds.

In the dragon's cramped chamber, deep under the castle, it was getting hotter. She dozed, gathering her strength. She was dreaming of long-ago days, when many more of her kind lived in the world, and they were content, she and her beloved.

After she had destroyed Castle Reynald and all who dwelt within it, she had been free, for a little while. But then the mortals returned and refused to leave, and she had sought shelter deep in the rock beneath the castle. A prisoner in her own land.

The witch of the between-worlds looked for her and could not find her, but she'd always known the witch would send someone to face her. She just hadn't realized that someone would be Reynald.

"Thank you, cariad," she mocked the witch. *"It will be my pleasure to kill him again. I will make it even more excruciating this time. I will boil him alive in his own blood."*

Fourteen

Reynald was climbing the stairs as Amy was coming down. The stairwell was narrow, and he was big, blocking her way. Intrigued, his gaze lingered on the tight clothing she was wearing on her shapely body, until she gave him an exasperated look and squeezed around him.

Her hip brushed his thigh, and his arm knocked against the soft roundness of her breast. For a heartbeat, he was overcome by sensation and longing, then he turned and followed her.

"You have forgotten your clothing, damsel," he said, quietly. "Or is it usual in these times to go about so?"

"Ha-ha! Still working on your cover story, Rey? If you were really the Ghost, wouldn't you be speaking in Latin or . . . or . . ."

"I speak French, damsel, as do all nobles, but I also speak English, and a little Welsh. Your English is strange, and you use words I do not know, but I am learning quickly."

"I'll bet you are."

Sometimes he didn't understand the inflections she used, and this was one of those times. He thought about asking her to explain, but her face was closed.

"Where are we going?" he asked, instead.

"I'm going down to the gym."

She strolled through the big room downstairs, gathering interested looks from the men in the vicinity. Reynald slowed, scowling at each and every one of them, but then he realized she was vanishing down another set of stairs.

"I have Julius's chronicle to show you!" he called, as he clattered after her. Why was she visiting the food store? In his time, it had been stacked to the ceiling with barrels of salted meat, ready for the winter.

"Julius's chronicle will have to wait." Her voice floated back to him.

The air was much cooler down here, but that was always so, and it was only as he reached the bottom step that he saw the drastic changes that had been wrought since his time. What had been a maze of passages and smaller chambers, was now a single, large room. There was soft cloth on the floor—Amy called it wall-to-wall carpet. But what really startled him were the shiny machines, with their workings of chains and metal. One appeared to have a long narrow seat upon it, as if to lie on, and where a person's head might rest there was a metal bar with discs of lead attached.

Reynald thought he recognized this room for what it was. He had never resorted to torture, although his father had believed in the virtue of using pain to get the result he wanted. Or there was always the oubliette, deep and dark, where prisoners could be forgotten.

"This place," he said to Amy, horrified, "is it a chamber for torture?"

Amy actually laughed. "You could say that."

As he stood, frozen, she stepped onto one of the machines, pushed at the flashing buttons on the front of it, and began to run upon the thin, moving path beneath her shoes.

Reynald watched her in amazement. That such a thing existed at all was barely comprehensible, but soon he was asking himself "why?" There seemed to be no purpose for it when there was a world outside to run in. He opened his mouth to ask her, and became distracted by the sight she made.

Her legs were slim and strong, and as she ran she swung her arms, and her breasts bounced. The tight clothing hugged her body, outlining every curve. He moved closer, circling the device, and trying to understand how it worked. It wasn't a torture machine, he knew now; it was a machine to exercise her body.

"There are some weights over there," Amy pointed out. "Do you pump weights, Rey? Is that how you got those muscles?"

There was admiration in her voice. He already knew that she must like his appearance—Why else would she be jealous and want him for herself?— but there was pleasure in confirming the fact.

"I do not need to 'pump weights,' " he said arrogantly.

"Come on, admit it, Rey. How much can you lift?"

"I can lift you, damsel."

She smiled.

Satisfied, he went to inspect the rest of the room. There was no one else here, and he could prowl to his heart's content. He tried out a few of the machines and found them interesting, but they were no substitute for the training yard or riding his stallion. By the wall, he found a large bowl with water inside it and small cups fixed to the outside. After poking and prodding at it, he discovered how to make the water come out, although not always into the cups.

Amy had moved on to another machine now. This time she was rowing as if she were seated in a small boat, except that she was not moving along.

Again, Reynald couldn't see the point. Surely to put so much effort into a thing, one should be moving along? She could be rowing in the river or fishing in the pond, instead of wasting her time going nowhere.

"Why do you do this, Amy?"

"To keep fit. To stay slim."

"You would not need to do such things in my time. No one is fat, unless they are too lazy to do their work. Or too rich to need to."

"The lady of the castle, huh? I don't know, that's a lot of responsibility."

"You are more than capable, damsel," he said, with quiet sincerity. "You would be a lady for all others to admire."

She glanced up at him, and he saw the startlement in her eyes, then she was smiling and pretending he was only teasing her. Reynald gave a mental shrug. So be it. He would bide his time a little longer then if she was not yet ready to hear the truth from him.

But he could not wait forever. Soon he would have to state his feelings, and she would have to respond.

"This chronicle," she began, changing the subject, "what does it say?"

"I do not know."

"You mean it's in another language? Latin or something?"

"No, I mean I cannot read it."

She gave him a look, as if she wasn't sure whether or not he was teasing her again. "You can't read?"

"Julius was my scribe as well as my priest. If I required a letter to be written or read to me, then he did it. A lord does not need to be able to read and write, not when he has others to do it for him."

She'd stopped rowing and was frowning up at him, her face flushed and her curls damp. There were wet patches on her clothing from her efforts. Reynald could smell the warm, sweet scent of her body and tried not to groan aloud.

It was all very well to speak of her fine qualities, but in his heart he wanted her in the way a man wants a woman, in a manner that was entirely carnal. Even now he was undressing her from her tight clothing, and laying her down on the wall-to-wall carpet so that he could touch her, taste her . . .

"But wouldn't you like to be able to read the letters for yourself?"

She was speaking, and he had to think a moment to remember what they'd been discussing. He pushed away the image of her bare breasts and his hands upon them.

"I-I could not, so I did not concern myself with what I could not do. Like my father, I had my servants to help me and advise me."

"Did you trust this Julius? What if he was

working for the enemy? He could tell you anything he pleased, and you'd believe him."

"He was a man of God," Reynald retorted, amused she should even suggest Julius might be a spy.

"So?"

"Do you not trust those around you, Amy?"

"I've learned it's safer not to."

"That must be an uncomfortable way to live."

"At least I *am* alive," she said, then stood up, stretching, before wandering over to the water and pouring a drink.

He followed, and stood watching the curve of her throat as she swallowed. That he could feel such pleasure in something so simple was amazing, and worrying. He needed his wits about him, he needed to concentrate on his task. Amy Fairweather was a distraction, one he'd be better off without, but he couldn't wish her away.

"Sometimes, Rey," she went on, "you have to think for yourself. You know what I mean? Other people have their own agendas and, although they mightn't mean to do it, they can skew the story for their own benefit. Julius, for instance, might see a dragon as a sign from God that he must be punished for some sin he'd committed or had failed to atone for. Others might see it as a pagan sign that the old gods had come to drive out the new. And others would view it differently again. You see what I mean?"

"I always weigh up the advice I am given," he retorted. "I am a Marcher Lord, damsel, and not a fool."

"I know that. I just ... you seem to prefer to trust others' judgment rather than your own. Why is that, Rey?"

He couldn't tell her. Not about Morwenna and the terrible mistake he'd made. If it was true that he didn't entirely trust his own judgment, then that was the reason.

She finished her water and cast him a sideways glance. "I could teach you, you know," she said.

"Teach me?" Once again she'd left him bewildered and confused.

"To read." She seemed almost shy as she made the offer. "That's what I'm studying to be, you know. A teacher," she explained, and it was as if she was afraid he might ridicule her.

One moment she was so strong and sure of herself, and the next so vulnerable. "A teacher of reading?" he asked, puzzled.

"Yes. Is that so strange!" Now she was defensive.

"No, it is just that ... In my time it was only wealthy, learned women who could read and write. My mother read poems and romances, and my father said that was why she was always unhappy, because they misled her in some way." He shrugged. "I think they gave her some happiness in a life that was not happy."

"Reading can do that. Transport you to somewhere else, just for a while." She appeared pensive. "But ordinary men and women did not read and write?"

"No."

"So . . . none of your people can read? None of the children?"

"They ask Julius."

"And this Julius character could tell them whatever he liked, and they'd have to accept it?"

"Julius is a good man—"

"What if your cook was feeling miserable, and wanted to read a poem or two to cheer herself up? What if the butcher wanted to check his profits against his losses? What if the tavern wench wanted to write her lover a letter, to tell him not to come on Saturday because her father would be there?"

His mouth twitched. "They would ask Julius to do it for them."

Amy gave him a look of disgust as if this lack was his fault. "It's wrong. It's not fair."

"Fair?"

"Oh, I forgot. You're a feudal lord, no one gets to vote. Still, I would have thought, as a Marcher Lord, a king in his own kingdom—to quote you—you'd have been a bit more innovative, Rey. After all, if your people could read, they would begin to think for themselves, they wouldn't be so dependent on you. But that's it, isn't it? You're worried that if they think too much for themselves, then they'll rebel against you and . . ." She took a breath. "Well, it'd be the end for men like you."

As usual some of her words were strange, but he understood her meaning well enough to disagree with it. He shook his head. "You are wrong, Amy. I do care for my people. I did not want them harmed. I wanted peace and prosperity, not just for myself but for them, too. My father believed in the glory of war, and I grew up looking at suffering faces and ravaged land. By the time I inherited, I had seen more than enough of starvation. I was determined to take a different road, whatever it cost me."

Amy felt tears sting her eyes and looked away so he wouldn't see how affected she was by his words. He had touched some deep intrinsic belief inside her. The endless fight of right against might, of strong against weak. She had grown up with it on the Parkhill Estate, seen the daily struggle of people to make some sort of life for themselves in difficult conditions.

Now, hearing how Rey felt was like looking into her own heart. Rey wanted to use his power and position to make sure everyone had a fair go; Amy wanted to teach them to read, to think. She wanted to inspire. If she'd had that influence in her life early on, then maybe she wouldn't have had to wait until she was twenty-two years old to turn her life around.

Thrown dangerously off-balance, her only defense was humor. Somehow she dredged up a flip comment.

"A perfect world, eh? I wish you luck then, Rey. In my experience perfect worlds exist only in books and movies."

He seemed to see right through her. "I do not believe you are so cynical. You say you wish to be a teacher, to help children to read? Damsel, you are a good person who wants to help others."

"Rey, you are so wrong!"

He folded his arms. "Then what is it you are striving for?"

"There's a question!"

Until she started the teacher training, Amy hadn't really striven for very much of anything. Her past had been like a dark stain in her life, and it was only recently she'd begun to escape from it. Did anyone really have such high moral goals as Rey? In her experience, people only cared about themselves and their immediate gratification. Which led her to the conclusion that he was either a liar . . . or a rare man indeed.

"Cannot you answer me, Amy? Are you afraid to?"

Amy shook her head. "No, I'm not afraid to. I was thinking that, given our differences—you being a Marcher Lord and all—we're actually quite similar. I think the world would be a far better place if the strong looked after the weak. I don't know . . . the older I get, the more cruelty I seem to see around me, and I want to make a difference. I want to change things for the better."

"You *are* the woman I thought you to be."

"I assure you, I'm not!"

But he didn't believe her; she could tell by the glint in his eyes.

Time to change the subject.

Amy cleared her throat. "Where is this chronicle you were talking about?"

Annoyingly, he smiled, as if he'd won some contest between them, and reached inside his tunic. The thin, magazine-sized book he pulled out had been photocopied from the original. The back section was a translation of the Latin into modern English. Amy cast a wary eye over it.

"I'm no expert, but I think it's a bit like a Book of Days. He writes about what was happening in spring and summer and winter and so on . . ." She read to herself for a moment.

Lord Reynald de Mortimer ordered that the crops be sown in the northern fields this year because of the dampness of the meadows along the river. He gave grain to those who were in want, and instructed his stonemasons to begin work on the new hospice for the old and infirm, to provide them with some shelter when the snows come.

"Does he speak of the dragon?"

She swallowed her emotion, and met Reynald's

eyes. There was impatience and anxiety lurking beneath his usual calm. His pale hair seemed to glow in the subdued lighting of the gym, almost like a ghost.

The Ghost.

Hastily she flipped through to the final pages. "Ah . . . Here's something.

> *"Reynald said that there would be peace, but even as the ink was drying upon the papers of agreement between him and the Welsh, death was approaching on the wind. When the 'dragon' came, it took all before it. Those who could stood and fought. Lord Reynald did not run from his enemy, and was consumed. I, Julius, was struck down and lay like one dead for two days before men arrived from Shrewsbury, but I could not walk and never did again."*

"Aye," Reynald said decisively, "I see where the problem lies. He speaks the truth, but that truth was been twisted. *Dragon* has been taken to mean the Welsh arriving to deal death by battle, and that is not right."

"Maybe whoever translated couldn't accept that there really was a dragon, so they decided it was a metaphor. I can understand that, Rey. It *is* hard to swallow. I don't even know if I can swallow it."

"You still do not believe me," he said, bleakly.

"Rey, I just don't know . . ." Amy glanced at the

clock on the wall. "I'm sorry to be boring, but I'd better get changed for the cocktail party. Jez will never forgive me if I don't turn up and charm Nicco."

Rey caught her arm to stop her. For a moment she was only aware of his strength, the heat of his fingers; then his words brought her back to reality.

"Why must you flatter such a man, damsel? What is it your brother wants from him that he must use you as the sacrificial goat?"

Amy felt her face flush. "That's my business," she said angrily, and pulled away. Her heart thumping, she started up the stairs.

She heard him begin to follow her, then stop. Tempted as she was to leave him there, something made her turn and look down at him. He was staring back into the gym, rigid.

"Rey? What is it? What's the matter?"

Slowly and unwillingly, sensing more trouble, she retraced her steps. "Rey?"

"Look, damsel," he said hoarsely. "Can you not see?"

She followed his pointing finger, then she saw it, too. On the far side of the gym, by a door with a sign that read STAFF ONLY.

The monk with the lantern.

Fifteen

"You again!"

Furiously, Amy started forward, but Reynald grabbed her around the waist, swinging her back into his arms. She felt vibrant and warm, but he couldn't afford to be distracted again.

"Take care," he warned. "This creature almost led me to my death."

Amy tilted her head to stare up at him, her curls brushing his chin. "When?" she breathed.

"Last night. I followed it out onto the walls, and I almost fell from them."

She drew a deep breath. "Rey, a few hours ago the same thing happened to me. I thought it was a . . . a monk, but whatever it is, it took me into a disused part of the castle and tried to send me down through a hole in the floor."

He stared back at her. Amy had almost died, too? His eyes narrowed and he felt an anger such as he'd never known flare up inside him. She was his, how dare anyone try to hurt her! His arm tightened around her, and he gazed down steadily into her pale and anxious face.

"You were not injured?"

"No, of course not."

His mouth twitched. "Of course not," he echoed. The apparition was swaying slightly, the light pulsing, as if waiting for them.

"Who is it? *What* is it?" Amy demanded.

"I thought it was Julius, but what reason would he have to hate me?"

"You'll need to give it some thought, but in the meantime . . . do we go after it?" Her hands rested on his arm, and she seemed to nestle against him.

The apparition was at the open door, seemingly about to slip through.

"Yes, we go after it. But very carefully, Amy. You must stay by me."

She nodded, and he heard the echo of his words in his head. *Stay by me.* He liked the sound of them. If only she *could* stay by him. But it was impossible. He and she were from different worlds.

With a sense of inevitability, he opened his arms and let her go.

She set off across the gym, then paused, glancing behind when he didn't follow. "Rey? Aren't you coming with me?"

"Aye, I am," he said, and wished he could say more, as he strode after her.

Beyond the door, there were more steps, dropping away into the shadows. Amy fiddled with a switch on the wall, then swore softly, and said, "The light isn't working."

"Then we will move slowly and carefully, and you will keep behind me."

"Will I?"

"Yes." He sensed she wasn't one to take orders without good reason, and this was how it should be, but he needed her to listen to him. She wasn't a fool, and she didn't disappoint him.

"Lead on then, my lord."

He smiled as he moved forward. After a moment he felt her hand press to the middle of his back. "You know," she said quietly, "I can usually take care of myself, but I'm glad you're here. In fact, I'm *really* glad you're here, Rey."

Reynald was watching the light. It had steadied, as if whoever was holding it was waiting for them to catch up before moving onward. Unless the apparition had laid another trap?

"Together we are safe," he said, reassuring her.

Her hand turned into a finger, and she gave him a gentle poke. "You have a way with words," she whispered. "I like it."

He was tempted to stop then and take her into his arms. He wanted to kiss her like a man suffering from thirst drinks from a stream. It required all his long years of training to enable him to resist.

"You said you thought it might be Julius," Amy murmured behind him. "What would he have against you? From what I read in his chronicle, he sounded to me as if he admired you."

"We were not always in agreement," he admitted. "He did not like Angharad, but he did not understand her and why I needed her. Julius did not trust the word of the Welsh. I tried to explain to him that I needed to understand them, to speak with them, so that I could persuade them to make peace with us. Angharad helped me do that, but Julius would not listen."

"So he didn't like her because she was Welsh, is that what you're saying?"

"He didn't like her because he didn't trust her."

"You said that you speak a little Welsh. Couldn't you have negotiated with them yourself? Then you wouldn't have needed Angharad—cut out the middlewoman, I say."

"Julius suggested that, too, but I felt Angharad was a wiser choice. It was just that she and Julius clashed over his religion. Angharad prayed to a god other than Julius's."

"She was a pagan," Amy said. "Well, I can understand a priest not liking that."

The stairs came to an end, and they found themselves in another of those long, narrow corridors. Behind him Amy gave a groan. "What *is* this place?" Her hand had tightened on a fold of his tunic, clinging tighter, as if afraid he'd leave her behind.

"This is the tunnel from the keep to the garrison," Reynald explained calmly. "If we were ever under attack with arrows, or trebuchets hurling fire—"

"Trebuchets?"

"Catapults."

"Ah, go on."

"If we were ever under attack from the air, damsel, then it was safer to use this tunnel than run across the open bailey."

She thought about that for a moment, then she said, "It smells like rotten meat."

Reynald nodded in agreement. "It does. Perhaps something has died down here." He reached back to touch her arm. "Remember, damsel, stay by me."

And heard her murmured reply, "Oh, I will, Rey, believe me, I will . . ."

The light from the apparition was fading into the distance, and Reynald quickened his pace and set off after it. All his senses were alert for danger, although some of them were all too aware of Amy's small, warm hand on his back. Around them, the tunnel walls were rough, hewn into the rock that formed the base of his castle, but it looked as if the floor had been kept clean and clear of debris. Apart from the guiding light ahead of them, everything was dark. And silent. Aside from their footsteps, and Amy's soft breath at his back, Reynald couldn't hear a thing.

Could the figure they were following really be Julius? It did not seem to fit. Julius, although strict and at times difficult, had been a good man at heart. Reynald couldn't imagine him wanting to hurt anyone in this underhand way. And why? What would it gain him? Revenge for his afflictions? Julius would be more likely to use his inability to walk after the attack as a reason to count his blessings in other areas of his life. He had been a most devout man.

"Where's he going now?"

Amy's voice intruded on his thoughts. He looked ahead and saw that the light was moving upward. "There are steps leading up into the gatehouse where the garrison is . . . was. Where I nearly fell last night."

"Maybe he's going to try again?" She was pressing to his side—the tunnel was narrow, but she'd squeezed in beside him. "Rey, if you are who you say you are, then I can understand why your life might be at risk. But why me?"

"Because we have been joined together by the witch." He looked down at her, and saw both fear and courage at war in her eyes. "Whatever is up there doesn't want me to succeed, or you to help me."

Inside the gatehouse it was just as gloomy as the tunnel. Reynald moved slowly and cautiously, aware of Amy. She'd taken his hand—not his sword hand, he noticed—and he let her. He could not remember the last time a woman had held his hand like this. Certainly not since he grew from a child.

He liked it.

They reached the top of the wall, feeling a blast of frigid air as they left the shelter of the gatehouse behind them. As Reynald peered ahead through the growing darkness, sleet stung his face, and he began to shake with the cold. Not surprisingly, the weather didn't seem to be impeding the movements of the apparition.

"We're going to die," Amy muttered. "Although you're probably used to the elements. You'll be telling me that this is nothing compared to the weather you've been out in."

He laughed. "'Tis true, I am not one to feel the cold—"

"You're hot," she said, and then for some reason blushed, as if she'd embarrassed herself.

"—but even I would not go out in a blizzard if I could avoid it."

"I think you're capable of anything."

She meant it, he could tell. She believed him to be a heroic figure. Rey wished it was so, to please her, but the mere fact of her believing it was sweet. An ember of warmth in the pit of his stomach.

She startled him by grabbing his arm with her other hand. "Rey! He's stopped."

She was right, the light had stopped. Reynald

watched as it appeared to hover just beyond them, on the other side of the battlements. Fifty feet down below was the drawbridge and the moat. It was impossible for any living thing to be suspended in the air without ropes or chains, or without falling to its death.

"Is it Julius?" Amy's teeth chattered beside him.

Reynald peered closely, but could not distinguish the figure's identity no matter how he tried.

"I think it's a woman," she said suddenly.

"Why do you think that?" Such a thing had not occurred to Reynald.

"I don't know . . . Just a feeling."

The light began to get brighter, dazzling them, just as it had before. Reynald put up his hand to shield his eyes and turned his head aside. If the apparition was tempting them to step out into nothing and fall to their deaths, then it would fail this time. He was about to call out to it jeeringly that it could not hurt them, when there was a thunderous roar.

The glowing light had formed a ball, and now it was moving toward them at high speed. Amy screamed, and he pulled her into his arms, bending to protect her with his body as the light came at them, crackling and hissing. He ducked to one side, just as it passed, and could feel the intense heat radiating from it. The skin and hairs on his arm felt seared. He looked up in time to see the ball tumble forward over the wall and down into the bailey, out of sight.

Fearing the apparition might be preparing another attack, he turned his head to face it again, only to realize that it seemed to be spent. It was shimmering, silhouetted against the darkening sky, and it began to fade and return to wherever it had come from. In another moment it was gone.

Amy had gone to peer over the battlements, and he followed. There was a scorched circle where the ball of light had struck the ground, but no other damage. Still, if it had struck them, it might have been a different matter. He had felt the heat of the thing as it passed.

"That could have killed us," Amy echoed his thoughts, and her voice was higher than usual. She stepped into his arms, and suddenly he was holding her. But she was holding him, too, her arms fastened about his waist, her cheek pressed hard to his chest.

"It tried to kill us, but it failed," he reminded her. "We are safe, Amy."

"But it will try again?"

"Yes, I believe so." There was no point in lying to her. "Whatever it is, it seems determined to stop us."

In the past few minutes the weather had grown even darker and colder. Amy's body was shaking uncontrollably, and he drew her still closer against him, trying to infuse her with his own heat.

She snuggled in with a sigh, then lifted her head to look up at him, her sharp chin digging into his breastbone. He knew then that he was going to kiss her, but the question was whether he'd fight with his conscience first, or not bother.

"Rey?" she whispered.

He decided not to bother, and bending his head, covered her lips with his own. She tasted sweet and clean, like springwater, and her lips were chilled. Her mouth wasn't, and he gave a ragged groan at the first mating of her tongue with his.

She circled his neck with her hands, clinging on, and he drew her even closer into his body. It occurred to him that any number of his enemies could have crept up behind him then, and he wouldn't have cared. Every part of him was fully concentrated on the feel and taste of Amy.

Her body fit so neatly into his, and despite his greater height, he didn't have to strain his neck to bend down to her. He wanted her. The need was overwhelming. Unstoppable. Amy was no Morwenna, and he was no innocent youth. They were woman and man, and for the first time in his adult life, he had found both the desire and the opportunity to mate with a woman. The woman of his dreams.

* * *

Amy tried to collect her thoughts, which was difficult when she was being kissed so wonderfully and held by a big strong man like Rey. The lust that had been simmering in her veins ever since she first saw him was intensifying to an unbearable pitch. She knew if she didn't make a move soon, she wouldn't be going anywhere.

Rey drew her closer, his big, warm hands clamped onto her back. She pressed her palms flat against his chest, telling herself she needed to push him away now, before this went any further. There was Jez to consider, and Nicco, and her sanity . . .

And then she heard a sound behind her.

"Rey," she breathed shakily, withdrawing her mouth from his. Her palms weren't pressing him away after all, they were caressing him. His eyes were still closed, and his lips sought hers, like a man in a dream who didn't want to wake up.

Amy probably would have let him kiss her again, she was already closing her own eyes. And then she heard it. The dry rustling of wings and the soft, sinister scraping of claws on stone.

Sixteen

"*Rey!*" *she shrieked.* "*There's something* behind us!"

His trance dropped from him instantly, and he was himself again. He'd pushed her behind him, as if to protect her, as he turned to face the threat. Amy, at the back of him, couldn't see a thing.

"I'm interrupting you, Ghost."

The voice was softly feminine and yet immensely powerful. It brought the goose bumps up on Amy's arms. Cautiously, she peered around him, then wondered if she was now completely insane.

There was a large eagle with glowing blue eyes sitting on the crenelated battlements, and it was speaking.

"My apologies, my lady. I didn't hear you."

Rey answered the bird as if that was perfectly normal. Amy stared, openmouthed.

"I have come to see how you are progressing, my Ghost. Your time is limited; you cannot waste it." At this, the eagle flashed a sideways look at Amy and seemed to smirk with its beak. There was another freezing gust of wind, and it shifted its feet and ruffled its feathers. Somehow seeing the cold make it uncomfortable made Amy more comfortable. She edged a step away from Rey.

"I know my time is short, lady, but this is a very strange world you have sent me into," Rey was saying in an even voice. Amy, glancing at his hand by his side, where it was clenched into a tight fist, thought he was probably understating the matter.

"And yet it appears as if you have made some friends?" The eagle chortled. It turned its blue eyes to Amy, leaving them there, and suddenly she felt very exposed.

"Eh, hello," she managed.

"Amy Fairweather."

It knew her name!

"Do not fail me or my Ghost. It is important that he completes his task so that he can return to his own time and try again. So that he can right the wrong."

"You mean . . . so that he can change history?" Despite herself, she sounded accusing.

"Of course. Why not?" the bird retorted. "Reynald de Mortimer was a great man, but he was meant to be far greater. A man ahead of his time, with ideas that will inspire others far into the future. He must succeed."

"And I am here to help him with this?" Amy confirmed. "A bit old-fashioned, isn't it, the submissive, little woman and the big, strong man? What do I get out of it?"

The bird's eyes flared so brightly they were like the approaching headlights on an express train, as it roared toward her. She felt dizzy, her legs wobbly, and instinctively reached out for Rey. He caught her, holding her upright.

The bird was lecturing her in a voice that seemed to reverberate in her brain. "Are you so mercenary, Amy Fairweather, that you can do nothing without payment? Are you so smug with your position in the world that there is nothing lacking? If you say yes, then I will know you are lying!"

The eagle was absolutely terrifying, and the power coming from it was playing havoc with her senses. Shaking, her head swimming, she looked upon it, and for a moment thought she saw a woman's face imposed upon the bird's. Young and sweet, but with an awe-inspiring strength. In another moment it was gone as if it had never been, and Rey was holding her up, his breath comfortingly warm against her temple.

"No, I am neither smug nor satisfied," she said croakily. "If you know me at all, then you know that. And you must also know that I'm not the right person for this job!"

The eagle's voice grew gentler, but it was no less frightening. "I do know you. I know everything about you. That is why I have chosen you, Amy. You have a part to play in something far greater than most mortals ever experience. Do not disappoint me."

The bird rose with a flapping of wings.

"Do not disappoint yourself!" it shrieked.

In a moment it was gone into the dark night. There was silence, apart from the faint sounds of music coming from the cocktail party on the far side of the castle, as Rey and Amy caught their breath.

"I think I've seen everything now," Amy whispered. "Was that . . . ?"

Rey knew what she meant, which was just as well because she doubted she could have finished her sentence.

"Aye, that was the witch from the between-worlds."

"You really are Reynald de Mortimer, aren't you?"

He smiled down at her, and his pale eyes glowed with a gentle light. "Damsel, you knew that," he said quietly.

"Did I? Maybe I did, but most of the time I told myself I was just humoring you."

It was as if she were looking at him for the first

time. Really *looking*. Because this was a man who had walked and talked and lived seven hundred years ago. A great and powerful lord, who controlled the destiny of many. Who had an ability to think far ahead of his time and beyond the casual brutality of his peers. And here he was, with her, and a moment ago she'd been in his arms, and he'd been kissing her.

Amy turned away. She felt shaken with doubt and guilt. "I should have made it plainer to the witch. This really is a mistake."

He frowned, puzzled. "Why should it be a mistake? The witch does not make mistakes."

"Well, she has this time!" Amy set off along the path on top of the wall. She hardly noticed the flurries of snow around her, or the bleak night landscape. The lights, fixed at irregular intervals on the crenelations, began to blur as tears filled her eyes.

"Amy? Where are you going?" he sounded worried.

"Away."

"But . . . why?"

"I'm not who you think I am, Rey. Really, I'm not!"

"I need you." He was right behind her. She should have known he wouldn't let her get away that easily.

Amy turned to face him and could have wept. The expression in his eyes was everything she wanted to see, but she had to destroy it. For both their sakes.

She could never be the kind of woman he needed by his side. The enormity of it was mind-blowing. Better to put an end to it now than to pretend that maybe it would be all right.

He was still looking at her, and somehow he had her frozen hands in his. Had she given them to him? She didn't remember. She had to do this thing, now, before she stepped forward and into his arms.

"Listen to me, Rey."

"I do not need to listen. I know you, Amy."

"You don't! Rey, for God's sake, listen . . ."

He was obediently silent, watching her, waiting with a faint smile.

She started speaking, almost babbling, because she was afraid that if she didn't she'd never say what she had to.

"My father was a thief. My brother is a thief. He's here this weekend to steal Nicco's priceless diamond—it's called the Star of Russia, and it belonged to Queen Catherine the Great. Jez asked me to help him find out where Nicco keeps it hidden. I said yes. Do you understand what I'm saying? I said yes!"

She could see the confusion in his face. "Your brother . . . ?"

"Jez and I are here to lie and cheat our way into Nicco's life. He has something Jez wants, and I'm the bait. I'm the lure, Rey, and I'll do anything to get that jewel."

He shook his head. "Jez has forced you to do this—"

"He hasn't. You're thinking this isn't my fault, that I'm a poor weak-minded woman who's been persuaded to agree to something that goes against her principles. But you're wrong. I agreed to do this. And I've done it before. I've lied and cheated, *and* stolen. I've done worse. I'm no innocent. I . . . I've used myself to get what I wanted. I've slept with men. So I'm not the person you think I am, Rey. I'm not good or honest or fine. I'm someone else altogether."

His face seemed to have flattened out, losing all expression. Apart from his eyes. They were bleak and icy. She kept her chin up, so he wouldn't see how much it was hurting her to shatter his good opinion of her.

This is for the best.

"No," he said, but all feeling had left his voice. "You are lying now, damsel. Tell me you are not the person you have just described. Tell me!"

"Yes, I am," she whispered. He turned away from her, and she couldn't help but cry out, "Rey, I'm sorry!"

He didn't even pause in his measured stride, just kept walking back the way they had come. Shivering, not knowing what else to do, Amy set off along the wall. Ahead of her, she knew, was the warmth and noise of the cocktail party, but it didn't make her feel any better. Tears ran down her cheeks as she accepted the truth, that she wasn't the woman for Rey.

But that's all right. I'm doing okay, and after the weekend this part of my life will be over with. No more Nicco. No more of Jez's schemes. I can start again.

Except Rey wouldn't be with her. And she'd never have the chance to help him to return to the past and make right his wrong.

Seventeen

She was a liar, and she'd lied to him. She wasn't who he thought she was. Amy meant to steal from Nicco, and to do it she was willing to do, and be, whatever she had to. He understood what she'd been trying to tell him.

To get what she wanted, she'd give Nicco her body.

The knowledge made the Ghost feel very hollow inside. As if he had suddenly lost something very important to him, even though he wasn't sure exactly what it was.

He strode back through the tunnel, not seeing what was in front of him, seething with anger, aching with pain. No matter how he tried to rationalize what he was feeling, to tell himself she was a stranger who meant nothing to him, he couldn't shake off his dark melancholy. The woman of his dreams was nothing but a lie. The cold, dank passageway seemed to fit his mood perfectly.

He tried to refocus his mind on his task.

The figure with the light appeared to be Julius, but Reynald didn't believe it. The monk was a trick, a deceit, behind which the real culprit was hiding.

Just like Amy.

He'd turned full circle, and the melancholy washed over him again. As if he were trying to outpace it, he climbed the steps into the gym two at a time. The medieval cocktail party was being held in a place called the Long Gallery, and he set off toward it, thinking he might as well drown his sorrows there as be alone with them.

The Long Gallery had once been divided into a series of chambers, with Julius's chapel at one end. Now it was one long room, the walls hung with the painted images of stern men and their sterner women. None of them looked particularly friendly, he thought, peering into their faces. He didn't know them, they were strangers, apart from the large figure in the position of honor—an alcove with draped curtains.

The portrait was meant to be him, but the representation wasn't a very good one. Apart from the fair hair and gray eyes, it could have been anyone.

If he didn't die in 1299, he thought, glancing once

more down the long lines of strangers, then those faces would have been his descendants. Men and women with gray eyes . . . and red curls.

He groaned. *Jesu, am I going insane?*

"Champagne, sir?" The boy with the drink tray arrived at exactly the right time.

Reynald snatched up a glass and downed the liquid in two gulps. It fizzed in his nose and throat. He took another glass and downed that, too, before the boy edged away.

"You looked like you needed that."

Reynald narrowed his eyes at the unfamiliar woman beside him with her frizz of gray hair and sharp eyes. Another stranger. His castle was full of strangers.

"Miriam Ure," she introduced herself. "Sans the wig."

It was the "authority." He almost groaned aloud for a second time.

"Have you changed your mind about the dragon?" she asked, with a smirk. "I believe Mr. Coster lent you the copy of Julius's Chronicle, with my translation."

"Yes, I have it." The potion in the glass had made him feel more at ease with his surroundings— dangerously relaxed. "And your translation is right. Julius said there was a dragon, because there *was* a dragon. It is the meaning you place on the word that is wrong."

Miriam tittered.

Reynald leaned closer. "A huge dragon, breathing fire and smoke."

"Perhaps you should write fiction."

He reached over her head as the boy with the tray passed by on the other side and plucked up another glass, taking a swallow. "Was the castle burned?" he asked abruptly.

Miriam blinked. "Yes, it was."

"Completely?"

"No, not completely. The battlements and some of the upper rooms were damaged, but the great hall and the lower areas were untouched."

Reynald smiled. "Tell me then, Lady Authority, how that could be? How is it that the upper parts of the castle are burned and the lower parts are untouched? What if a dragon flew over and blew fire over the castle, would that explain it?"

"Or a flaming arrow could have lodged in the roof."

He threw up his hands in disgust, spilling champagne. "Have it your own way!" As he moved from her side, a couple of smiling women started toward him but, seeing the grim expression on his face, changed their minds. *Good.* Reynald didn't want to be nice to anyone. Why should he be? This was his home, and these people were not welcome.

He wasn't in a good mood. He feared that something inside him was broken; if not his heart, then some other important organ. He wanted to smash something, or sweat it out of himself in the training yard. He wanted to be himself again, cold and emotionless, with no thought of wrapping his arms about a woman and holding her . . . Holding her tightly, safely, against him, and kissing her soft lips until he died of the pleasure.

Reynald cursed and strode over by the curtained alcove, the portrait behind him, and stood watching the interlopers at their foolishness. If only he could order them all to leave, or threaten them with his sword and send them running from his presence, how much happier he'd be. Why should they enjoy themselves when he was suffering?

"Have you seen my sister?"

This time it was Jez who interrupted him. Reynald glowered back at him. This was the man who had destroyed Amy's life. She might have tried to tell him differently, but Reynald didn't want to believe her. In his experience, young women were the prey of any male relative who could find a use for them, so if anyone was to blame for Amy's predicament, then it was her brother.

Jez didn't wait for an answer. "She was supposed to be here by now." His eyes slid past to the portrait, and he nodded toward it. "Nasty customer."

"What do you mean?" Reynald demanded, suddenly feeling protective about the painting, even if it was poorly done.

"I mean he looks like he'd lock you in the dungeon before he'd give you the time of day."

Reynald shook his head. The speech of these people was utterly confusing. Why could they not say what they meant in plain English?

"He looks a bit like you, you know," Jez was continuing. "Around the eyes. Not much, though. You should be grateful for that, I suppose."

His bad mood ratcheted up a notch, and suddenly he wanted . . . he *needed* a confrontation with this man, who in his heart he blamed for Amy's situation.

"Why are you your sister's whoremaster?"

Jez stiffened. "Her what?" There was fire in his eyes.

Good! thought Reynald. He wanted a fight, and if he couldn't have it with Amy, then Jez would do very well in her stead.

"That is what I call a man who uses his sister the way you use Amy. Whoremaster."

Jez took a step closer, getting into his face. "My sister is her own person. I'm not using her in any way. Though what business it is of yours, you bastard, I—"

"Liar."

Jez's face tightened around the eyes and mouth, but he had remarkable self-control. "You're an arrogant son of a bitch, aren't you?"

Their exchange had been quiet until now, but as the people around them became aware of the developing situation, they stopped their own conversations to listen.

"You are a cheat and a liar, and you have made of her the same."

"I haven't done anything to her. She chooses her own path."

"You have no honor!"

The two men's faces were now only an inch apart. Jez's eyes were glittering, and his nostrils flaring like a warhorse scenting blood. "I'll break your neck for what you've said."

Reynald grinned. *This* was the real Jez. Not the calm, controlled man, but the assassin with the sharp knife. "I could spit you like a pig," he said softly. "Just say the word, and we will fight to the death."

"I'm saying the word then," Jez said.

"What the hell is going on here?" It was Amy.

Reynald had been so absorbed in his verbal struggle with Jez, he hadn't realized she was here. Startled, he looked up, quickly sobering. Amy was standing with her hands on her hips, glaring furiously from him to Jez and back again. It didn't help that she was wearing a tight black dress, cut low at the front and exposing a swell of bosom. Reynald swallowed.

"Amy," Jez tried a smile, his temper reined in. "I was, eh, beginning to, eh, wonder where you'd got to . . ."

"Well, I'm here now," she snapped. "Is someone going to tell me what's going on?"

Clearly, Reynald thought, she wanted an answer.

Her gaze turned on him, green eyes flashing, and he understood Jez's stammer. An angry Amy was certainly formidable. But at the same time his heart leapt at the beauty of her.

"This is talk between men," he said, all the colder because he didn't want her to know how much her presence affected him.

She snorted. And then she poked him, hard, in the chest with her finger. "That is just so much crap, Rey!"

Her finger hurt, and he winced, rubbing his chest.

Her eyes were even greener than before. "This is about me, isn't it?"

Neither of them answered.

"Well? Are both of you cowards?"

"We were planning a fight to the death, actually," Jez said, with a smug sideways glance at Reynald. "It was your boyfriend's idea. I wouldn't know one end of a sword from another."

"A fight to the—" For a moment she was too shocked to carry on.

"Your brother wishes to break my neck." Reynald could tell tales, too.

"Stop it!" she gasped. "Just stop it, both of you. Don't you understand? My life is none of your business."

"Sweetheart—"

"Don't you dare 'sweetheart' me," she hissed at her brother. "Just leave me alone!"

"Amy," Reynald moved to touch her, but she flung her hand out at him, knocking his away.

"Both of you!" she burst out. Suddenly, as if it was too much for her, her eyes filled with tears. She pushed her way through the interested circle of observers, hurrying away down the room.

Reynald stood, feeling the place where her finger had touched him. It was aching deep inside his chest, as if she had bruised his heart.

Jez took a shaky breath and turned to Rey, ready to rip into him again. But the expression on the other man's face stopped him. Rey looked as if he were suffering from a broken heart. And now he remembered Amy's pale face.

Were they in love?

It seemed incredible, or maybe he was the fool because he hadn't noticed earlier. Did Amy really care for this man after such a short acquaintance? It was infatuation, he decided uneasily, that was all. It must be. Love wasn't going to fit in with his plans.

"Jez!"

Nicco had arrived in a beige suit, simpering, thinking himself the most admired man in the room. Listening to his list of petty complaints about the hotel and life in general, Jez smiled and wished he could tell Nicco what he really thought of him. He deserved to be brought down off that pedestal, to be kicked in the teeth—metaphorically speaking, of course. Once Amy would have loved to take on the job, she'd have reveled in it. What had happened to her?

Jez refused to believe he was using her in the way Rey accused him. He loved his sister, and he always had. When their father was drinking and violent, it was always Jez who'd taken Amy away from the flat, waiting until things quieted down again. It was Jez who looked out for her when she wasn't his sweet, obedient little sister anymore, and she insisted on coming along on his more reckless escapades. She'd said she didn't want his help then, but he'd always been there, in the background.

It had been to get her out of the wild life she was drifting into that he'd offered her the job as his partner in his first scheme. She had to worm her way into the confidence of an "importer of fine arts" and find out the date of his next shipment— stolen antiques from the Cairo Museum. Even then, Jez wasn't an ordinary criminal.

Amy had come through with flying colors, and their partnership continued from there. Until recently, when they'd drifted apart. He'd been aware of it, but he'd been busy himself, and besides, Amy was a big girl now. But Jez would never hurt her. He truly believed his schemes were as much for her sake as his. And what about the Star of Russia? He was depending on her to find out where Nicco had it hidden, and she'd promised to help. Was she really about to back out of a promise for the sake of an arrogant bastard she'd only just met?

An image of her face flashed into his head, tears filling her eyes, her mouth trembling. She'd looked heartbroken.

She'll be fine once it's finished, he told himself, plucking out the seed of guilt that was trying to germinate inside him. *Besides, I need her.*

If Amy's promise to him was causing tension between her and Rey, then surely that was for her to sort out? And if Rey was such a bastard he couldn't love her for herself, then he didn't deserve her, did he?

As far as Jez was concerned it was business as usual.

He put a friendly arm around Nicco's shoulders, walking him as far away from Rey as he could. "Amy's around here somewhere," he assured him. "Can I get you some champagne, Nicco? It's the good stuff."

"Thank you." Nicco smiled. "Tonight I hope to celebrate. Do you think Amy will celebrate with me?"

"She talks of nothing else," Jez assured him. Suddenly, out of the blue, he felt disgusted with himself. He knew Amy disliked Nicco just as much as he did. Maybe he *was* the sort of man Rey had accused him of being. He opened his mouth, within seconds of telling Nicco to screw himself, because obviously that was who he really loved, when he was interrupted.

A group of acrobats dressed in costume had

come running into the Long Gallery. They were calling out and clapping their hands, then they started to build a human pyramid. Jez watched them, knowing he was secretly glad he hadn't been able to say anything and hating himself for it. Suddenly he longed passionately for London. He wanted to go home. He was sick and tired of this miserable place in the middle of nowhere.

But that was the trouble wasn't it? He couldn't go home, not unless he knew where the Star of Russia was. The people he owed money to weren't the kind you let down.

He told himself he didn't have a choice.

Eighteen

Amy stood by the bar in her slinky black dress and high heels, simmering. She was furious. How dare they fight over her like that! As if she was some sort of prize in a raffle. She'd agreed to Jez's plan, she'd been prepared to do it, no matter what it cost her where Rey was concerned, and now they'd humiliated her with a public brawl.

She was sick and tired of them both! Jez and his schemes and lies, and Rey with his eagle girlfriend and the seven-hundred-year wrong he had to right. Serve them right if she walked out on them here and now and never—

"Amee . . ."

Oh God, it was Nicco. How could she possibly play her part now, after what had happened? She clenched her hands around her glass and wished him far, far away.

Nicco slid his fingers over the bare skin of her back, making her want to cringe and shrink away from his touch. Somehow she forced herself to turn and face him.

"You are so beautiful tonight." Nicco was oblivious to her emotional state, but that made sense—all he ever thought about was himself.

She was about to tell him she had a headache, when she noticed Rey, watching them from a safe distance. For a moment she was disoriented, struck dumb by him, just as she'd been the first time she saw him. Perhaps she could go over to him and explain, make everything all right, perhaps . . .

It was no use. No explanation would ever change what she was. Amy hardened her resolve to destroy completely any feeling he had for her. And there was one way to do that, wasn't there? She looked at Nicco and gave him her sultriest smile.

"Nicco, babe, where have you been?"

He leaned one hand against the bar and smiled back. "A little injury."

"Oh, does that mean you're out of action?"

"It is nothing."

"Jez said you hurt your back. I hope it isn't too painful?"

"When I see you I feel no pain," he announced, gallantly.

"I'm sure that's not true. I have some antiinflam-matories in—"

"I am fine," he cut her short with a hint of impa-tience. He moved closer, his thigh brushing against hers. "I want you, Amee," he murmured huskily. "You are a woman who can drive men wild."

With Nicco's drawling, affected voice in her ear, Amy found herself looking up again, toward Rey. He was still watching, and he looked angry. Very angry. But whether he was angry with her or Nicco, she wasn't sure.

At least he couldn't slice them in two with his sword—it was safely upstairs in her room. Or send them to his dungeon—the dungeon wasn't in use these days, except as an all-night coffee shop. In fact there wasn't very much he could do at all, which was probably why he looked so cross.

Nicco was still whispering sweet nothings into her ear, but now he had his hand on the curve of her hip, sweaty and heavy.

This is your chance. Ask him about the diamond now. Tease him, go to his room, let him make love to you. You can do it. You've done it before, and you can do it again.

He leaned into her, kissing her neck, and she felt his erection prod her in the belly. A wave of panicked sickness washed over her, and she knew, as she'd known all along but wouldn't admit it, that she couldn't do it.

Not for Jez and not for anyone.

"Nicco," she said, knowing he wasn't going to

take this very well, "I'm worried about your back. I don't want you to do any more damage to it."

"My back is fine," he said, his mouth still cruising.

"Nicco, this will sound strange, but I think I've changed my mind."

He chuckled. "Amee, I will change it back again."

"Nicco, I'm not in the mood. I need to be alone for a while, just to think. A man of your experience would be understanding, I know."

"You don't need to be alone, Amee," he drawled, unconvinced. "Not when I can make you feel so much better."

"Nicco, honestly, I don't want to do this."

"Babe," he groaned, "I'm hard for you." His hand was creeping up her ribs, stroking the underside of her breast.

"Nicco, I'm warning you," she gasped, pulling away and almost falling over in her heels. He caught her arm to steady her.

"You're warning *me*? Oh, I'm frightened." He giggled like a girl.

"Nicco, this is not—"

"You are fire, and I long to burn in your arms. Come to my room, Amee, I have something to show you." He wiggled his eyebrows suggestively. "Something you will like very much."

Oh God. "Thank you for the offer, but I don't want to go to your room," she told him, very clearly, in case he tried to pretend he misunderstood.

"I can make you feel things you have never felt before."

Amy opened her mouth. It was no use, he wouldn't listen. He didn't want to listen. Nicco heard only what Nicco wanted to hear. She was wasting her time.

"Good-bye," she said, and turned to walk away.

Nicco reached out and caught her elbow, stopping her in her tracks. "Oh no, you don't. You are going the wrong way," he said, in a tone that was meant to be playful. "Paradise is over here."

Amy laughed in disbelief and began to walk away a second time.

This time he didn't bother with foreplay. He pulled her back against him, his hips hard against her bottom, and thrust against her as though he thought it was his right to handle her in front of everyone, right there in the middle of the Long Gallery.

Right there in front of Rey.

Amy lost it. In her best self-defense-class move, she grabbed hold of his arm and his hip, and tossed him. As he flipped over, she felt a rush of intense satisfaction. But as he hit the floor with an "Oomph" and lay flat on his back among the startled guests, satisfaction was replaced by horror. What had she done?

"Nicco?" she cried, moving to help him up. But it was too late. He slapped her hand away and crawled crablike away from her, all the while cursing her in a mangled mixture of Russian and English.

She'd failed Jez and Rey, and herself. She felt like a child again, knowing she could never please her father no matter what she did.

Amy turned and ran from the room.

Reynald could hardly believe his eyes. He'd seen Amy and Nicco together, talking. He'd watched them, knowing he shouldn't, but somehow drawn to them and unable to help himself. It was like burning in the fires of hell, but he wanted to prove that he was right, and she wasn't the woman she said she was. That she was his good, sweet Amy.

At first it seemed he would be disappointed. Amy had seemed very happy to see Nicco; she'd even let him press his hands and mouth to her. Reynald had clenched his fists, sick and furious. This was worse than any torture, he'd told himself. He'd been about to walk away, when he sensed a change in Amy. She was glancing toward him, and she was growing agitated.

Then Reynald had seen Nicco grab hold of her. He started toward her with the intention of saving her, but she hadn't needed saving. She'd taken hold of Nicco and thrown him to the ground as if he were nothing more than a bag of straw. He'd never seen a woman do such a thing before, but he'd forgotten that Amy was like no other woman he had ever known. He wanted to cheer for her.

But then he'd seen her face as she ran past him.

She was suffering. Perhaps she really was everything she had told him she was, a liar and a cheat and a woman who used her body as a means of gaining what she wanted. But right now she needed him.

Reynald knew that it was he, of all the men in her life, past and present, and he alone who could soothe her pain. Just as it was only Amy who could save him from an eternity in the between-worlds. They needed each other, and he must make her understand, and accept, that truth.

Reynald strode after her.

She'd left the door ajar, but Reynald didn't allow himself to believe she'd done it on purpose. For him. As he stepped quietly inside, he could hear her, sobbing.

Until then he hadn't thought of her as a woman who wept when her pain was great. His mother had often cried, but she was not strong like Amy. He knew now that Amy was forged in fire, like a sword, and she would never break. Or so he had thought. And now here she was, sobbing as if her heart was in pieces.

He couldn't bear it.

The sound was tearing him in two.

"Amy?" he said, venturing another step inside, and then another.

She stopped crying. "Go away," she ordered in a husky voice.

"I cannot go away, not while you are upset."

"I'm not upset."

"Oh, Amy . . ."

"Don't you understand? Can't I get through to you? I don't *want* you, Rey. I never have."

He sighed. "Whether you want me or not, damsel, I will stay by you. Just as you stayed by me."

She groaned and pounded her fists into the mattress with such fury that he thought she'd injure herself. "Why do men never listen?"

"If you really want me to leave, then you must throw me out," he told her. "Come, I will not struggle."

"I could throw you out, Rey. You saw what I did to Nicco."

"Aye," he replied, with great satisfaction.

She chuckled wetly. "Oh God, what a mess." Then she flopped over onto her back and wiped her face with her fingers, like a child. "Did you see the look on Nicco's face? I've blown it now; he'll never forgive me. And neither will Jez. He trusted me, and I've let him down. All the times he got me out of trouble, and I couldn't even do this one last thing for him."

All amusement had fallen from her, and she lay there, very sober, her eyes filled with misery.

"Your loyalty is commendable, damsel."

Carefully, Reynald sat down beside her on the bed. He didn't want to frighten her, and he didn't want her to send him away. He felt her need of him, tight, in his chest, and it overruled his confusion. He didn't know how he could feel this way about a woman who, in his own time, would be so unworthy of him. He just knew he wanted to stay.

After a moment she spoke again into the silence.

"You hate me, don't you, Rey? Look, I don't blame you. You are so . . . so good. Honorable, that's how I think of you. I could never be like you. I admire you, though, Rey. I really do. You have no idea how much I wish . . ." Her lips trembled, and she shook her head. "Well, what's the point in wishing for something I can't have?"

Reynald shook his head, too. "Amy, I apologize. You love your brother, I see that now, and you want to help him. You have set aside all that is right, to do so. That is a sacrifice of the greatest kind. I don't think I would have the courage to do such a thing."

Reynald felt as if his head was pounding, torn apart by the conflict within him. He had seen with his own eyes the sort of woman Amy was, and she had told him she was a bad person. And yet . . . his heart was telling him something else, to look beneath the words and her past actions, to the woman sitting before him right now.

Amy was looking up at him intently, biting her lips to stop them from trembling. Waiting.

"It's okay, Rey," she whispered. "I don't expect absolution. I don't want it; I am what I am."

He shook his head and said what was in his heart rather than in his head. "I find that I do not care what you have done in the past, Amy. That is behind you now. What is important is what you do from this moment. And I *know* how fine and good you are, Amy. I feel it here." He touched his chest. "Surely that is all that matters?"

It was as if he was trying to convince himself.

She knew it, too. "Rey . . ."

He reached out and stroked her cheek with his fingertip, tracing the warm dampness left from her tears.

Amy reached up and entwined her fingers with his. "I wish that was true." She rubbed her cheek against his hand, and he felt her soft skin against the scars and calluses that came from a lifetime of fighting. "But you're right about one thing. Whatever I did before, this time I don't want any part of Jez's scheme. I know I'll be letting him down, but I just can't—"

"Then you must tell him."

"How can I? He's relying on me. He won't understand."

"He will understand."

"No, Rey, he won't. He needs Nicco's diamond so that he can sell it. He owes money to some dangerous people, people who can hurt him. He's in trouble and he asked for my help and I promised to give it. How can I tell him I've changed my mind now? After all he's done for me?"

"What has he done for you?"

"He looked after me, when we were kids. And later. He protected me from our dad. He was a violent drunk. If it wasn't for Jez, I'd have been on the receiving end of his rages far more than I was." She smiled wanly. "So, you see, I can't let him down, though in my heart I want to . . ." The smile turned into a frown. "Do you think that was why I lost it with Nicco? To make certain he wouldn't want me near him? Oh God, now I'm psychoanalyzing myself. What a mess."

"Damsel . . ."

As if suddenly aware of his hand in hers, she snatched it away and sat up, arranging her dress rather primly. "You don't have to be nice to me, Rey. I'm a disaster, my family is a disaster, and I have a feeling things are only going to get worse after tonight. Feel free to walk away. You have far more important things to worry about than me."

"I want to worry about you, Amy."

She glanced sideways at him, then she sighed and looked him full in the eyes. "There's something special about you. I knew it from the first moment I saw you." She reached out slowly, tentatively, to stroke the ugly scar on his neck. Reynald sat very still, enjoying the feel of her fingers on his skin, so warm and gentle, as if they would heal him after all these years.

Normally, Reynald didn't think about his scar. It had been so long, and he preferred to forget. But now, as she touched him, he remembered that long-ago night, and the fear and horror that accompanied it. That was when he had made his vow, and he'd never had the urge to break it, not once in sixteen years.

Until now.

"Tell me about this," she said, caressing him where the dagger had sliced through his flesh and very nearly ended his life.

"It was a long time ago." But he needed to talk, and she knew it.

"Tell me," she said softly.

Nineteen

The girl's name was Morwenna, and she was young and beautiful. Lithe and fair, she had slanting black eyes and a shy smile that also had a fascinating knowing quality to it. As if she possessed a wisdom far beyond her years.

He was smitten the first time he saw her. But then he was at an age to be smitten by love. Not lust. Reynald was the sort of boy who lifted women above mere receivers of his baser instincts. Perhaps he had inherited something of his mother's romantic nature, but he was firm in his beliefs: that a lord must be pure and good to all those of lesser standing than himself; that he must abide by the rules and laws of the world he lived in; that he must love God and try to be fair; and that he must always be honorable.

Morwenna was his mother's new serving maid, and from the little glances she was sending him, he knew she admired him, too. Reynald started stammering in her presence, and his face would flush bright red. If she didn't know how he felt before, he told himself, then she knew it after that.

And so she did.

Her shy smiles grew more frequent, and her glances lingered, and sometimes he was sure that she brushed against him apurpose as she was moving by.

Then, one memorable night, she came to him in the darkness.

"My lord," she whispered, standing by his bed. She was wearing a robe made of dull wool, but she made it beautiful.

He took her in his arms, a little clumsy and inexperienced, but he loved her truly and was eager to please and be pleased. There was no resistance, she came willingly, melting against him, and their mouths fused in a hot, mindless passion he would never forget.

He was so bound up in the pleasure of the moment—his first love—that at first he didn't feel the pain. Only an unpleasant stinging at his throat, and then a sudden warmth as liquid began to spill over his chest and shoulder. He reached up to touch it, and held his fingers up to the light of the rush.

Blood.

He didn't believe it, but he knew at the same

time that she had hurt him, and he had to stop her. With a cry, he flung her off him and the bed. He heard the dagger clatter to the floor.

She began to scream like a banshee, as if she were the wounded party. But by then Reynald was clutching at his throat, wondering if the spinning in his head and the gathering dark lassitude meant he was dying. There was blood everywhere.

Servants came running. And his mother, wailing, with terror in her eyes when she saw her son. The last thing he remembered, before the blackness swept over him, was the girl he had loved being held by two men, her face twisted with fury and hatred. She looked like a stranger.

"Why did she do it?" Amy's voice was bringing him back. "Apart from the fact I can't imagine setting out to seduce someone, then trying to kill him, she must have known she'd be punished."

"She was acting under orders."

"You mean she was—"

"Aye, an assassin."

"Oh Rey, Rey," she breathed, her fingers fluttering over him, until he caught them and stilled them in his.

"My father had many enemies, damsel. We never found out which of them realized that the best way to deal my father a mortal blow was to murder his only son and heir. Me."

Amy was resting her head on his shoulder, and

her breath warmed him. "What happened to the girl?"

"My father had her killed, or maybe he killed her himself. He was like a madman, they told me afterwards. Morwenna was tossed from the north tower, down into the ravine. They searched for her body, but it was never found. Her bones are probably still there, somewhere. No one could have survived such a fall."

She shuddered.

"Sometimes in the night I hear her screaming. I knew nothing of what was happening at the time, so it must be a dream, although it always seems very real."

"I've seen the ceiling painting. I didn't realize what it meant."

"Morwenna floating through the sky with the birds? Aye," he said grimly. "I think the artist was drunk at the time."

She chuckled.

"I was close to death, for many weeks I struggled to live, and even then I recovered very slowly. So slowly. It took me a long time to heal."

She murmured sympathetically, snuggling closer, and her curls tickled his throat.

"I made a vow as I lay in my bed. I swore that I would remain chaste until I met a woman I could trust completely."

"And did you? Remain chaste?"

"Aye. There has been no one I have lain with

since. There were women I have kissed, even embraced, but we have never given our bodies to each other. I haven't broken my vow, damsel."

She stroked his scar, and he knew her fingers would be gentle, although he could barely feel her touch. Although his flesh had closed over the wound, healed in a fashion, he had never regained all sensation in the area. He would never be as he was. He was scarred in body and mind and heart; Morwenna had seen to that.

"I can't believe you haven't been tempted, Rey, even a little bit," she said, a smile in her voice. "You're still a man. Even if you are just about perfect."

He smiled, too. Her body against his was arousing him, and the sound of her voice was like an aphrodisiac. "I am very much a man, damsel," he said, his voice dropping, "and I have met many beautiful women. But whenever I thought of breaking my vow, I swiftly remembered Morwenna, and it was enough to sober me. No matter how beautiful those women were, in my heart I didn't trust them."

Amy shifted away so that she could look up and meet his gaze. It was almost dark in the room, apart from the light from the lamp, and he could see the gleam in her green eyes and the shine of her lips. He wanted to kiss her and put a stop to the talk, but there were things to be said before they could take the next step forward.

"Do you trust *me?*" she whispered.

There was so much unspoken in her question. The reasons she was here with Jez, what she had done in the past, her murky confession. It was as if she was asking him how it was possible for him to trust her, after all that.

Reynald wanted to tell her that he trusted her more than any other woman he had ever known, that despite what she had told him of her reasons for being here—or perhaps because of it—he believed in her completely and forever. The words were there, in his head, but he couldn't utter them—he would be lying. There were too many conflicting emotions pulling him one way and then another. In the end all he said was, "In this moment, damsel, yes, I trust you."

He knew it wasn't the answer she wanted, but to heal the sadness in her eyes, he began to kiss her, his lips gentle, seeking, and felt her instant response. She made a little sound of contentment, and perhaps anticipation. Her hands slid around his neck and clung here, as she wriggled herself up onto his lap. His rod was rock hard. She must have been able to feel it. But, apart from another little murmur of pleasure, she didn't speak. He cupped her shoulders with his hands, then slid them to her waist, lost in the wonderful sensation of Amy.

Her fingers were gliding across his broad shoulders, then they delved into the opening of his tunic, enjoying the exploration of bare chest and hard muscle. She reached for his cuffs and tugged the tunic off him, then removed his shirt, too, so that he was naked from the waist up.

She didn't know where to start, her hands hovering, fingertips barely brushing against his warm skin as she tried to explore all of him at once.

"So many scars," she whispered in wonder. "So many close calls, Rey. It frightens me to think of what your life has been like."

"I am the Ghost," he reminded her, amused. "No one can kill me."

"Don't get too cocky," she retorted, tapping his chin with her finger. "There's still the dragon."

Serious Reynald chuckled, even though it wasn't funny. He felt light-headed with happiness. Amy began to press little, biting kisses to his skin, and he groaned with the sheer pleasure of it. She shoved him back, so that he was lying across the bed, and climbed on top of him, tugging at the waist of his trousers. She followed its descent with more kisses, each one longer and hotter, her mouth open. And then her tongue . . .

"Amy," he gasped, his body lurching up.

"Do you want me to stop?" she whispered, staring back at him, her face flushed and beautiful.

"Jesu, no."

She smiled, "Good, because I don't want to either," and went back to her kissing. She was stroking him through the cloth of his trousers, as if he were a gift she couldn't wait to open, and he was caught between not wanting her to stop and wanting her to stop so that he didn't lose complete control.

"Damsel . . ."

"You said not to stop." This time when her fingers closed on him, it was flesh to flesh, with nothing between them.

He'd never lost his ability to maintain control before. Always the memory of what had happened with Morwenna had stopped him from going any further than his vow allowed. But this time it was different. This time, he didn't want to stop, and he didn't have to.

Is Amy the woman I've been waiting for?

He reached down and drew her against him, rolling over so that she was underneath him. His breath was coming quickly, and he knew he was heavy on her despite the soft mattress and the weight he was taking on his arms and legs.

Suddenly, the man who was always in control was afraid of what he might do. He didn't want to frighten her, but it was as if the part of him that had been able to halt his baser instincts had vanished. The years peeled away from him, and he felt hot and wild, like the youth he had never allowed himself to be.

Looking up at the big, naked man on top of her, Amy was wondering if she'd done the right thing. Physically, Rey was probably the most masculine man she'd ever encountered—strong and powerful. Even dangerous. Should she be afraid of what she'd unleashed inside him?

She wasn't. She wasn't afraid at all.

Amy was looking forward to it.

With agonizing slowness, he ran one shaking finger over the full curve of her breast, stopping when he felt her nipple erect through the silky black material of her dress.

Amy whimpered.

Fascinated, he rubbed her nipple between his thumb and finger, sending delighted shivers through her. She arched her breast into his hand, just to let him know she was enjoying what he was doing, and he reached for her straps and slid them down her arms.

Her breasts popped free so dramatically that Amy giggled. He smiled back, but he wasn't about to be distracted from his main focus. His hands came down, hot against her skin, cupping her firm, rounded flesh and squeezing just enough. Then, as if he couldn't wait any longer, he bent his head and licked her with his tongue.

Her breath caught in her throat in something that sounded like a purr, and she ran her fingers through his short hair, petting him as he caressed her. To encourage him further, she rubbed her thigh against his hip, but the dress she was wearing was so tight that it was awkward to move her legs at all.

Impatient now to feel him against all of her, Amy struggled to get the dress off, but the bodice was caught about her waist and the straps were still halfway down her arms, imprisoning her.

"Rey," she gasped.

He seemed to know what she wanted. Easing back, he rose up onto his knees and caught hold of the hem at her ankles, sliding it up. It peeled off her like a second skin, uncovering her knees, then her thighs, and finally the tiny black panties that were all her underwear consisted of. Reynald drew in a shaken breath and dragged his eyes upward to hers.

"I want you," he said, and it was a promise and a warning rolled into one.

Trembling, Amy took him in as he knelt at her feet, every inch the virile male. "Yes," she told him.

It was all the encouragement he needed.

With a soft growl, Reynald reached for her panties and ripped them off. *Well, that's a first.* Next he closed his big hands around her thighs and lifted them, and her hips, clean off the bed, and buried his face between them. Amy shrieked. But he hadn't finished yet. His mouth on her was hot and greedy, taking her by surprise. She bucked, crying out in mindless pleasure. *Orgasm Number One.*

When she came to, he was kissing his way up her body. She gave a languid wriggle and moaned, as he reached her breasts. She could feel the head of his erection against her, and it felt so big she wondered if she should panic. But she didn't feel like panicking; the opposite in fact. She wanted him, and to prove it to them both, she arched upward and tried to slide herself onto him.

His turn to groan. He eased inside her, taking his time, and she turned her face and kissed his shoulder. He was panting, trying to be gentle, but she didn't want gentle. Amy reached down and grasped his buttocks, and the momentum lodged him fully inside her.

The head of his penis touched something, and her eyes widened. She'd never believed in G-spots, but there was definitely something going on. Rey moved, pressing deeper, stroking her inside, and . . .

Orgasm Number Two.

"How did you know about that?" she gasped, coming back to earth. "I thought you said you'd never done this before!"

He looked genuinely puzzled. "Know about what?"

Hmm, she thought, perhaps it would be better to keep him in the dark, for now. Amy wasn't sure how much pleasure she could cope with. "Oh," she breathed, as he began to move again, and he grinned. Too late, he'd worked it out for himself.

He was pressing into her harder now, the muscles in his arms and shoulders standing out with tension. She rubbed her hand over his jaw, feeling the rough texture of stubble, then he was gasping out her name, lifting her hips in his hands so that he could go even deeper inside her. And then he let go with a roar, and . . .

Orgasm Number Three.

Was she still alive? After such mind-blowing pleasure, she could quite happily die.

"Amy," Rey panted. He was lying on his back beside her, his chest rising and falling as if he was having trouble breathing. He dragged himself up onto one elbow and leant over her. "Did I . . . ?" he seemed to be trying to ask her if he'd hurt her.

"Oh Rey, you're good," she said huskily. "You're *very* good."

That made him laugh, and warmth flooded his normally cool, gray eyes.

"I'm glad you waited for me," Amy added, and she was only half-joking. "Maybe chastity is underrated these days."

"Perhaps not everyone has my incentive," he replied wryly.

"No." She frowned. "I suppose a would-be lover who cuts your throat can be a life-changing experience." Amy hesitated. "Sorry, that was a terrible thing to say."

"I do not mind, damsel. I want to hear about your life. But first . . ." He bent his head to nibble her earlobe, and his arm slid around her, turning her and drawing her against him until they were pressed together, skin to skin.

"Is that your sword?" she joked weakly.

He gave her that smile, as though he knew exactly what she was thinking. "Aye, it is. Can I use your scabbard to sheath it in?"

"Oh God, Rey," she groaned, "that's a terrible metaphor."

His smile broadened. "Terrible or not, what is your answer, damsel?"

And Amy leaned closer, gazing hungrily at his lips. "Be my guest."

Twenty

Reynald felt a new lightness. As if his body might just float off the bed if Amy wasn't there to hold on to him. It wasn't just the physical release of their mating, there was much more to it than that. He'd made a joke about his sword and her sheath, but there was a truth in his words that went far beyond the surface crudity.

They fitted together. They were made for each other.

Together, he and Amy were complete, and for a moment his inner conflict was stilled.

He stroked her bright curls as she dozed against his shoulder. If he could have his way right now, he would take her back with him to his own time, and together they would create the world he had always dreamed of. But time was not his to meddle

with, and besides, she mightn't want to go. Ulti-
mately, frustratingly, Reynald knew he had no
control over what happened to him.

Having found Amy, it seemed unjust that he
would soon be leaving her, but Reynald had
grown up in a world where justice was something few expected. Crops failed, wars erupted,
disease spread. A man prayed to God to save his
family, but he did not expect his overlords to do
so. Love was but a dream, to be looked forward
to in the next life rather than this one. *That* was
reality.

To have a woman like Amy at his side, a woman
he desired, to walk with him through the years
ahead. To lie down with her every night, be held in
her arms and to hold her. To be content and *happy* . . .
Aye, Reynald would give much for that.

Outside in the darkness the snow was falling
again, blown against the glass by savage gusts of
wind. He admitted to himself that he would miss
things such as double-glazing and air-conditioning,
but he could live without them. He would have to.
There were other matters he would certainly not
miss; the crowd of fools who were currently inhab-
iting his castle, for instance.

I need to be in control of my destiny again.

The words lingered in his mind. Something the
witch had said to him had been nagging at him
ever since.

I always did what was right.

But how did you know it was right?

I asked questions.

What was wrong in asking questions? Advice was important in making decisions, and Reynald liked to hear what others thought. His father had been single-minded, always believing he was right, but Reynald wasn't so arrogant. He knew he had been wrong before, and nearly died for it. He could not afford to be wrong again.

But he had been. He had been wrong about the dragon. And his aim with the longbow, that fateful, terrible day, had been astray. Because even as he was preparing to shoot his arrow, he hadn't believed he was capable of destroying such a creature. He hadn't listened to himself, to what was in his own heart. Was that what the witch had been trying to tell him, in her oblique way?

After Morwenna, Reynald had found it difficult to believe in himself. Such a mistake—almost fatal—shook him to the core. He'd begun to listen to others, growing more and more cautious of his inner voice. All great men, even kings, had advisors, there was nothing wrong in that. And he didn't always take their advice; Reynald was an intelligent, clearheaded leader. He knew what was right and what was wrong.

But gradually, over time, he'd stopped listening to the voice of his own heart. He'd stopped believing it.

"Rey?"

Amy was staring up at him, her curls rumpled, her eyes sleepy, and her lips swollen. He had that light-headed feeling again, as if he was floating with sheer happiness.

"I'm hungry," she complained. "Starving, actually."

"Hungry?" He examined his own feelings and discovered an emptiness in his belly, too. "Do you think there is any roast beef left from the feast?"

Amy rolled her eyes. "I'll ring for room service," she said.

Amy made the call, and they sat up in bed and ate roast beef sandwiches with fries—American style, she told him, and he smiled even though he didn't understand. She knew he probably didn't understand half of what she was saying to him, but it didn't seem to matter. They were communicating perfectly in the ways that were important.

When they made love again it was just as good as before. She'd half thought that last time might just have been the emotion of the moment—Rey's seven hundred years of chastity coming to a climactic end—that had made it seem better than any sex she had ever experienced before.

But she was convinced now; to her, it really was special. A forever-after situation. And comparing Rey to her other sexual partners was like comparing the sun to a twenty-five-watt bulb.

Did Rey feel the same? He certainly enjoyed

making love to her, he couldn't hide that, but did that mean he wanted to stay with her forever? Perhaps it was just the novelty, after being celibate for so long. Perhaps it didn't really matter who she was, as long as she was a woman and had the required parts.

Rey hadn't made love to any woman since Morwenna. She wanted to believe that made her special, but Amy wasn't sure. And she was practical enough not to build up her hopes. But she knew her life could never go back to what it'd been before, and the realization was wonderful, and bleak, at the same time. Because when it came to boyfriends, Rey was as short-term as it was possible to be. She believed that the eagle was right. They were meant for each other in every sense of the word, and it seemed cruel and unfair that there was no future for them and never could be.

She lay, listening to Rey sleeping beside her and wondering what she was going to do. Outside, she could hear the wind moaning around the castle walls, and she shivered, wondering if the roads would be open in the morning. It sounded like a blizzard out there. She might never get back to her flat in London, and the life she had planned out for herself.

Just at the moment she didn't really care.

"Are you cold?" he asked, his voice husky with sleep.

Amy glanced at his closed eyes and snuggled

closer. "Are you awake? I was listening to the storm outside."

"We are safe in my castle," he said dreamily, drawing her in against him, one arm heavy about her waist. "The walls are strong, they can withstand sieges and storms, and my garrison is well trained. I promise you, damsel, nothing can harm us."

He seemed to have forgotten where he was, as if just for a moment he'd slipped back into the past. Amy opened her mouth to remind him, but then changed her mind. Maybe it was kinder to let him dream, and, anyway, it was nice to pretend. Who knew how much longer they might have together? Reality would raise its ugly head soon enough without her raising it for him.

"I know I'm safe with you, my lord," she whispered.

"In the morning I will send some of my men out to see whether any of the villagers are in need. The winter is difficult for those who are old and young in years. I will need your help, Amy."

"So it's the lady of the castle's job to supply hot soup and blankets?" she asked, curious. In her ignorance, she'd always thought of the lady as someone who was unlikely to soil her hands with anything more strenuous than embroidery and a little singing.

"The lady is the heart of the castle. It is she who makes of it a place of warmth and joyfulness, or misery and darkness. It is the lady who must look to everyone under her lord's roof, and beyond it, making certain they are fed and cared for. She must make a tally of every morsel of food in the storerooms, and every jug of ale in the great hall. She must know exactly how long the castle can last under siege, or through a bad winter. She must kiss her lord without tears when he rides out to battle, even if she knows he may not come back again alive. To those she rules she is the lady, but when she and her lord are alone in their bed at night, she is a woman, and she opens her body and her heart to him, and him alone."

Amy chuckled. "You're a romantic, Rey. I don't know about the tallying up the food bit—math was never my strong point—but I get your meaning. I could do most of that. But I think, if I were the lady of the castle, my first job would be to teach the children to read. Their parents, too, if they wanted me to."

"Julius will look upon you with disfavor." He said *will*, as if it was actually possible.

"Well, Julius *will* just have to bite his tongue, won't he?" Amy could play the game, too.

"He can be intimidating to those who do not know him well."

"I'm not scared of him. Anyway, I'm the lady of the castle. I'll tell send him to clean the privies, or something."

He opened his eyes and looked a little shocked. "Julius is the youngest son of a baron, damsel. He has never cleaned a privy in his life."

"Then maybe he should."

He smiled again, then laughed softly. "Ah, Angharad will like you. She is strong and speaks her mind. Julius calls her . . ." His voice trailed off.

"Pig-headed?"

"Aye, that's it," he said lazily, grinning at her.

"Angharad meant a lot to you, didn't she?"

"I trusted her, and offered to protect her, but I failed her, and she died, in the end, because of me."

"Are you sure she died? You said that you didn't actually see it happen. Remember, you thought Julius was dead, and he turned out to be alive. Angharad might have gotten away. Who knows, she might have lived out her days quite comfortably in her, eh, hut."

"I don't think so," he said, and he was bleak now, the playfulness gone.

The Ghost was done with pretending.

Amy pulled a face. So it was back in the real world now. As if on cue, she heard someone ringing the bell, calling the guests to breakfast. Jez had probably spent all night waiting for Amy to explain herself. It was a wonder he hadn't come looking for her.

It was a confrontation she could have done without.

"I'll go alone," she said.

"Very well."

It was only after he answered that she realized she'd spoken aloud, following her own line of thought, and he had answered as if he was quite easily able to read her mind.

Twenty-one

Jez answered his door on the third knock. Silently, he stood leaning against the jamb. There were dark circles under his eyes, his hair was untidy, and his shirt, usually immaculate, looked as if he'd spent the night in it. Amy wondered what he thought of her own dark-circled eyes and whether he'd guess her reasons for not sleeping were probably a lot more pleasant than his.

"Hiyu," she said, a little warily.

"Hello, Amy."

"I wanted to talk."

"I don't know if I want to listen."

"Can I come in if I promise not to yell and scream?"

"Or toss me onto my back on the floor?"

"When have I ever tossed you onto your back on the floor?"

At least she'd made him smile. He stepped aside and allowed her into the room.

The remains of his breakfast was still on a tray in the middle of his unmade bed, and he shifted it to the table. "There's some coffee left in the pot if you want a cup while we talk?"

"No, thanks."

"I think I will. I need all the caffeine I can get before I face Nicco today."

Amy sank down into a chair. So much for preliminary chitchat, they'd already got to the unpleasant part. "I'm very sorry, Jez . . ."

"I don't understand," he said, raking a hand through his hair. "Couldn't you just have said no?"

"He wouldn't listen," she murmured, staring down at her hands, held tight together in her lap. "I was being candid, but he thought I was playing games with him."

"I suppose he had a right to think that. You were playing games, Amy."

There was enough justification in that to stop her from arguing with him, although she still believed Nicco was as much in the wrong as she. The silence dragged on, and she shifted uncomfortably, saying in a small voice, "Do you think I can make it all right with him?"

"Do you want to make it all right?" Jez had poured himself coffee and was watching her over the rim of his cup. "It's just that I got the impression you weren't keen to go on with it."

This was the moment she'd been dreading. Whatever she said it was going to be difficult . . . No, *horrible*. It was a no-win situation for her.

Jez set down his cup. "Tell me the truth," he said gruffly. "I always thought that between us, at least, we could be honest."

"All right." She met his eyes. "You're right, I'm hating this weekend with Nicco. But I know how much you need the diamond, Jez. I don't want to let you down."

"Amy—"

"No, listen to me. Now I've started talking I have to finish." She took a breath. "I owe you a lot, Jez, more than I can ever repay, and I want so much to do this for you. But it's tearing me to pieces. If I sleep with Nicco—and that's what it'll come down to—I'll rip away all the good things in my life that I've been building up for the past four years. I'll be right back where I started."

He seemed flattened. "I didn't realize you felt like that."

"I should have said. I'm sorry. I know how much you love all this, but I don't, Jez. For me, it was over a long time ago."

He nodded. "So, what are you going to do?" he asked, and his smile was painful. "Take a trip around the world? Climb mountains and fly planes?"

"No, Jez," she whispered. "That's what *you* would do. I don't want or need that sort of buzz. What I'm doing is something that doesn't involve lying or cheating or stealing."

He stared at her as if he didn't believe her. "You'd miss it, sweetheart. Whatever you say, you'd start to get bored, then you'd give me a ring and—"

"I wouldn't, you know."

"What about that diplomat with the dodgy bank account and the taste for young girls? Don't you remember him? When we took off with his cash and left those photos with the cops, you said we'd done a good job."

"I know I did. But there weren't many days like that. I want to be a grown-up, with a grown-up job, and a life where I'm not waiting for the authorities to come pounding on my door in the middle of the night. I don't want to be looking over my shoulder all the time, wondering if I'm being followed by that pal of yours, what's his name."

"Detective Inspector O'Neill."

"Yep, him. When someone offers to give me a body search, I want it to be my lover and not some constable with a smirk. When I say I've done ten years, I want to mean my job and not prison. Do you see what I'm getting at here, Jez?"

She was breathing quickly. Amy realized she'd

been close to shouting at him with frustration. It surprised him, she could see that, and upset him. He'd had no idea she felt like this; he'd been oblivious to everything but the game.

"I should have told you a long time ago," she admitted.

"No, no, I should have seen it. I just never . . ." He slapped his hands on his thighs and stood up. "I just never thought we were that different. Two of a kind." He gave a weak half laugh that made her heart ache.

There was a silence while he went to peer out of the window at the falling snow. He'd done that, she remembered, when they were children. It was as if there was always something more interesting beyond the room he was standing in, while she'd been content to stay put. She wanted to go to him now, but she didn't quite dare.

"Will you be all right?" she asked him softly.

"Sure, why not?" He shrugged, hands in his pockets.

"So . . . what are you going to tell Nicco?"

"I'll think of something."

"Jez, I have some savings. I can help you to pay off these people."

He turned to her, pulling a face. "Sweetheart, your savings wouldn't even make a dent in what I owe them. Don't worry. I'll get hold of the Star somehow. My lucky star, hey?" And he laughed, sounding like their father when he was in trouble, as if he expected her to join in. Amy didn't even smile—it was beyond her to pretend this was anything other than an awful moment.

"Jez, please . . ."

"Better get moving," he cut through her briskly. "What's on today? My memory is still recovering from those cocktails."

"I don't know," she said quietly. "I think there might be a service in the chapel, and then some sort of battle reenactment. That's just this morning. Oh, and a fair."

"Rustic handcrafts with four-figure price tags. Wonderful," Jez said, smiling and showing his teeth.

Amy hesitated. She had the urge to explain herself again, but he clearly wanted her out of the room as soon as possible. "Okay then. I'll talk to you later."

He closed the door and left her standing there in the muted luxury of the corridor.

Amy felt sick. Whatever her justification, the truth was she'd failed her brother. Disappointed him. Left him in a dangerous position. There was the possibility that he was playing up his situation, overreacting, but she didn't think so. The truth was, she hadn't seen him that shattered since they were children, and their father had smashed his skateboard to pieces for some imagined transgression.

On the way back to her room, Amy could see through the glassed-in windows that the snow was falling harder than before. It was piled up everywhere, covering paths and roofs. When one of the kitchen staff approached her, wheeling a trolley, she asked whether the roads were closed.

"Yes, madam, the main highway into London is closed, and most of the minor roads are shut, too. They say there's more snow on the way, too, so it's not going to improve just yet. Is there a problem?"

As far as Amy was concerned there wasn't a problem. Here she was, trapped in a snowbound castle, with Rey. If it were just him and her, then she'd be celebrating, but there were also Jez and Nicco. And, she reminded herself, an apparition with a lantern who seemed to want to kill them. Would the snow help Rey discover where he had gone wrong in 1299, or would it hinder him?

Maybe if he didn't find out, he could stay a little longer?

It was a nice thought, but Amy didn't think the witch from the between-worlds worked like that. Once the clock ticked down, that was probably it, and he'd either return home to the past or be locked away forever.

She'd reached the corridor to her room and started to walk toward it. For some reason, the closer she got, the more she began to worry that Rey might be already gone. How did she know how much longer he had? He could vanish as suddenly as he'd appeared.

Amy picked up her pace. By the time she opened

her door, her heart was thumping, and she was breathing hard. "Rey?"

The room was empty. Sheets and quilt were tumbled over the floor, and clothes were everywhere, but no Ghost. In that instant she felt as if she'd died. And then she heard the shower.

Laughing at her own stupidity—it was better than crying—she opened the bathroom door. She could see the shape of him through the stream and the glass, and her heart began to beat to a different tune. She didn't even bother taking off her clothes, just opened the shower door and stepped in.

The surprise on his face turned to pleasure, then quickly to desire. "Damsel," he said, his voice deepening as he reached for her and drew her beneath the water.

Amy lifted her mouth to his, and he tasted like heaven.

"You bathe in your clothing?" he whispered, kissing her, hands stripping her of her sopping-wet garments.

"Only when you're here," she gasped, as he found naked skin and began to stroke her. She arched against his fingers, every nerve ending concentrated between her legs as he touched her with a certainty that belied his inexperience.

"Amy," he groaned, lifting her, her thighs clasped about his waist.

"I don't . . . think . . . there's . . . enough . . . room . . ." she managed, as he filled her. She

231

gazed down into his face, both of them wet, hair dripping and skin flushed from the warm water and their desire for each other.

He was perfect.

"You are so beautiful," he whispered. "I wish—"

But Amy didn't want to hear whatever it was he wished for. She had a horrible feeling he was wishing she was someone else, another Amy who hadn't been brought up on the Parkhill Estate with a violent drunk for a father, and a thief for a brother. An Amy who was pure and saccharine sweet.

Not her at all.

So she kissed him, their lips clinging and sucking, as their bodies began to move together.

And that was perfect, too.

Twenty-two

Reynald had always found peace in the castle chapel, and this morning was no different. He sat, letting the voice of the priest wash over him and trying to pretend he was in his own time. The Latin service helped, but it wasn't the same, and this man lacked Julius's intensity and passion. He also lacked his steely eye when it came to those of his flock who did not show the appropriate level of piety and concentration.

The structure of the chapel was different, too. There were alterations, and someone had built an appalling stone plaque on one wall, to commemorate something called WW II. But, if he closed his eyes, and breathed in the smell of incense, then he could pretend he was home again.

He could hear some other members of the

congregation stirring about restlessly on their seats. Amy had told him they were tetchy—her word—and that it was because the roads out of the castle had been closed by the bad weather. People were worried they might have to stay on after tomorrow instead of returning to their lives elsewhere, as if a day or two would mean the end of them. Reynald thought it was ridiculous and told her so. He could remember many such days during his winters here, days when both horse and rider could fall into a drift and perish, and not be found until the spring thaw.

He didn't understand these people. They rushed about blindly, with never a moment to spare. Their cell phones rang, they had to check their e-mail, they had to network. Ridiculous words Amy had taught him. She said that they were frightened, that if they stopped rushing, they might have to *think*. And if they had to think, then they might realize how empty and pointless their lives were.

So what, Reynald thought, if they had to stay on another day or two? They had warmth and food and shelter. At times such as this there was nothing else to do but make yourself comfortable and wait it out. There were others far worse off. And in seven hundred years no one would remember them or what all the fuss was about.

That was one thing he had learned from the between-worlds. Mortal life was short, and you had to make the most of it.

Amy's fingers were intertwined with his. He glanced sideways at her and found her staring intently at the priest. But she wasn't listening; he could tell she was far away. He thought he knew what she was thinking. Amy was worrying about her brother and the choice she'd made.

"Jez and I have agreed to part company," she'd said earlier. "He says he understands, but he doesn't. He can't imagine a life that doesn't involve balancing on a knife-edge and waiting to fall."

"You did the right thing," Reynald assured her. "You told him the truth."

"Yeah, I did."

Now Reynald wondered if she regretted it. Perhaps she wished she had given her body to Nicco for this Catherine's jewel, so that Jez could be saved from his own mess. But Reynald was glad she hadn't. Such an action would have destroyed her. She had taken her own advice and listened to what her heart was telling her rather than to the persuasions of others.

Rey looked down at their fingers, joined, his and hers, and felt the peacefulness of the chapel stealing over him. In this place he had believed that one day he would be wed. But now, even if he was able to return to 1299, he knew he would not want a wife who wasn't Amy . . .

A ripple disturbed his peace. How, he asked himself, could he marry her, even assuming he could, without remembering what she had been and what she had done? Was it possible to want a woman so much that your body ached yet be unable to accept her for what she was?

He sickened himself with his own thoughts. He was clearly no Julius, who was able to forgive any transgression, although sometimes he thought Julius was more saint than man, while Reynald was very much a man.

"Is it okay to make wishes in a place like this?" Amy whispered beside him. "It's probably silly, but I feel like I'd like to make a wish."

He drew a deep breath before he turned to look at her, trying to regain his equilibrium. Her eyes were wide and serious. "You can say a prayer, but I thought you were not sure you believed in God?"

Amy shrugged one shoulder. "I'm not sure I do."

Reynald had been horrified—again—when she'd told him her views on religion and that she had never been inside a church in her entire life. In his time, life revolved around religion—saints' days, holy days, the bells for prayer ringing throughout the day; the two were so tightly entwined there was no separating them.

"What do you want to wish for?" he asked softly.

She smiled, and he felt like his heart would burst. She was beautiful, with her red curls and green eyes, and the pink she had painted on her lips.

"It won't come true, will it, if I tell you?" she teased. When he looked puzzled, she bumped his shoulder with hers. "See, Rey, you shake your head at my failings, but you're as ignorant as I am. Haven't you ever heard that before? I thought every child knew about not telling their wishes if they want them to come true."

"While you were making wishes, I was learning to use my sword and ride my stallion," he said evenly.

The expression in her eyes changed, turned to pity. "Poor Rey. No child of mine would miss out on being a child."

"Even if he was a Marcher Lord's heir?"

"Even then."

Their gazes tangled, clung, then she looked away and bowed her head. He could see her lips moving and realized she was making her wish. And he wondered if it was the same as his.

Jez stood at the back of the chapel, but his eyes were on Amy and Rey rather than the service. He'd come here to see his sister and try and talk her into changing her mind.

After Amy had left him, Jez had felt bitter and angry, but he'd had no intention of crawling to her. After all he'd done for her! How could she have turned her back on him? There was no way he was going to ask her for any favors.

And then he got the phone call from reception.

It was the sweetheart with the big blue eyes, the girl he'd made a point of befriending from the moment he arrived. He always did that. It was a trick of his to have an ally who could let him know if anyone was asking for him.

Never leave your back unguarded. That was a saying of his dad's, one of his better ones, and Jez had never forgotten it.

The girl said that someone had just rung to ask if he was staying there, and when they learned he was, they asked to speak to the manager. She'd put the call through, and Mr. Coster had been on his phone for ages, then he'd come out and told her not to mention the call to Jez, or anyone else.

"You're a treasure," Jez had said warmly. "Probably one of the newspapers trying to track me down. Did they say who they were? *Daily Mail?* The *Telegraph?*"

"It wasn't the newspapers," she said, her voice dropping to a whisper. "It was a policeman. Detective Inspector O'Neill."

Jez's first thought, after he'd thanked her and hung up, was that the dodgy paintings he'd sold a couple of months ago must have been hotter than he'd thought. O'Neill had been poking around him for years, watching him, asking questions about him, tracking his movements. Maybe he finally had some piece of evidence he could use to bring Jez to justice?

In the beginning O'Neill's obsession had seemed like a joke, a bit of a laugh, and he got a buzz out of keeping out of the policeman's reach. But now . . . it just didn't feel funny anymore. O'Neill was circling closer and closer, and Jez had the nasty feeling that he was just waiting for the moment to strike.

So he'd come to find Amy, to beg her to change her mind and go after Nicco for him. Once he knew where the Star of Russia was, he could get it, pay off his debts, and go somewhere where O'Neill wouldn't be able to touch him. Spain, maybe, or Italy. Have a holiday.

Amy was right; this was no way to make a living.

But now, as he watched her and Rey, he began to remember all the years they'd been together, good and bad. And he knew he couldn't do it to her. She was happy; he could see it shining from her, as if a light had been turned on inside her. Jez hadn't seen Amy smile like that for a long time. He realized, with a strange sort of calm, that she really was in love with Rey, and she didn't deserve for him to come and spoil it for her. She didn't need him to protect her anymore, probably hadn't for ages, but he'd refused to believe it. Maybe he had needed her more than she had needed him—she was his only link with the past, the only one who really understood.

But now, painful and difficult as it was, he needed to let her go, for both their sakes.

Jez went out of the chapel, closing the doors as quietly as he'd opened them.

* * *

The tunnel leading from the underground chamber was too narrow, and the dragon was having difficulty dragging herself through it. Her hard scales scratched against the rough-hewn walls, and once, when a small pile of debris fell down onto her, she roared from rage and frustration.

But gradually, inch by inch, she was moving forward.

For too long she'd been interred in the darkness beneath the earth, but soon she would be in the light of the outside world once more. She'd be able to breathe, and the fresh air would make her strong, make her feel young.

If only my beloved was here, with me. If only I could turn time backward, like the witch of the between-worlds, and make my decision over again.

This time she wouldn't have been so careless of the life of the one she loved. This time she would have guarded that life with all her strength and cunning. But the decision had been made long ago. It was done, and there was no undoing it.

Exhausted, she rested, dreaming of flying through the crisp dawn air, the green forest laid out below her, and the blue sky above. She would stretch her wings wide and sail on the wind. She would bathe in the river and gorge herself on the fish she caught with her talons. It would be like it used to be.

But first she must kill Reynald and his mate.

What right had he to be happy? She hated him with a burning fire in her belly. If not for him, she wouldn't have had to make the fateful decision. If not for him, her beloved would still be here beside her.

The dragon had seen Reynald's mate in her mind. She had green eyes that saw much, and the bond between the two of them was very strong. She well knew that if she killed one of them, then the other would die of grief.

Aye, she knew all about grief.

Twenty-three

The mock-battle was to have been held
outside in the bailey—a medley of jousts and tour-
naments, and a local historical reenactment
group giving an exhibition. But the weather had
changed that. Now, instead, there was a rather ram-
shackle affair, with men in armor charging up and
down the pavilion, or else trying to knock each other
out with an assortment of medieval weapons—clubs
and battle-axes, lances and maces. All replicas, of
course.

Rey kept a stern demeanor for some time, but
eventually it was too much for him, and once he
began to laugh, he laughed until his eyes streamed
with tears.

Amy shook her head at him, but she was pleased

to see him so happy. From what she could gather, she didn't think he had much time to be happy where he came from, and although he talked about Julius and Angharad, he hadn't had anyone to love, either. Not to really, truly *love*.

And everyone needed love.

Mr. Coster had asked him to participate in some of the "jousts," and he'd agreed good-naturedly, even though there were no horses and the lances were made of cardboard. After he knocked down every one of his opponents in quick succession, Amy suddenly understood why he'd been laughing. What was just a game to the other men was a question of life and death to Reynald. He was good at it because he had to be.

He hadn't had a childhood where he made wishes, and that was because he needed to learn to fight to stay alive. His world was full of people wanting to kill him or people he had to protect with his own life.

Amy wanted to take him in her arms and hold him, but she knew he would laugh at her. Or make love to her. He didn't want pity, he didn't need it, and she didn't pity him. She admired him. She— oh God—loved him.

I love him.

"You are making more wishes, damsel?"

Amy blinked. Rey had returned to his seat, and she'd been too stunned by this new realization to notice. As usual when emotionally pressed, she made a joke. "I was wishing for you to win, and you did. You're a champion, Rey!"

He gave her his most arrogant smile. She was sure he was going to say he always won, or something equally macho, but he never had the chance. Just then the pavilion started to shake.

The whole building was moving from side to side, and people were shouting and screaming, and trying to run. For a moment all was pandemonium, then it was over.

It took a few minutes for everyone to realize they were safe and unhurt, and that despite the violence of the shuddering, there was little sign of damage.

Amy was standing within Rey's arms. It felt so natural she hadn't even noticed, and she stepped away reluctantly, already missing the feel of him.

"That's the second earth tremor we've had this weekend," a precise voice said beside them.

"Ms. Ure." Amy recognized the woman who had sat opposite her at the feast.

"It's quite strange," she went on, ignoring Rey and focusing on Amy. "According to Julius's Chronicle, there was a similar occurrence in 1299. 'The earth shook violently,' he says. As far as I know we're not on a fault line, so I can't imagine why—"

Rey grabbed Amy's hand and made for the door.

"It's all right," she said, wondering why he was in such a panic. "Rey, it's stopped now . . ."

"No." He halted and clamped his hands on her

shoulders, gazing intently into her eyes. "It is not all right, Amy. It is very bad indeed." Excitement, anger, trepidation . . . they were all in his face.

"What is it, Rey?"

"I remember. The 'authority' is right. The earth did shake in 1299. In the days before the dragon came, it shook often."

Again, he was pulling her along, making no allowance for her smaller steps and shorter legs. Amy did her best to keep up, glad she'd forgone medieval costume this morning for slacks, sweater, her boots, and a thick jacket, as well as a bright blue woolen hat and the matching scarf she'd flung about her neck.

"They're connected then? Is that what you're—"

He spun around to face her, just outside the door, and she crashed into him. He hardly seemed to notice. "The dragon came from the west that day, from over the border, but could it be that its lair was closer to home?"

"Surely if it was living in the castle someone would have seen it?" she pointed out the obvious.

"Not if it was underground."

"Rey . . . you don't mean to tell me you think it's still here? That after seven hundred years the dragon is starting to wake up again?"

She was frightened, and she couldn't hide it.

"Aye," he spoke grimly. "I do. I think this is meant to be."

"But . . ."

There was a sound, an echo, like a woman screaming down a long tunnel. Amy lifted her head, eyes wide. Rey was frowning, staring toward the north tower.

"What was that?" she said.

"I do not know." But he did.

"Rey . . . ?"

But he shook his head, as if to dismiss it.

"Rey . . . that was a scream we heard. It was Morwenna's scream, wasn't it? You told me her story, and how your father had her thrown from the north tower. Why do you think we can still hear her screams seven hundred years later? Can her death have something to do with all of this?"

"Why should it? That was before the dragon came, before I was Lord de Mortimer. I did not order Morwenna's death, and I did nothing to make her hate me. Although she did," he added, remembering the expression on the girl's face as his father's men dragged her away.

"It was just a thought."

He rested his gaze on her contemplatively. Amy was prone to saying things like this, and he had found them to be useful. It was as if she had a way of seeing through to the heart of a matter without having to take the slow, logical steps. Reynald hadn't given much thought to Morwenna, not for many years, but since he'd met Amy, he had spoken of her, and now he was remembering her. Could she be important?

"My father told me that she confessed under torture to being sent to us by one of his enemies, but she gave no names. No matter how they tried to extract them from her, she would not name them. She did ask for someone, though."

"Her master?"

"No. Her mother."

Amy blanched. "Poor girl," she whispered.

"Aye."

He slid an arm about her, drawing her against him and cradling her there. He rested his cheek on the top of her head, breathing in the sweet scent of her hair, feeling the soft spring of the curls that had freed themselves from beneath her hat.

"She made her choice," he reminded her. "She must have known that her failure to kill me would mean her death."

"I know," Amy murmured. "And I'm very glad you're alive. It just seems so brutal."

"I live in brutal times," he reminded her.

"But you're a good man, Rey. I would trust you to do what was best and fairest. I don't think I'd trust your father."

He chuckled. "My father would have liked you, damsel."

"Hmm."

"My mother, too. You and she could have read poems together, about beautiful ladies, and men who prefer to gaze upon their faces and compose songs to them, rather than take them to their beds."

"Not like you then."

She grinned up at him, and he bent to kiss her. The kiss grew hotter, lingering, until he broke it off regretfully. He took a deep breath to clear his head.

"We must concern ourselves with the dragon, Amy. If it has been sleeping, then it will be vulnerable to attack. If I can find its lair, I can finish it before it reaches the outside." And he turned and set off again.

He's going to go down into the tunnels, Amy thought, running after him through the snow. *He's going dragon hunting.*

And God help me, I'm going with him.

As he walked, Reynald was trying to map out the nether regions of the castle in his mind. There were so many tunnels, and some of them he had rarely traversed, if ever. He knew that when the castle had been built after the Norman conquest of the English, it was constructed on an old burial site. There were already tunnels in existence, and it was decided to turn one of them into an escape route—in case the occupants ever needed to send out a messenger during a siege or get away themselves.

Escape had not been necessary during his father's days, or his own. His family had a tradition of taking its battles to their enemy rather than skulking at home. And then the escape tunnel had been more or less forgotten when the postern gate was built. But the Ghost remembered it now.

What better place was there for a dragon to hide than under the very noses of the enemy?

These people are pagans. There are no dragons, my lord.

Angharad's scornful voice rang in his head. He'd accepted what she said, merely thinking it strange that anyone still believed in such arcane creatures. And yet, even as he'd agreed with her, there was something. Some doubt that plagued him. It plagued him now, but Reynald knew it would come forth when it was ready. For now, he had enough to do.

The antechamber outside the great hall was no longer empty. There was a table set up with coffee and tea, and a half dozen guests were chatting or admiring the ceiling painting. They all seemed very calm.

As Reynald and Amy passed through the reception area, they heard Coster assuring everyone it was over.

"There's nothing to worry about!" he said.

Reynald knew that for a lie. There was everything to worry about.

The door he had come through when he first awoke was the one he wanted now. He knew that it led down into the tunnels, a starting point for the maze beneath his feet. The dragon was in there somewhere, moving, shifting in the earth, and he had to find it. He reached out to turn the door handle, already deciding on various strategies and counterstrategies, as he formulated his battle plan.

The door was locked.

Angrily, he wrenched at it, but it would not budge.

"Rey!" Amy shook his arm to get his attention. "You need a key. Coster probably has one."

"This door was not locked before!"

"He probably locked it after the, eh, the Santa incident."

"I need that key," he shouted, "or I will smash it down."

"Rey," she hissed, glancing over her shoulder. "You know what'll happen if you do that. Coster will send some of his security guys after you, and you'll never complete your task and right the wrong."

As much as he wanted to ignore her warning and crash his way through the thick wooden door, he knew she was right.

"We must find him then," he said urgently.

She clung to his arm, refusing to let go as he tried to march away. "You can't just ask him for it! He'll ask you why, and he doesn't think you have any business poking around in the dungeons or whatever else is down there. We'll have to steal it."

He turned to stare at her.

"And don't look down your nose at me." She sighed, impatient with him. "Do you have a better idea, my lord? Maybe you could *order* him to give it to you?"

He didn't have a better idea.

"I thought not," she said, with her familiar eye roll. "Come on then, we'll find his office. Maybe it's empty, and we can just sneak in."

But the office was locked, too.

Seething with frustration, Reynald watched as Amy crossed to the girl at the reception desk. When she returned, she took him by the arm again and led him away toward the elevator. He was too busy listening to her explanation to be nervous of the small moving box.

"She says Coster will be back soon, and she'll tell him you need to see him."

"I need to see him now!"

"Rey, you can't. Surely half an hour isn't going to make a difference?"

He looked at her in amazement. She didn't understand. Perhaps she didn't even believe it, not really. She hadn't seen the creature as he had. Reynald took her face between his hands.

"The dragon is waking," he told her with a deadly seriousness. "It is making its way out of the tunnel. That is why the earth is shaking, because it is moving down there beneath the castle. Soon it will be free. I need to find it before then, so I can kill it."

"Kill it?" she repeated, flinching.

"Aye, it will be easier. Once it is free . . ."

"I don't like the thought of killing it," she murmured. "I can't even squash a spider—I always catch them and put them outside."

"Then it will kill you," he retorted. "And me. And your brother. And everyone else in this place. You can have no pity for the dragon, damsel, for it has no feelings for us. Its only wish is to see us dead."

"But how do you know that?"

"I have looked into its eyes."

He stood upon the north tower and watched it come. This was the second time it had swept down over his castle. The first time it had killed hundreds, among them his important guests, and turned to flame and ash the tents he'd ordered to be set up on the grounds beyond the moat. The village outside his walls was a cloud of black smoke as everything and everyone in it burned.

He had his Welsh longbow and bodkin arrows ready. He could fire at an object over two hundred yards away and usually hit it, and chain mail parted like butter before the steel tips of his arrowheads. Up here, on the highest point of the castle, he would be able to see the dragon as it flew toward him. He might be able to kill it, or at least wound it. He was arrogant enough to think his aim was better than that of anyone else in his domain, including the Welsh. He believed in himself. Or at least he had done, until Angharad seeded her doubts into his head.

The dragon flapped lazily toward him, its body cov-

ered in heavy scales that shone in the sunlight like the plates of steel of his own armor. The creature's underbelly was unprotected though. Reynald had seen the soft flesh when the dragon came over him the first time. If he could send his arrow into that vulnerable place and wound it mortally, it would not matter if he died. At least he would have saved what remained of his people and his castle.

Still it came on.

He set the arrow in place and bent the six-foot-six-inch bow with all his mighty strength. He had been practicing ever since he was a boy, and been inspired by stories of the Welsh bowmen, who were so deadly during the skirmishes in their leafy green forests. For Reynald, there was something mystical about the longbow, with its legends and superstitions. He'd persisted with his attempts to master it, although his father laughed at him and said it was the weapon of peasants. "Learn to wield a sword, boy! Forget the bow and arrow!"

But his father did not realize the potential of such a weapon. Reynald saw a time when the English lords would be sending their own bowmen to Wales so that they could learn the deadly accuracy of their enemies. If a man could gain some edge over his opponents in battle, then it was worth the effort.

"You have not the talent for the longbow," Angharad's voice whispered in his ear, sending him back in time to a year ago, when he'd been practicing at the butts, and she had come by. She'd spoken in her usual way, with no regard for his lordly status. Angharad said what she *thought, without fear or favor, and that was why so many disliked her.*

"Perhaps not," he'd answered her, "but I hope one day to be proficient in it."

"You haven't the mind for it," she went on. "When the crucial moment comes, you will always miss. You think too much, my lord, and a bowman cannot afford to think with his mind, only with his hands and his eyes and his heart."

Why was he remembering their conversation now? Why were the doubts circling him when he least needed them? Anghared was probably dead, he reminded himself. He must put her out of his mind and concentrate on saving the living.

Reynald stood and waited, feet planted apart, his bow drawn back, and his arrow pointed.

The dragon was close now, its huge body shading the sun, its talons outstretched as if to receive him into an embrace. Reynald looked up into the creature's face—the long snout, the obsidian eyes. He stared into those eyes, but he saw nothing there to make him believe this foe would offer him the slightest kindness. There was only hatred, and death.

The Ghost's muscles began to shake with the tension of holding the bow steady, but he forced them to still. Waiting, waiting, until the precise moment when the underbelly was visible. Exposed.

You will miss.

"I cannot."

You think too much. You will miss, my lord.

The dragon was so close now that he knew he could wait no longer. He released the arrow. It went hissing through the air. But even as he watched its deadly flight, Reynald's experience told him that he had missed, and there was no time to nock another arrow.

He felt a terrible sadness.

The black eyes appeared to mock him. And then the dragon opened wide its mouth and vomited out deadly gobs of flame. If he thought of anything in that last moment, it was of Morwenna, the girl who had tried to assassinate him all those years ago, and her fall from this very same tower. He thought he heard her voice, screaming.

And then there was nothing.

Twenty-four

Jez had arrived late at the pavilion to watch the mock-battles. He'd thought about going to visit Nicco to see if he could do any better than Amy when it came to discovering the whereabouts of the Star of Russia, but he'd changed his mind. Nicco wasn't a fool, he'd laugh in his face. And if he thought for one moment that Jez was planning to steal his treasure, he'd be on the first flight back to Moscow.

Anyway, Jez didn't feel like putting up with Nicco's ego this morning. The news about O'Neill had considerably shortened the time he thought he had to deal with his creditors. If O'Neill was watching him, hoping for a slip-up, then he needed to be extra careful. And yet, at the same time, he needed to be quick, to get things moving if he wanted to keep his fingers and toes attached.

Amy had been with Rey at the joust, too. Jez kept his distance from them. He was still coming to terms with what Amy had said to him; he was still feeling hurt and angry. But he was also aware of a growing acceptance. When they were children he'd protected her, but she'd been there for him, too. All these years she'd been there. If Amy had ever been indebted to him, then she'd well and truly paid it off.

She didn't need him anymore. She was a big girl, who could stand on her own feet. She'd shown that last night when she dealt with Nicco.

Despite himself, Jez smiled, remembering Nicco lying flat on the floor. Amy had upset Jez's plans, and at the same severed their professional relationship, but she'd done it spectacularly, and in a way he'd always remember with pleasure and pride.

After the earth tremor, they left so suddenly that he didn't have time to speak to her, but he set off in the direction he expected the two of them to have taken. Back to their room. Shame to interrupt them, he told himself mockingly, as he stepped out of the elevator, but it couldn't be helped.

Rey was slumped against the wall outside Amy's room, and Amy was struggling to get the big bastard to his feet, but he was much too heavy for petite Amy.

"Rey," she was wailing, "please, come on. Wake up."

"What happened?" Jez said, as he ran toward them.

Startled, Amy turned, and then relief filled her face. "Jez, oh thank God."

Amy held Rey as best she could, to stop him sinking farther toward the floor, while Jez propped his shoulder under one of Rey's arms. "He weighs a bloody ton," he muttered, trying not to stagger as he waited for Amy to fumble her door open.

"He collapsed." She was wide-eyed and frightened. "Lay him on the bed. Rey?" Leaning over him now, her hands brushing his face, his chest, fluttering about like crazed moths. Amy was in a state.

Jez took her fingers in his and squeezed them, then pushed her gently aside. "Let me," he said, and proceeded to do a check of the big man's vital signs. "He seems okay," he said. "Maybe he just passed out. I can slap his face for you, if you like, to bring him around . . . ?"

She gave him a glare. "No, I don't like."

Jez gave the big man on the bed a curious look. "Why did he faint? What did you say to him?"

"Nothing. He went quiet, but I just thought he was remembering the . . . the past, then he collapsed. Rey?" she whispered, her fingers gentle as she stroked his cheek. "Wake up. *Please*."

"I'd better call for the doctor." He moved toward the phone, and picked up the handset.

"Jez, I don't think we can. Rey isn't supposed to be here, and if they ask for details, then . . . They'll find out he doesn't exist."

There was something going on. Something other than his sister's grand love affair. Carefully, Jez set the phone back in its cradle.

"Amy, come clean. Are you involved in a scam of your own? Is that it? You're running your own operation, and you didn't want to tell me about it." Suddenly he was excited, thinking he hadn't lost her after all.

Her mouth dropped open, and she stared at him as if she couldn't believe her ears. "No! I'm not. I told you, I'm not interested in scams or cons or anything like that. I don't do that anymore, Jez. I don't want to."

His mood swung back the other way, and Jez knew she was right. He'd let himself believe it because he wanted to. For an uncomfortable moment he remembered his father's face, that last time he went into prison. Confused and lonely, uncomprehending of the feelings his children had toward him. Jez had thought then: "You don't even know what you've done to us, do you, you stupid bugger? You can't see past your own nose." Now, uncomfortably, he wondered if he was just as self-centered as the man he despised.

"If I told you the truth, you wouldn't believe me anyway," Amy was saying, peering into Rey's unconscious face as if she'd like to give him mouth-to-mouth.

"Oh?" Jez replied without much interest.

"We need a key. The key that opens the door from the room with the paintings into the underground tunnels. Coster has it somewhere in his office—or at least, I suppose he does. We need to open the door and go down there."

Jez considered her request. "Why?"

"I can't tell you. You wouldn't want to know anyway," she grumbled. "And if I did tell you, you wouldn't believe me."

"Amy, if you're going to be mysterious . . ."

"We have to find the dragon."

The voice was Rey's. As he spoke, he opened his eyes and tried to sit up, but Amy wouldn't let him. After a brief struggle between them, Rey pulled her down to him, kissed her hard on the mouth, then sat up while she was still getting her breath.

"The dragon," Jez repeated calmly, but it was an act. Now he was really worried. It sounded as if Amy was involved in some dangerous shit—God, he should have known it!—and he wasn't going to leave her alone with this character again. He'd be glued to his sister's side from now on, O'Neill or no O'Neill. In fact, maybe he could get the inspector to arrest Rey for him, and get him locked away somewhere safe. Safe for Amy, that is. It might even give him some points with O'Neill, or he could make a deal . . .

"Rey, he won't believe you," Amy said, her lips still tingling from his kiss. She could see from the expression on Jez's face, and the glances he was giving Rey, that he was going into protective mode. He was working out how he could get Rey arrested and taken away, without putting himself or Amy at risk.

Rey stood up, and she only just stopped herself from reaching out to stop him. But he didn't seem dizzy or unsteady on his feet, and when he didn't fall over again she relaxed a little. She'd never been so scared in her life as when he collapsed against the wall. She'd been calling his name, but it was as if he couldn't hear her, despite his eyes being wide open, and then he'd just fainted. He was so big and heavy. If Jez hadn't come along to help, she didn't know what she would have done.

A sock hit her in the face. Rey was going through the mess of clothes on the floor, searching for something. Another sock floated through the air, then a pair of panties.

"Rey, what are you—"

He gave a grunt of satisfaction as dragged his sword out from under some towels and began to buckle it around his waist.

"What happened to you a moment ago?" she

asked, watching him uneasily. He had the look of a man preparing to do battle, and she was reminded uneasily of what he'd said, about the lady allowing her lord to go off to fight with a smile on her face, neither of them admitting they might never see each other again.

"I was remembering," Rey said, meeting her eyes and fixing her with a look that meant he couldn't tell her in front of Jez.

"Remembering what?" Jez didn't have any such qualms. "The dragon? Tell me about the dragon, Rey. Is it a friend of yours? Is that why you want the key, so that you can go and visit it?" His eyes narrowed and he smiled. "Its name wouldn't happen to be Dorothy, would it?"

Rey looked at him sideways, as if Jez was the one who was insane.

"I want the key—" he began.

"No, Rey!" But Amy was wasting her breath, he couldn't be stopped.

"—so that I can find the dragon, and kill it."

Jez's mouth pursed. "Hmm," he said, "not your friend then."

Amy lost any temper she had left. "Jez, really, this has nothing to do with you. Just go. You must have important things to do, people to avoid, plane tickets out of the country to buy—"

"I'm not leaving," he said, and she knew he meant it. This was the Jez she remembered from her childhood, protective, watching over her, and while it was lovely to see him again, it was the worst possible moment for him to reappear.

Rey had no such qualms. "Then you will have to come with us," he said. He strode toward the door, then paused and turned back to face Jez. He looked grim and serious, his hand resting on the handle of his sword, his back straight. "How fast can you run?" he demanded.

Jez eyed him warily. "I used to be the sprint champion of our school when I was ten years old. Does that count?"

The Ghost smiled without any trace of humor whatsoever. "Good, because you might need to run for your life."

Amy followed him out the door, hoping that Jez would stay put, but he was right on her tail. Her nightmare was getting worse, and they hadn't even found the dragon yet.

Twenty-five

Reynald took the stairs. He knew he had no time to waste, and this time he was determined to listen to his own heart rather than the well-meaning advice of others. He had never fainted before in his life, and the fact that he'd done so now, while remembering the dragon, made him suspicious that the dragon had something to do with it.

He had his suspicions about the dark apparition with the light, too. At the time, he'd thought it appeared to be Julius, then he'd grown wary and realized it wasn't. Julius would never do something like that. Whoever . . . *what*ever it was, was cunning and devious enough to lure them into a dangerous place and try to kill them.

Was that the dragon's doing, too? Was such a

creature capable of getting inside his head and sending him into a swoon? Was it able to re-create itself as a spirit, to protect itself from those it knew were the most dangerous? Seven hundred years ago, when he'd fought it for the first time, Reynald had believed he was pitting himself against a physical monster. Now he knew there was far more to the dragon than that. Like the witch from the between-worlds, this creature was magical, able to perform feats no mortal could begin to imagine. To have lived so long it must have a strength and cunning far beyond anything he'd faced before.

But he had no choice. Running away and playing the coward was not in his nature. Whether this was the task that had been given him or just an unpleasant consequence of his return to the mortal world, he had to save these people, to save Amy and her brother and, if it was possible, to save himself.

Behind him, Amy and Jez were arguing again. The verbal sparring seemed to be a part of their relationship, and he sensed that it helped them to cope with their emotions. He knew that Jez didn't believe him, but he didn't care. Jez could come along, or Jez could stay safe in his room, but Reynald would do what he had to.

"We *need* the key, Jez," Amy said, and without turning to look, Reynald knew her pretty face would be all flushed and cross.

"You're not going down into the tunnels with

that character," Jez retorted, his whisper just loud enough to be heard. "I won't let you."

"I am. With or without you. Now, are you going to get that key?"

"I shouldn't have waited," Rey said, silencing their bickering with a glance over his shoulder. They stared back at him, Amy looking worried and Jez stubborn. "I will smash open the door. There is no time to find the key."

"But Rey—"

The ground began to shake.

A potted plant on a wooden stand fell over at the bottom of the stairs. As Reynald steadied himself with one hand against the wall, the voice spoke inside his head. He recognized the strange husky tones with a mixture of triumph and dread.

Ah, it is you, cariad. You can feel me, too, can't you? You know I am coming for you, Reynald.

"Prepare to die, foul creature!"

It is you who will die.

"Bloody hell," Jez muttered, "he talks to it."

The tremors had stopped as suddenly as they'd started. Reynald continued on his way to the antechamber. The table with the strange drinks upon it, and the little crowd of people, were gone. There were broken cups and saucers on the floor, and a spreading stain from the overturned hot-water receptacle. He paused, then changed direction, turning into the great hall.

The weapons were where he remembered, hanging on the wall by the dais. Swords and shields and pikes. He saw the crossbow and smiled. Aye, that would do. His longbow was too large and un-wieldy for the tunnels, but the crossbow, although not as powerful, would be better in such confined quarters. He could disable the dragon with a well-aimed arrow, then move in with his sword for the final blow.

At least, that was the plan.

Reynald collected the crossbow, wrenching it off the wall, pleased to see there were also bolts, and that the weapon appeared to be well cared for. He laid a bolt into the groove at the top and aimed it carefully at the tapestry on the opposite wall. It was a hunting scene, with a stag and hounds and men on horses. Reynald pressed the trigger to re-lease the bolt, and it sprang through the air and struck the tapestry, and stuck there.

He grunted his satisfaction.

"Rey?"

When he turned, he saw that both Amy and Jez were watching him from the doorway. He forced a smile. " 'Tis in working order," he said.

Jez nodded toward the bolt. "You hit the stag in the heart," he said. "Lucky shot, huh?"

But it wasn't a lucky shot, and they both knew it.

The Ghost slung the crossbow over his shoulder and walked quickly back through the door. Two servants were passing by—staff, as Amy called them—hurrying in the opposite direction.

". . . only here," one of them was saying. "No other part of the county has been affected at all."

"Coster should evacuate the building. This isn't right."

Jez was walking backward, trying to listen to them and still follow Reynald and his sister. "It's the dragon," Amy whispered loudly. "This is what happens when it wakes up and starts crawling out of the tunnels."

"Well, of course, all earthquakes are caused by dragons."

"Oh, forget it!" She caught up to Reynald, grasping his arm in both hands, as if she wanted to make sure he didn't get away from her again.

He stooped and kissed her brow, breathing in her scent. "You have my heart, damsel," he murmured. "Always."

Her eyes filled with tears. "Rey—"

"This thing must be done, Amy. Perhaps this is why I am here. I must face my foe once again, and this time I *must* succeed."

They reached the door, and Reynald bent to inspect the lock. It was strange and unfamiliar, and very shiny. He would need to break it. Determinedly, he began to slide his sword from its scabbard.

"Oh, for God's sake," Jez muttered, and pushed in front of him. He knelt, reaching into his pocket, and brought out a small device. This he set against the lock, fiddling with dials and watching as lights flicked on and off. There was a clicking, whirring noise, and Jez reached out and turned the handle, trying not to look too smug.

The door opened with a puff of very cold air.

"Thank you," Amy said, turning to hug her brother.

Reynald was already entering the room he remembered, with the boxes stacked against the walls and the stairs leading down underground.

"Brrr, no heating in here," Amy murmured, following him in and flicking on the lights. They were very dim, barely throwing forth enough light for them to see their feet in front of them.

Suddenly a voice called out from behind them. "Excuse me!"

Reynald heaved a sigh. He knew that voice. Unwillingly, he turned to face her. "What is it?" he asked Miriam Ure.

She was wearing her wig again, and it slipped over one eye as she hurried toward them. "You're not meant to go in there. It might be dangerous."

Reynald snorted a laugh. "Go away, lady," he advised her.

"You are very rude. I don't know who you think you are, but as a well-known historian, I am—"

Another tremor, a smaller one, started shaking the castle. Reynald slid his arm around Amy, protecting her from the falling dust and small pebbles of stone from the roof above.

"This is dangerous," Jez protested, glancing

nervously toward the tunnel at the bottom of the stairs. "She's right," with a nod toward Miriam Ure. "We shouldn't be here."

"This shaking is the dragon trying to stop me," Reynald retorted. "We must not allow it to succeed."

Miriam was peering at them from the doorway. "Come back at once," she demanded bossily.

"No," Reynald retorted.

The tremor was almost stopped, and Reynald went quickly down the stairs, plunging into the tunnel. He ducked beneath a reinforcing beam, glancing back at Amy to make sure she was safe. He knew he couldn't prevent her from coming with him, but he swore to himself that he would make her turn back before the danger became too great. Jez would help him. He knew now that Jez would protect his sister. That was the only reason he had allowed the other man to accompany them.

He peered ahead. The tunnel branched into two, and he took the left fork, negotiating the uneven ground as it began to slope downward, sending them deeper into the earth. There was an unpleasant dank smell here, and the lights were flickering and fizzing. Reynald almost smiled when Jez cleared his throat as if he was making an announcement, then produced some sort of lighting device from his other pocket.

The beam it threw out was, though small, very bright. Enough for them to see their way. "I hope you know what you're doing, Rey," Jez said. "You know what will happen to you if anyone gets hurt."

"Jez, it's true," Amy tried again. "The dragon is waking up. We need to find it."

"Cannot wait . . ."

There was a strange humming through the air, and the tunnel began to tremble. It quickly grew much worse, until the shaking was so violent that Reynald found it impossible to keep walking. Even to stand upright was difficult, and he crouched with his arms around Amy, her face buried against his neck, waiting for the tremors to stop. Choking dust billowed around them, and there was a hideous grinding noise, as the centuries-old timbers moved and stretched.

"Amy, for God's sake—" shouted Jez.

And that was when they heard it.

The dragon's roar.

It was unlike anything they'd ever heard before. Animal, yet with overtones of emotion that were almost human. And most of all, terrifying.

Jez had frozen, his mouth still hanging open. "What the hell was that?" The light beam in his hand jerked, swinging crazily around the tunnel. Reynald saw that his face was coated in dust, and his suit was torn at the shoulder, where he had caught it against the uneven wall.

"Do you believe us now?" Amy asked him, her voice rising hysterically.

"You mean *that* was a dragon?" But Reynald noted that his skepticism wasn't quite as whole-hearted as it had been. It sounded more like bravado now.

"No, Jez," Amy said, shaking the dust from her hair, "it was a bat."

"Amy, you can't truly believe—"

She sneezed.

Reynald was already up again and walking. The tunnel narrowed in front of them. With one hand on the wall at his side to guide him, he kept the other on his crossbow. The thought of firing a bolt in the half darkness at a creature who wanted to kill him was not a pleasant one, and he knew he wouldn't have much time. Even if he didn't succeed, he might be able to keep the dragon distracted while Amy escaped.

As she entered his thoughts, he felt her come up behind him again, then her hand was clinging to a fold of his tunic. Several paces back, Jez grumbled to himself, the light in his hand moving jerkily from side to side.

"It's freezing," Amy said.

There were more stairs cut roughly into the rock, and Reynald waited for the other two to come up beside him before he moved on. Jez's light shone down the shallow steps, barely penetrating farther than three yards and finding no end to the staircase. The darkness was so intense, it was as if it sucked up the bright beam, reducing its effectiveness.

Was this another of the dragon's tricks? the Ghost thought, as Jez shook the device and swore, saying he didn't understand it, that the batteries were almost new.

"It is the dragon. She is protecting herself in every way she can. Keep watch and be careful. She will have more tricks as we draw closer."

For once Jez didn't argue or make a sneering comment. Since the dragon's roar, he had been far more subdued.

Carefully, Reynald began to descend the steps, not knowing how far it was to the bottom. It seemed unlikely that many people in this present time would wander down here. The place was chilly and damp, and there was a very bad smell.

"Rotten meat."

He glanced over his shoulder, where Jez was much closer than he'd thought. "Aye," he agreed.

"Why can I smell—" Jez began, uncertainly.

This time the roar was louder, or they were closer. It rushed down the tunnels, echoing all about them, as if it were surrounding them. Amy gasped, trying not to scream, and Jez swore again. Good English words! It was nice to know that some things had not changed, Reynald thought with a smile.

A moment later the earth began to shake again.

"How close are we?" Amy said, her fingers rigid as she clutched his tunic.

"Close," he murmured, and reached around to touch her and give a comforting squeeze.

It has been too long, Reynald. Come to me and let me kill you again. I have been hungry for your flesh. Sweet, sweet flesh. I wonder what your mate will taste like? I will enjoy crunching her bones.

The dragon was back inside his head, its voice deep and soft, with that lilting Welsh accent distracting him from the horrors of which it spoke.

"You will never know. I am going to send you to the between-worlds. The witch is waiting for you, *cariad.*"

It wasn't gloating now. Was it afraid of the witch? Had he found something that even a dragon feared?

"Rey?" Amy whispered. "Who are you talking to?"

"The dragon. She speaks to me inside my head. She thinks to frighten me away." He threw back his head and shouted at the top of his voice, "I am coming to kill you!"

His words echoed, fading. He waited to see what would happen.

"What's that light?" Suddenly Amy was peering in front of him. "There, up ahead!"

"There's someone in the tunnels with us!" Jez began to push past. "Dragon," he sneered. "I told you it was all crap, Amy."

Reynald could see the light, too, like a ball of pale moving color. It was very familiar ... And then he realized what it was.

"No!" he shouted. But it was too late, Jez was past him and running eagerly forward.

"Jez!" Amy screamed her brother's name, her voice echoing back and forth down the tunnel.

Reynald caught her as she, too, went to run, holding her tight as she struggled, and more tremors shook the ground and walls, sending down a shower of fine rubble. The dragon roared furiously, a roar that turned into a high-pitched scream of frustration.

Amy changed her mind about running after her brother, and dived into his arms. He held on to her, enclosing her, protecting her.

"Rey," she said, and her voice was oddly calm, as if she'd gone beyond fear. "I'm s-so frightened. I've never been so frightened."

"Stay by me," he murmured the familiar words into her hair, kissing her, soothing her with his hands and lips and voice. "We must stay together, damsel. If we do that, we cannot be harmed."

He didn't really believe it, but if his being invincible helped Amy, then he would finally learn to tell lies.

She recovered herself, taking a deep breath, then another. "We have to find Jez," she said. "Let's go."

Reynald realized that the ground had stopped shaking and straightened up. The dust made them cough, and the foul smell was even stronger. The dragon had been feeding down here for centuries. He wondered what it had been feeding on, and decided he did not particularly want to know.

"Rey," Amy said dully. "Look."

He did look. Ahead of them, at the far end of the tunnel, the ball of light no longer glowed, but the bright beam that belonged to Jez was lying abandoned upon the ground.

There was no sign of Amy's brother.

Twenty-six

"*Where is he? Where's Jez?*" *Amy knew* she was asking the same question again and again. She couldn't help asking it. Ever since Jez had run off, and they'd found his flashlight, they'd been searching for him. "Surely, if he was knocked out or . . . or hurt, he would've been near his flashlight? Even if he could walk, he wouldn't get far in the dark. Would he?"

"I do not know, Amy."

"He only came down here because of me. He wanted to protect me. And now he's gone."

The tears ran down her cheeks, and she couldn't stop them. She put her head in her hands and sank onto the floor. The whole weekend had been imbued with a sense of unreality, as if at any moment she might wake up at home in bed and discover it had been a dream. Except that now it had turned into a nightmare.

Rey crouched beside her, stroking her face, and murmuring that they would find him, he promised, that everything would be all right. She wished she could believe him, but she knew he was saying that to comfort her. How could she have been so deliriously happy only a short time ago, and now be plummeted into the depths of despair?

"I hate this tunnel," Amy said, her voice vibrating with emotion. "It's worse than anything I've ever known. Worse than running away from a father who beats you. Worse than losing the brother who kept me safe when no one else would. Worse than knowing *you're* going away and I'll n-never see you again. W-worse than anything."

"My dearest heart," he whispered, gathering her into his arms. He was holding her so tight she could hardly breathe, but she liked it. She wanted to become a part of him, she thought, as she cuddled up against him. She wanted to be with him always. "I will never let anything hurt you again," he went on. "I will be your lord and your love, and wherever I go, you will be in my mind and my heart."

It was nonsense, of course. In a minute, an hour, a day, they might be parted and never see each other again. But she was exhausted, physically and emotionally, and she let his words form a soothing shield between her and reality.

They stayed like that for a moment or two.

"Amy?" he said, his voice gentle but firm. "Are you all right now?"

And she knew it was time to pull herself together again. There were dragons to slay.

"I'm all right," she replied, and gave an embarrassed laugh. "Sorry. I don't usually freak out like that."

"You have a right to 'freak out' from all that has happened to you. I think you are the most courageous woman I have ever known."

"Rey," she whispered, "you always know what to say. If I didn't already love you, I'd love you for that."

His lips brushed hers, then moved in gentle exploration. She rested her hand on his cheek, drawing him nearer. His mouth was hot, and she tried not to moan as his tongue brushed hers.

She didn't take any notice of the first tremors, but she felt the next ones. The floor began to move, and they huddled together until it stopped.

"I thought for a moment we were responsible for that," she said, when all was still again.

"Moving the earth?" He chuckled. " 'Tis possible."

"Do you really think it's the same dragon, Rey? Don't dragons have little dragons? Maybe this is a whole new generation."

"No, it is the same dragon. I know that voice."

Nervously, she found herself going off on another tangent. "I always thought I'd like a big family. Lots of children and dogs and cats, and whatever else came along. I imagined myself on a farm, with space all around me, lots of open ground and trees and meadows and . . . well, as different from Parkhill as it could be. Now look at me! I'm living in a tiny flat in inner London, with the underground beneath me, planes overhead, and lorries rumbling by outside. And not even a cat or a potted plant to my name."

"I, too, would like children," he said quietly. "In my position, I have much to give to them—wealth, power, privilege. They would need to work for it, fight for it, but the rewards would be worth the reaping."

"I think you'd make a good father. Of course, you'd have to learn to laugh more often and to kiss them good night."

"I can laugh and kiss, damsel," he said, "if you can give me the children."

Her heart ached too much for her to answer him. Because she'd never be able to have children with Rey. There was no future for them.

"Look, you're better off without me anyway," she spoke at last, trying to sound matter-of-fact when she wanted to cry again. "You've seen how untidy I am. I'd drive you mad. And how could I run a castle of this size when I can't even run my flat? I lose things all the time, you know. My keys, my cell phone, my purse. How would it be if I lost the keys to the storeroom? Everyone would starve to death over the winter. And I'm always forgetting to pay the bills. We'd be out of candles in no time."

He laughed, and if it wasn't quite as hearty as she would have liked, it was a good effort. "No more, Amy, you have convinced me," he said. He held out his hand to her and helped her to her feet.

Neither of them said much as they continued on their search. The flashlight grew dimmer and dimmer, and eventually died altogether, but Rey would not turn back. Amy found the darkness almost a tangible entity, and as she put one foot in front of the other, she never knew what was before her.

And yet Rey remained confident that they would find and defeat the dragon. She couldn't help but admire him for it.

Jez was never far from her mind. She kept hoping that they'd turn a corner and there he'd be, but they didn't find him. How could he have vanished like that? As far as she could tell there were dozens of other tunnels running off the main tunnel along this stretch. If he hadn't gone another way, then maybe he'd caught up with the monk and lantern?

Amy hoped not.

The tremors came and went, but each time they were worse, and the sequences were closer together. Amy lost count of the number of times they were forced to stop and cling together, while she expected the roof to collapse on top of them. And then that terrible roaring would sound out, as if the earth itself was in agony.

The dragon.

Until now she'd half thought of it as something like an illustration in a children's storybook; a quaint, colorful creature with cute little wings and a kindly heart, who just wanted to be left in peace and didn't really mean any harm.

The thing that roared in the darkness was neither quaint nor kindly. Rey was right. It was a simple question of their lives or the dragon's.

"What is your plan, Rey?"

"I want to get close enough to use my crossbow and wound the dragon while it is still restricted by the tunnels. Then I can go in with my sword. In such cramped quarters I do not have many choices, but perhaps that will work in our favor."

"Is it possible? To get close enough without . . . ?"

"It is the best I can do," he said gently.

Amy lost track of time. They could have been down here for hours or days. And then, gradually, as they shuffled forward, her eyes began to detect a change in the light. She realized that it wasn't totally dark after all and that there was a faint glow coming from somewhere.

They began to move more quickly, and soon the tunnel had widened out, the ceiling so high she couldn't see it. This was more like a natural cavern than a man-made tunnel. The only problem was that the rotten smell was stronger, so bad that she pulled her scarf up over her nose and mouth and tried not to breathe too deeply.

Rey had taken the lead, despite there being room for them to walk abreast, and his hand was clenched about his crossbow. Amy didn't argue with him. She trusted him to know what he was doing, and it made sense for the man with the weapon to go first.

And then she felt it. Movement in front of them. A shuffling, swishing noise, as though something very large was forcing a passage through the earth.

Reynald stopped. "We are close," he whispered. "I can hear her voice."

Amy couldn't hear anything, but she believed him. "What does she say?"

"She welcomes me to my death."

"Nice," she murmured.

Reynald loaded a bolt into his crossbow. "Amy, you must stay behind me," he said, "and if I tell you to run, then you will."

It was an order; Amy didn't fool herself into thinking it was anything else. "What if I don't want to run away and leave you to face that thing alone?"

"I cannot do what I must if I am worrying for you. I have to know you will obey me."

"What happened to 'stay by me'?" she said sulkily, sounding close to tears. She didn't want to leave him; she loved him.

"You are my brave lady," he went on. "A lady must help her lord to do his duty. I cannot do it without your help, Amy. I fear if I were to see you hurt, I would abandon everything to carry you to safety."

He meant it. Her heart ached for him and her, and the words he had spoken and which she'd never forget.

"I'll do as you say," she promised.

He kissed her, his mouth hard and passionate, then he turned away and began to walk forward again, but very slowly and cautiously. After taking a moment to catch her breath, Amy followed.

The smell was much, much worse, and she added a fold of her jacket to the scarf. She couldn't remember anything in the storybooks about dragons smelling this bad.

The roar came again, so close now that the sound swallowed them up. Luckily, the covering over her mouth muffled her scream. The ground began to quake.

Reynald stumbled and fell to one knee, holding the crossbow up and ready to fire the bolt.

And that was when Amy looked beyond him, into the tunnel, and saw it.

An enormous dark shape, it filled the tunnel entirely with its bulk. She could see that it was moving, and as it moved the earth groaned. It turned its head, and she saw the shine of its eyes. Black eyes. Full of hatred.

Bitch, it hissed, the voice invading her head. *I will show him what it is to lose the one you love. Let him suffer as I have!*

Amy was still recovering from her shock when she saw that the dragon had taken an almighty breath, opening its mouth like a furnace. It was going to fry them both to a crisp.

Reynald knew it, too. He was up and running, taking her with him, before she could even begin to shout a warning. They fled for their lives, back the way they'd come. Behind them there was a brilliant burst of red light, and the smell of burning, then Reynald swung her around with him, and she struck the tunnel wall. Dazed, the next thing she knew, he had flattened himself over her, and she couldn't breathe.

The flames rushed past them like an intercity express.

Amy heard it happen, although her eyes were closed, and she couldn't have seen anything anyway, because her face was pressed tightly to Rey's chest. Her head was spinning, and she thought for a moment she was dead, because how could anyone possibly survive a dragon's fiery breath? And then, when she realized she wasn't, she thought Rey must be dead, because he had shielded her with his body.

"Rey?" she croaked. "Rey!"

He wasn't dead either. Just before he finally stepped away, she felt the strong beat of his heart against her cheek.

Amy peeled herself off the wall and staggered a few steps. She realized then how they'd survived. There was an outcropping of rock, just wide enough to protect them from the hot blast. Even so, when she touched Rey's back, his tunic felt singed.

"Where is it?" she asked, strangely calm for someone who had nearly been sautéed.

"Stay here."

He looked at her as he said it, to make certain she knew this was not a suggestion but an order to be obeyed, then he walked to where the dragon had been. Amy stayed, waiting, and trying not to shake.

She couldn't help but think that, if Jez had come across the dragon, then he must be dead. Maybe that was why they hadn't found him. There was nothing left to find.

She felt numb at the thought.

"Amy?"

She hadn't heard Reynald return, and she jumped as he touched her arm.

"There is a tunnel ahead of us that crosses the one we are now in. The dragon was passing through that other tunnel when she saw us."

"Did you fire your crossbow before . . . ?"

"No. I didn't have a chance. I dropped it, and I fear it is ash."

"Then what are we going to do, Rey? You can't fight that thing with a sword!"

"I must. Once she gets out . . ."

"So we keep following?"

"I want you to stay here."

"No," she begged, "not yet. Please, let me stay with you a while longer. I promise I won't get in the way, and I'll obey your orders. I want to be with you as long as I can."

He hesitated, and Amy knew she was taking unfair advantage of his feelings for her. But she couldn't leave him yet, when every second together was precious.

She heard him sigh and knew she'd won. "Very well. Just a little longer."

The tunnel that crossed theirs was even wider and taller, or maybe the passage of the dragon had done that. The rock sides seemed smooth, shiny, and warm to the touch. Amy grimaced.

"There is light up ahead." Rey's voice brought her back to herself.

She blinked, stiffening, thinking he meant the lantern they had seen before. But then she realized that this was a different kind of light.

"It's daylight!"

The tunnel had an entrance to the outside world, and they'd almost reached it.

"The dragon will escape," Rey groaned.

He began to run. Amy, taken by surprise, was slow to follow. Despite her fitness, her legs were burning with fatigue, and she wondered how it was Rey could keep going.

The daylight was getting brighter, and now, against it, she could see the dark silhouette of the dragon. A huge, lizardlike creature, with wings folded onto its back, four muscular legs with claws that scraped the rock with each step, and a long, trailing tail. It was moving swiftly now, half-slithering, half-crawling in a desperate effort to get to the tunnel entrance.

"Stop!" Rey shouted. "Fight me, damn you!"

But the dragon didn't stop, and again Amy heard the voice inside her head.

I am free, cariad! *Why should I stop? But don't fret, we will meet again. Soon, very soon.*

The dragon unfolded its wings, stretching them out so that the leathery tips brushed the sides of the tunnel. It began to flap them, slowly and strongly. As it reached the entrance to the tunnel, it rose into the air. Clumsy at first, it seemed to be having difficulty remembering the technicalities of flight. And then, as if it had got the knack, it began to move more gracefully, wings beating rhythmically, and soared beyond their limited vision.

Rey staggered to the entrance and knelt, shading his eyes and gazing up. Amy followed him. The day was ending. Dazed, she stared at the sky of blue and gold and apricot, the sun's rays streaming down. The snow had passed, and although there was little warmth in the sunshine, it felt so good on her face.

"Beautiful," she murmured, and understood completely what the dragon felt after seven hundred years alone in darkness.

It was simply good to be alive.

Twenty-seven

Reynald knew where they were. Soaring high above them was the north tower of his castle, and below them was the dangerously sheer side of the ravine. He straightened, sheathed his sword, and began to climb out of the tunnel. There was a narrow path running around the entrance, leading up the rocky hillside to the base of the tower.

"This way," he said, holding out his hand to Amy. She came willingly, obviously very glad to be free of the darkness and the stench of dragon.

"Is it possible the dragon will be happy enough just to be out of there?" she asked, panting slightly as she climbed. "Why would she come back and risk everything?"

"Because freedom is not enough," he said,

pausing to gaze down over the ravine and the trees that clustered deep within it.

"What does she want then, Rey? Why is she so bitter and angry?"

"It is a woman, is it not?" he said, turning his gaze to search her face. "You feel that too, damsel?"

"Yes, it is a woman."

"She wants me. And you. She wants revenge for something she believes has been done to her by me, or in my name. And she wants this land. She will come back." He shook his head. "I have failed."

"No, Rey, you haven't failed," she said. Her hand was warm and comforting in his. "When the dragon returns, that will be your chance. This idea of yours, hunting it down in the tunnels, it was never going to work, the dragon was always going to win. But next time, that really will be your turn. You can prepare, you will have the advantage."

Reynald felt his mouth twitch. He couldn't help it. She had stripped the sense of failure and melancholy from him, and instead he felt confident and alive. His blood was singing. He had missed his chance, yes, but Amy was right, next time would be better. More fitting. The dragon would come again, and next time he would succeed.

With her beside him, how could it be otherwise?

"Come," he said, and squeezed her fingers in his.

She followed him in silence for a few steps, then she said, as if she couldn't hold the words inside any longer, "What about Jez?"

"We'll go back to the beginning of the tunnels. We need lights and men. Now that the dragon is gone, it is safe for others to help in the search."

"Yes," she brightened. "You're right. We'll find him, won't we?"

Reynald wasn't so certain, but he let her keep her hopes. Amy did not deserve to lose her brother, and Jez did not deserve to die, but the Ghost had seen many injustices in the world.

"What will happen after you kill the dragon?" Amy asked, as if it were a foregone conclusion.

"I do not know."

"Will the witch send you straight back to 1299?"

"Amy, I do not know. I am not even certain whether or not that is the task she has set me."

"It's just that I want to be ready. If I know how it works, then I can be prepared for you to disappear, or whatever happens. I don't want to make a fool of myself. I want to be the brave lady of the castle, with a smile on my face."

"I will not go without saying good-bye," he said gently.

"Do you promise?"

He smoothed her cheek with the backs of his fingers. "I promise, my heart."

"I'll be disappointed not to be able to teach those children to read," she murmured, with a wistful smile, "but I imagine the present day has its compensations over the thirteenth century. I don't suppose anyone bathes more than once a year, and all you eat are pigs' insides."

He threw back his head and laughed.

She watched him irritably, but her eyes were sparkling. "I didn't mean to be funny."

"Amy, we bathe often," he lectured her. "And we eat well. But you are right, we do not waste anything. I promise you, though." And although he was still smiling he was serious now. "If you came back with me to the thirteenth century, I would never insist you eat the insides of any pigs."

He wanted her to go with him.

"It isn't fair," she breathed. "Why is this happening to us?"

"Julius would say it is to make us better people."

She sniffed, as he knew she would. "What would Angharad say?"

"She would say we are wasting her time with such nonsense, and that there is no rhyme or reason to anything that happens in this world."

Amy pondered on that, and Reynald let the silence grow.

They had walked around the base of the castle wall, and now the gatehouse was just ahead. Once they'd crossed the drawbridge over the frozen moat, they would be back inside.

Back inside!

For the first time, Reynald realized he was

actually outside the castle walls. Whatever the witch had put in place to keep him a prisoner within his own home was gone. He was free.

Did that mean the witch was pleased with him? That he had passed some test?

He turned to tell Amy his news, just as someone shouted from directly above them.

"Who goes there?"

They looked up, and Amy shrieked, "Jez!"

Her brother was leaning over the battlements, his face a pale blur in the dusk, but it was definitely Jez. He was alive.

"Where did you go?" she called, and she was smiling.

"Let me come down and I'll tell you." His face disappeared.

Amy turned to Rey and threw her arms about his neck. "Jez is alive," she gasped. He picked her up and swung her around, then he was laughing because she was laughing. And then she was crying, and he kissed her to comfort them both.

Jez told them that he'd followed the ball of light for a time. "But it was a trick. It wasn't a real person, instead it was as if someone was projecting an image in front of me," he said in disgust.

They were sitting in Jez's room in the castle, and he'd rung room service to order food and drinks. Jez had already showered and changed, but Amy hadn't had time, and although she'd stripped off her jacket, she still felt as if she had the smell and feel of the tunnels clinging to her.

"And then it vanished altogether," he went on, "and I panicked. While I was running after it, I lost my flashlight, and I was all alone in the dark. I tried to turn back the way we'd come, but although I walked for miles, I never found either of you. Then I started to run again and fell over. For a time I just lay there feeling as if I'd never get out. I hadn't felt like that since Dad caught me selling his booze to the kids in the upper grades."

Sympathetically, Amy reached out to take his hand. "It was horrible down there."

"I really was starting to think I'd be lost in the dark forever, and the ground was still shaking, and that . . . that thing was still howling."

"The dragon," Rey said primly.

To Amy's amusement, Jez ignored him. "I must have taken a wrong turning, because the next thing I knew I was inside the castle wall. Actually *inside* it. A secret passage. There were arrow slits or peepholes, and I could see well enough. Anyway, eventually the secret passage led me to a room in the gatehouse. It was like a movie."

"Horror," Amy murmured.

"I was wondering whether you were okay, but I knew I couldn't go back into those tunnels. I just hoped that Rey would look after you."

He shuddered at the memories, and Amy knew he was shattered. She didn't blame him; she'd felt the same, but she'd had Rey to hold her hand.

"I was standing up there, trying to work out what to do, when you appeared." He glanced at Rey and gave a grimace. "Something else appeared, too, not long before you and Amy. I still don't believe it, but I think it was a dragon."

"Oh Jez . . ."

"I know I must be crazy, but I swear I saw it," he burst out, as if she was doubting him. "Flew up from the direction of the ravine. It was big, not quite jumbo-jet size, but bloody big. I watched it until it faded into the sun."

"So you do believe us now?" Rey said, looking down his nose.

"I have to whether I like it or not, don't I?"

"You don't sound very happy about it," Amy scolded him. "Not many people get to see a dragon, Jez."

He looked at her as if she was the one who was crazy. "And I envy them. So, what happens now?"

"Can't the castle be evacuated?" Amy asked.

"I heard that Coster had everyone outside while the shaking was going on," Jez updated them, "but once it stopped, everyone went back to their rooms. With the roads closed, and now the phone lines down, there's no help and nowhere else to go. Besides, the castle hasn't been damaged. It seems to be business as usual."

"The dragon will return," Reynald said with grim certainty. "She believes she alone has the right to all that is mine. She will return and kill everyone who stands in her way."

Jez sat up straight. "Then we should go. Now. Even if we have to ski out."

Amy gave him a bemused look. "And leave everyone else to die? Jez, you can't be serious!"

"We can warn them," he said feebly.

"And do you think they'll believe us? No, Jez, we can't just leave. I don't believe you're suggesting it. We have to stay. Rey has to kill the dragon this time, so that he can . . ." She stopped, aware she had said too much.

Jez's eyes narrowed. "Kill the dragon *this* time?" he repeated. "Rey? Is your name really Rey? How do you spell that?"

"He spells it R-e-y," Amy muttered. "Short for Reynald de Mortimer."

Jez's face went chalky. "Oh God, you're going to tell me that he's the Ghost, aren't you? Amy, that's impossible!"

"Like dragons, do you mean? It's not impossible, Jez, it's . . . it's wonderful."

He just shook his head as if he didn't want to know.

"Rey *is* Reynald de Mortimer. He's been sleeping for seven hundred years in the between-worlds, but he's back now to right the wrong and save himself and his people."

Jez's eyes seemed to have glazed over. "Don't tell me any more, please. I can't take it. I've reached my limit."

Amy sighed. "Please yourself. Although I don't know how you can find scheming to steal Nicco's diamond exciting and challenging, yet act like a nervous wreck just because Rey has returned from the dead. He needs help to kill the dragon so that he can go home to 1299."

"Amy, believe me, I'd rather O'Neill sent me to prison than help Rey kill the dragon."

Disgusted, Amy got up and went and sat by Rey, glaring at him when he put up his hand to hide his smile. "I'm trying to help," she said, "and Jez doesn't want to know and *you* think it's funny."

"I appreciate your help, damsel, believe me. I am smiling because I find the manner in which you and your brother argue amusing. It is strange to me; I was an only child."

"You were lucky, mate," Jez muttered.

"Thanks so much!" Amy aimed a blow at his shoulder.

There was a knock on the door. Thinking it was room service, Jez got up to answer it.

The door opened into the room, hiding whoever was standing in the corridor, but Amy recognized his voice. "Jez, I wonder if I might come in?"

"Nicco," said Jez. "I don't see why not."

Twenty-eight

Amy was desperately shaking her head and waving her arms, but it was already too late. Nicco was inside the room. He stopped, frozen, seeing Amy and Rey sitting cozily on the bed, then his face creased in distaste as he took note of the grubby state they were in.

"We were caught in the earthquake," Jez explained easily. "What about you?"

"I did not venture from my room," Nicco replied, implying that anyone who had was insane.

Amy watched him seat himself elegantly in a chair, smoothing down his sleeves, straightening his tie. Then he put his hand in his jacket pocket, before he looked up at her and gave a bland smile.

"You are feeling better, I hope, Amee?"

"Better?"

"Maybe you have not taken your medicine again today? Jez told me of your problems. I am sorry to hear you have an illness with your brain." He clicked his tongue and shook his head.

Amy shot Jez a furious look, but he was studiously ignoring her as he poured the drinks. "What will you have, Rey? What was the usual in 1299?"

Rey said nothing, his eyes on Nicco.

Amy wondered whether the Russian was religious. Did he have rosary beads in his pocket? The idea was a hard one to swallow, but he was certainly playing with something, his fingers turning the object over and over.

"This place," Nicco said, "it is lacking in sophistication. I can't believe someone of importance really lived here; it is fit only for peasants. Why would anyone want to take a holiday in such a cold and miserable castle? Next time I come here they should pay me! If the roads weren't closed, I'd drive back to where it is more civilized. Perhaps I should walk." He recrossed his legs.

"You'd die in the snow like an unsophisticated peasant," Rey said evenly.

Nicco gave him a look of dislike.

"You'd ruin your nice shoes," Amy added.

Nicco turned the look onto her, but now it was far more venomous. "I can afford more shoes," he let her know. "I am a wealthy man, Amee."

"You can always stay in your room and watch the porn channel," Jez suggested. "They won't be putting on this medieval rubbish now, will they?"

Nicco couldn't wait to give him the bad news. "Ah, my friend, but they are! That fool, Coster, told me it will take our minds off our predicament. The calling will be performed tonight, at nine o'clock. Sharp," he added, with a smirk.

"The calling?" Amy repeated, but there was a memory stirring in her head. Something she had missed; something she should have remembered before.

"The dragon-calling," said Nicco, and gave a scornful laugh. "Perhaps we can use its fiery breath to toast marshmallows. Isn't that something you English like to do, Jez?"

"Something like that," Jez said quietly, but he was staring over at Rey, and his face had lost all the animation it had gained since Nicco came into the room.

Amy turned to look at Rey, too.

His colorless eyes were blazing.

"The fools!" Reynald raged. "Lackwits, slimy frogs, turd-eating knaves."

He said lots of other things, too, but they were in French.

Amy and Jez were staring at him in silence. His uncharacteristic explosion of anger had shocked them both. Nicco had left after "shit-crawling worms."

"We have to stop them."

"But how can we?" Amy said reasonably. "No one will believe us. *I* wouldn't have believed us before I saw it for myself."

"Then we must try!"

Amy knew he had seen what a dragon was capable of, that he was a man who knew of these things, and he should be listened to. But this was a world where science and rational thinking were the new religion. How were they going to convince Coster and his guests that there really was a dragon out there and calling to it was a very bad idea?

"Rey," she began.

Jez interrupted her. "Amy, what was Nicco doing in his pocket?"

She frowned. "I . . . I thought he must have some worry beads in there, but he isn't religious, is he? Whatever it was, he was getting off on it, smirking and preening and—"

Suddenly Jez grinned. "I think it was the Star of Russia. I think he had it with him in his pocket!" He laughed aloud, pounding his fists on the arms of his chair. "The stupid bugger, he's brought it with him."

Amy laughed, too. "Jez, I think you're right! It'd be just like him, wouldn't it? He probably plays with it when he thinks no one's watching. What a turn-on for him, sitting there with one of the most famous diamonds in the world in his pocket and no one knowing."

"I can't believe my luck. I'll wait until he goes down to dinner—he's too greedy not to—then I'll get into his room and look for it. Shouldn't be difficult to find. Knowing Nicco, he probably has it under his pillow."

"Or in a sock in his drawer. Jez, do you think—"

"Stop it!"

The voice was loud and furious and cut through their chatter like a battle-axe. They both froze, then turned slowly to face the Ghost. If his eyes had been bright before, now they were burning with emotion. How could anyone ever have called this man cold? Amy felt her heartbeat speed up.

"You are talking of stealing a ring when we are all in danger of being killed?"

"I'm sorry," Amy murmured.

"Can it be you still don't believe in the dragon? But you have seen it. You have felt its power. It exists!" Rey shook his head in disgust.

Jez turned and made a face at her, making her feel like they were a couple of schoolchildren sent to the headmaster's office. "Rey," he said, matter-of-factly, "I hear what you're saying, and I know it's important. But I want that diamond ring. I need it. And this is my chance. A chance I never thought I'd have, by the way. Nicco isn't going to know who's taken the diamond, and he probably won't want to admit he's lost it. He'll be worried about his insurers. And I'll be long gone by the time he puts two and two together."

"You are stealing—"

"Think of it this way," Jez interrupted. "Nicco is the kind of man who'd starve his peasants just so that he could afford to go to Paris to shop. He probably sold his grandmother for that diamond."

"So you're going to give the money to the poor?" Amy asked innocently.

Jez stood up, opened the door, and cleared his throat.

"I don't mean to be rude, but I need some time to get ready."

"To slip into your Robin Hood costume?" Amy murmured.

"Ha-ha. I'll see you both later."

Reynald rose up to his full intimidating height, and he was not amused. "You are a fool, Jez," he said, and his words were all the more significant because of the quietness with which he said them. "This jewel is more precious to you than your own life."

"It isn't that," Jez protested. "I just figure I can kill two birds with one stone . . . eh, diamond."

"If you were brought before me at my manor court, it would be my duty to sentence you to have your hand chopped off."

"Lucky we're here then, isn't it?"

Rey stared at him a moment longer, as if hoping for some sort of enlightenment for himself or Jez, then he walked out of the door.

Amy followed, but as she passed, Jez whispered, "Are you really into the sheriff of Nottingham? Don't you find him a bit much?"

She smiled. "He's perfect."

Jez shook his head in bewilderment and closed the door behind her.

"He baffles me," Rey said, as they walked toward the elevator.

"It's just that you don't understand. You think he doesn't care, but he does. Jez and I lived through some terrible times when we were children. Humor helped us to survive. It was like we'd put things into compartments. The bad stuff was shoved aside for a while, and we concentrated on something fun. What's the point in wringing your hands and being permanently miserable? It never helped us. The bad stuff was still there in the morning."

He was listening to her, and she could see that he was trying his best to understand a concept that was completely alien to him.

"You're different, Rey," she went on. "You're a hero. I don't think Jez was ever a hero, except to me, and . . . I'm just plain, ordinary Amy."

He turned and his gaze swept her from head to toe. "There is nothing plain, or ordinary, about you, damsel."

She smiled. "Isn't there?"

"No." He frowned at her smile, and she bit her lip to make it go away.

"Maybe you can show me what's special about me, then?" she suggested demurely.

"Amy, we have to warn . . ."

"The calling isn't until nine sharp. For all we know you could be gone forever, and I'll be all alone. Let's spend some time together. Please."

He wanted to, she could see the longing in his face. Amy stretched out her hand and brushed her fingertips lightly over his lips. "Please?" she repeated, but now there was a sensual invitation in her voice.

Rey leaned forward and caught her index finger between his teeth, nipping it gently. Amy moved in close, pressing her body lightly to his.

Rey groaned in defeat, opened the door, and went inside.

With a smile, Amy followed.

He'd never get tired of the feel of her, so warm and vibrant. Amy was like no other woman, sweet and yet with a fiery passion that took his breath away. One moment he was raging with lust, and the next . . . he wanted to rock her in his arms and never let her go.

She kissed his jaw, tasting him, like a cat in a dairy.

"You need to start enjoying life, Rey," she purred. "You can't be a hero all the time. I know there are a great many people depending on you, but sometimes you just have to be a man."

He cupped her breasts as she leaned over him from her position astride him. The muted light from the windows made her skin pale as the snow outside, while her hair was a glorious halo of curls. She slid down over his rod, embracing him with the warmth of her sheath, and he moaned in ecstasy.

"You're mine, Reynald de Mortimer," she murmured, kissing his mouth. "Every inch of you."

It was true, he thought, he was hers. He let her ride him at her own pace, holding back, enjoying the sensation. She was gasping now, reaching for her peak, and he caught her hips and held her, thrusting upward, wishing the moment would never end.

While knowing, with an aching melancholy, that it must.

"Are you sorry now that you waited so long to break your vow?" she asked him, when they had their breath back.

He turned and kissed the tip of her nose. Her eyes were very green and he read the spark of longing and jealousy in them. "I did not break my vow," he reminded her. "I waited for the right woman. You. And no, I am not sorry that I did wait, for my time with you has been beyond mortal pleasure."

The corners of her mouth curved upward, pleased with his answer, and he wanted to take her again. The desire in him was so strong that he was reaching out for her when he heard the sound.

A scream. Like an echo from far away, and yet so clear and chilling in his head.

Reynald sat up, looking around him, despite the fact that he already knew the sound had not come from nearby. Not even from the time he was in now.

"What was that?" Amy whispered.

One glance at her anxious expression, and he knew that she had heard it, too. "I do not know. Some trick of the witch's, mayhap. Or the dragon . . ."

"Morwenna," she said.

He glanced at her sharply. "Again?"

She nodded. "I think we should warn Coster now."

"Aye." He began to dress, his mind already moving ahead to practical matters, to taking charge.

"Rey?"

It took him a moment to register that she was speaking to him again. He was already heading for the door.

"Damsel?"

"Wait for me," she said. "*Stay by me*. Remember?"

She was right. For a moment he had forgotten he was no longer alone. The realization was sweet. He watched her finish pulling on her sweater and jeans and boots before she hurried to his side. He took her hand in his.

"If I do return to 1299, I will instruct my stone-masons to carve that motto above my gate," he said. " 'Stay by me.' For you, Amy."

She stretched up and kissed his cheek. "I'd like that very much, Rey. "

Twenty-nine

Nicco returned to his room. He'd spent a pleasant hour in the bar, chatting up a fashion model with big plans and little talent, and basking in her hopeful smiles—he'd told her he knew people in the business. He invited her up to join him, but she'd suddenly turned evasive and made some excuse about needing to take a cell phone call.

Women are all bitches, he thought sourly, *and Amy Fairweather is the biggest bitch of all.*

He'd hoped to be able to persuade Jez into forcing her to be nice to him. Jez was like him, willing to reshape his principles to suit his situation. But it seemed that Jez was now in league with that big bastard, and was no longer willing to sacrifice his sister to benefit his friendship with Nicco. Maybe riffraff had something Jez wanted? He couldn't imagine any other reason.

Nicco would have to think of some way of getting Amy alone. She needed to be shown he wasn't a man to be easily forgotten, just because it was now expedient for Jez to do so. She'd humiliated him, and that couldn't go unpunished. Nicco was good at extracting revenge. It was one of his secret little pleasures . . . along with expensive jewelry.

He hadn't quite dared to take the Star of Russia with him into the bar, although he would have liked to have seen the model's eyes pop if he showed it to her. Now he needed to hold it in his hand again, to finger the magnificent diamond that had once belonged to the greatest queen the Russians had ever had.

Nicco took the key from his pocket, went over to the drawer, and unlocked it. The silver box was just where he'd left it, and he smiled. In his secret thoughts he rather fancied he and Catherine were of similar minds, both enjoying a variety of lovers, both ruthless and ambitious. She'd probably approve of his owning the ring.

Nicco flipped open the lid. And stared.

At first he couldn't believe it was empty. He reached inside as if the ring had become invisible, and he might still be able to feel it. His movements became more frantic, and he started searching toward the back of the drawer, but his fingers found nothing but empty space.

With a cry, he pulled out the drawer and emptied it onto the bed, banging it up and down until one of the side joints broke open.

Nicco began to rampage through his room. Searching wildly, throwing items around, swearing all the while in Russian. When he had searched every possible location he stood, panting, amidst the wreckage.

He had no choice but to accept it.

The ring was gone.

He tried to think. Someone had come in, seen the ring, and taken it. Maybe one of the cleaners had found it; surely that was the most likely explanation? He would complain to the hotel management and . . . But Nicco didn't want it known he had the ring in his possession. He would find the staff member himself and *make* them return his property—before he killed them.

He was on his way to the door when some elusive memory stopped him in his steps. The last time he had the ring on him was when he went to see Jez. It had been hidden in his jacket pocket, but he couldn't resist reaching in and running his fingers over it. Caressing the hard stone as he stared at Amy, and letting his imagination roam into the dark places he normally hid from others. He'd been so caught up in his fantasies of pain and perversion that he'd forgotten to be cautious.

Had Jez noticed?

Amy had been pestering him about the ring.

He'd accepted her story that she was obsessed with the sort of jewelry she could never afford to own. He'd accepted a lot of things. Suddenly he knew he'd been a gullible fool. Jez had thrown his sister out as bait, and Nicco had taken it. They hadn't been interested in him—they'd been after the Star of Russia all along.

Jez had the ring. It was the only explanation that made any sense.

Nicco gave a vicious smile. It would be a pleasure getting it back, especially when he explained to Jez, in detail, what he'd done to Amy. Just before he killed him.

Thirty

Amy was right about Coster, but it gave her no great pleasure. The man listened to their story, then smirked in their faces.

"What about the earthquake?" Amy said, trying not to show her desperation. "Explain that, then?"

"The tremors weren't serious. I've been on to some government seismologists in Cardiff by cell phone, and they've assured me that it wasn't an earthquake. It didn't register on their instruments at all. When the weather clears they want to come out here and do some tests. I don't know what they'll find, but I'm certain they won't find any dragons."

He laughed out loud.

"They won't find the dragon, because it is no longer under the ground," Rey retorted, his face like stone, his arms crossed over his chest. He looked formidable, and Coster's smile slipped.

"I know I'm going to regret this, but I have to ask. Where is it then?"

"Out there," Rey said, nodding toward the window. The day had long since turned to night, and it was dark outside. "The dragon is waiting. We must prepare ourselves for an attack. If we don't . . . we will all die, just as we did in 1299."

Coster gave him a bemused look. "I tell you what," he said at last, turning to his desk and fiddling with the papers on it, "leave this with me. I'll think about it and get back to you."

There was nothing more they could do.

"I don't like this," Amy murmured, as they walked away. "He's going to call the police."

"How will they get here through the snow?" Rey said, striding ahead in his usual lordly manner. "The roads are closed, Amy, and their horses would be lost in the drifts."

"Horses, huh? Well let's hope it stays that way." She found herself talking to his back and hurried to catch him up. Why did her role always seem to be following her man? First Jez, now Rey. Amy was sick and tired of being the follower; she wanted to lead for a change.

"Where are we going?"

"I need to fetch something," Rey said, without slowing down or turning to look at her.

Amy was slipping behind him again, but this

time she did it through choice. She was admiring his long legs and broad shoulders. She knew he was all muscle, every gorgeous inch of him.

With a start, she realized they'd come to the door that led down into the tunnels, and froze as Rey put out his hand to push it open.

"Oh no . . ."

He glanced back at her. In that moment there was no emotion in his eyes—they were as cold and gray as castle stone—then they changed and warmed. Like quicksilver. Amy realized that she had done that, she had changed him.

"Stay here," he said gently. "Wait for me. I will not be long."

"Do you swear it?" she whispered, darting a glance past him into the shadows. Even though she knew the dragon was gone, she almost expected to see it waiting.

"Aye, I give you my word, damsel. I am going to fetch something I left in a safe place when the witch first brought me back from the between-worlds. I am not going to fight any dragons. Not yet."

Amy nodded shakily, and watched with a sinking heart as he disappeared down the stairs and into the darkness.

I'll give him twenty minutes, and then if he hasn't come back I'm going after him . . .

The longbow wasn't far away. Reynald remembered the niche where he'd stashed it and the arrows on the day that the witch brought him back to life and sent him here.

To occupy his mind as he walked, he tried to formulate some sort of battle plan. It was obvious that Coster didn't believe him and wasn't going to take any part in preparing for the dragon. So that only left himself and Amy, and perhaps Jez. The Ghost knew that if he could draw the dragon to him and encourage it to concentrate its fiercesome energies on destroying him, then it was possible he could save the others.

Whether or not he could save himself, however, was another question.

A further turn and some more steps, and he reached the fissure in the wall. Reynald reached inside and gave a sigh of relief. The longbow was just where he'd left it. He ran his fingers over the smooth wood and linen string of the bow, as if he was greeting an old friend. And then he reached in again, hunting around for his arrows. They had been made for him by the best Welsh fletchers he could find, with ash shafts and gray goose feathers. The arrowheads were steel-tipped and deadly, able to pierce armor.

His hand closed on two arrows. Only two? His heart sank. He'd forgotten he had so few remaining. That only gave him two chances to strike the dragon where it mattered. That was, if he had time enough to aim and shoot the second arrow after he missed with the first.

You failed last time.

Maybe it is not meant to be.

Reynald knew he couldn't afford to think like that. He couldn't let the doubts and uncertainties of the past return to cause his hand to shake and his eye to falter. His life, Amy's life, depended upon him.

Reynald straightened, the longbow and arrows clasped firmly in his hand, and turned back the way he'd come.

There was someone behind him.

He had already raised his fist to strike, when his eyes told him that it was a disheveled and dirty woman with long, fair hair.

"Good God, it's you!" she cried. "I don't know whether to be relieved or angry."

He recognized her. It was Miriam, the authority.

She must have seen the confusion in his face, because she explained. "I followed you all down here and became lost. I've been wandering around every since. Appalling place! I thought I'd never find my way out, and then I heard you talking to yourself . . ."

"I was not talking to myself," he said in disgust.

"You were. I'm grateful for it. I mightn't have found you if you weren't."

He gave her another searching look. It horrified him to think of her lost down here. A grown man could go mad in this place, and yet, despite her grubby appearance, the woman was calm.

"You are unharmed?" he asked tentatively.

"Thirsty and hungry, but other than that, I'm quite unharmed. I used to go caving when I was younger and fitter. This place is nasty, but it's a picnic to some of the tight spots I got myself into. Lead on then!" She waved her hand bossily at him. "We'll miss the dragon-calling, and I particularly wanted to see it. Coster told me he's got some folklore specialist in from the wilds of Wales. Very old ritual. Complete nonsense, of course," she added, with a sly glance up at him, "or are you expecting to see a *real* dragon?"

"Aye," he said grimly, "I am."

After that she trotted along behind him in silence, although Reynald knew it couldn't last for long. The woman was in love with the sound of her own voice.

"I can see the fascination with them," she mused. "Dragons, I mean. The ancients were afraid of anything they didn't understand, so I suspect blaming a dragon was as good a trick as any when there was a suspicious death. They worshipped nature, the trees in the forest and so on. On a dark night, a fallen tree might look like a waiting dragon . . ."

"You would do well to take refuge, lady, when the time comes."

"Oh no, I don't think so. I want to see *everything*."

"Then do not say I did not warn you."

She chuckled. "I won't."

Reynald reached the final set of steps and began to climb them toward the room with the door.

"You know of Julius," he said, a thought occurring to him. "Do you know of Angharad?"

"You mean from the time of the Ghost?" she asked, but didn't wait for him to answer. "Angharad. Hmm, it sounds Welsh. No, I don't think I have heard her mentioned in connection with Reynald de Mortimer. Was she important?"

"She was a woman with a sharp tongue and wise counsel, who lived and died long ago. And no, she probably wasn't important, except to me."

"I thought you were going to tell me that Angharad was the dragon's name," the woman tittered. "A Welsh name for a Welsh dragon."

Angharad the dragon? The thought of it was as ridiculous as Miriam Ure's wig. So why did his stomach start to squirm and his head start to hurt?

"Beautiful weapon you have there," the woman was still yammering. "The longbow really came into its own after the Ghost's day, but he's credited, you know, with raising its profile among the Norman and English aristocracy. All the King Edwards were very fond of it. And without the longbow, where would the English have been at Falkirk, Crécy, and Agincourt?"

Reynald wasn't listening. There was something wrong, but he couldn't work out what it was.

You have not the talent for the longbow. You have not the mind for it.

That was Angharad, and although at the time he had not considered it purposely done, now he wondered. It was as if she had searched his inner self for weakness then set about working on it. As if she had wanted him to miss that fateful day.

Angharad . . .

"Most people forget what a victory Falkirk was, they only remember Agincourt, but the longbow was just as important—"

Reynald reached out to open the door, suddenly keen to escape her company and find somewhere quiet, where he could sort through his confused thoughts and memories.

As the door swung in, Amy jumped up in surprise, and he nearly crashed into her. She'd dragged a chair over to the door and been sitting there, waiting. Her relieved gasp turned to eyes-wide amazement when she spied Miriam.

"Ms. Ure!"

"I must look a sight," said Miriam, with a grimace. "Been down there for hours. Horrid place."

Amy nodded in agreement, speechless.

"I'd better go and get cleaned up." She gave Reynald a pat on the back. "Thank you again for your help. I don't agree with your dragon theory, but I'm glad I met you." And with that she set off across the room, heading for the door to reception.

"She was down there all by herself?" Amy said weakly.

"Aye, she found me." Reynald shook his head in

disgust. "She said I was talking to myself. And she does not believe me about the dragon-calling. I have the satisfaction of knowing she will be proved wrong, but there is no pleasure in what will happen after that. She will die, and many others with her."

"I suppose one thing we have in our favor is that the dragon hates you so much that it's likely to try and get to you first." Amy shuddered and hugged her arms about herself. "I can't believe I just said that."

"You are thinking practically instead of emotionally; that is good."

"No, it's not good. We should leave now, Rey, before anything happens."

But he wouldn't, he couldn't, and she knew it even as she spoke the words.

"I cannot leave, Amy. I can't abandon these people. I do not think you would want a man who could." He brushed her cheek with his fingers, and she felt the scars and calluses. Two of his fingertips were as hard as iron. "But you are right about the dragon hating me the most. The creature will come to me first, it will not be able to help itself, and that is what I want. It will give me a chance to kill it."

"That's why you needed the bow and arrows?" Amy nodded to the weapon he held in his hand.

He smiled. "You must pay proper respect, damsel. This is the Welsh longbow, and a formidable weapon. I have been practicing with it since I was a boy, but I am nothing to some of the men I have seen using it. They can fire ten arrows in a minute, at a distance of close to four hundred yards."

"Your fingers," she said. "I just realized why they're so callused."

Reynald held them up. "Aye, I use them to draw back the string to shoot the arrow. If you want to destroy the livelihood and the pride of a Welsh archer, then take him prisoner and cut off his drawing fingers."

Amy shuddered. "You're good at it then?"

He smiled. " 'Tis said by others that I am the best archer in England, but I do not claim so. I am certainly not the best in Wales. But I am training my garrison in the use of the longbow, and I hope one day their skills will protect my lands from those who wish me ill."

"You must go home, Rey," Amy said quietly. "They need you."

I need you.

But she was already pushing her sadness away, dredging up her wry humor. "What do you need to attract the dragon to you, so you can turn it into a pincushion?"

"I will be standing on the north tower."

"Okay then . . . what about a spotlight?"

"A spotlight?" he repeated.

"Don't worry, Jez can do that. It means you'll stand out very nicely when the dragon arrives."

She hesitated and her matter-of-factness faltered. "How can you be so sure it'll come?"

"I am. It will come, Amy, never doubt it. We must prepare," he said.

"I know. I'll have to find Jez."

As he followed her across the room, it occurred to Reynald that he was walking behind Amy. For the first time in his adult life he was following a woman, and for the second time in his life—since Angharad—he was prepared to do as she told him.

The dragon lay quietly in the darkness. Every now and then she gave a shiver, for it was cold after the warmth of her chamber, deep in the earth. But what did a little snow matter when she was free! And soon she would take back what had been stolen from her.

Reynald had to die, and this time she must be certain he stayed dead. His woman, too, with her laughing green eyes and fiery hair. They must both die.

Above her, the pine branches were still covered in green needles, giving some shelter, but elsewhere the trees were bare and would not regain their leaves until the spring. When that happened, she told herself, she would fly over the tops of them, as she used to. She would glide on the wind currents, and gaze upon her lands, stretching as far as she could see in every direction.

The dragon shifted and sighed, scratching her talons into the frozen earth, burying herself deeper to keep out the icy wind. She didn't want to admit it, even to herself, but she was lonely. There were no more of her kind remaining in the mortal world—the witch had gathered them all up. There was only her.

Her black eyes closed, and she dozed. Gathering strength for the confrontation with her enemy and dreaming of the past.

Thirty-one

It was Jez who found them. They'd returned to Amy's room so that Rey could put on his armor and other paraphernalia, while Amy dressed warmly for the freezing night ahead.

Although, if the dragon comes, I'll be warm, she told herself. *Warmer than I'd like.*

She opened her mouth to share her black humor with Rey, but one glance at his serious face and grim mouth changed her mind. He might die tonight; they might all die. It wasn't really something to joke about.

That was when Jez arrived at the door.

He was wired, his eyes bright and his smile brighter, and he couldn't seem to stay still. Amy knew then that he had it. He met her gaze and, with a grin, held out his hand and wriggled his fingers.

"You're wearing it!" she gasped. "Jez, for God's sake . . ."

He laughed. "Gorgeous, isn't it?"

Rey gave him a stern look. "You have risked your soul for a bauble."

"Yeah, well, my soul is pretty much a dead loss anyway, and the ring will get me out of trouble. Who knows, maybe I'll make a clean start. Get a proper job, like Amy."

"I wish you would. You could do anything you liked, Jez."

He calmed, and now his smile was rueful. "I heard that O'Neill was on the phone talking to Coster about me."

"He knows you're here?" Amy's eyes widened. "When he hears about the ring, he'll come after you. Jez, you know he'll see it as his chance to put you away!"

"He can try. I intend to be long gone by then."

But although he dismissed it so easily, Amy knew he was worried; otherwise, he wouldn't have mentioned it.

"So." Jez was rubbing his hands together. "What's the agenda?"

"Rey is going to be the bait this time," Amy replied evenly, pretending she wasn't petrified at the thought of it. "He's going up to the north tower, so we need you to rig up some sort of spotlight. Then, when the dragon comes, it'll see him and . . ."

She closed her eyes. "Isn't there another way?" she whispered. "Isn't there someone else?"

"No." It was Rey. "There is no one else."

She looked at him, seeing him as he was, and was overwhelmed with love for him. She'd never love another man like this. He was her soul mate, the husband of her heart.

"I can't bear it," she said, her voice trembling.

He reached for her and held her fast, despite his armor and padding, and all the things that made him a warrior lord in the thirteenth century. This, she thought, was what it must be like for those wives and lovers, when their men went off to battle. This was what it meant to send your man off, not knowing whether or not you'd ever see him again.

After a moment, she took a steadying breath, then another, and finally pulled away from him and stood alone. "I'm all right," she said.

He cupped her chin, lifting her face, and scrutinizing it with those quicksilver eyes. "You are brave," he told her. "Good. I need you to be brave, Amy, so that I, too, can be brave."

"You're always brave," she whispered.

"No. Not always. With you at my side, though, I know I can do this. I can defeat my enemy."

"So that you can go back to the past, and I'll never see you again."

He opened his mouth to say something, but she didn't let him.

"No, Rey. It's true. We must accept it. I don't

believe in miracles. These will be our final few hours together, and apart from dreams, what we say and do and feel now will have to last us for the rest of our lives."

After a moment, embarrassed at being a spectator to so much raw emotion, Jez cleared his throat. "Okay. Maybe we should get going. It's eight o'clock, and the dragon-calling is supposed to start at nine . . ."

Amy nodded and turned away. "Come on, then," she said, putting on her new brave face. "Let's show that dragon what we're made of!"

Jez caught up with her at the elevator.

"Amy, isn't there another way to do this?"

"No."

"I hate to think . . ."

"Yes, well, better if you don't. Can you do the spotlight?"

"Yes. You know I can. I used to be a lighting director at Drury Lane—in another life."

"You were good at it. Why didn't you—"

"I don't know. Saw a quick chance and took it, I suppose."

"You don't want to end up like Dad, Jez. You don't want to be a sad old man who's spent his best years locked away."

"Thanks for the vote of confidence."

"You know what I mean. You can't go on like this forever. I don't want my only brother to be someone I visit in prison every month."

"He really has got to you, hasn't he?" he said sarcastically, jerking his head back to Rey.

Amy frowned. "This has nothing to do with Rey. I've felt like this for ages. I just haven't had the guts to say it."

Rey joined them, eyeing the elevator uneasily. Ironic, Amy thought, that he was afraid of this convenience of the modern age, yet was ready and willing to face a fire-breathing dragon.

In the reception area, where the guests were already gathering, the drinks were flowing very freely, and they were in a boisterous mood.

As soon as they saw Rey step out of the elevator in his coat of armor, they gave a rousing cheer.

Coster, seeing them, hurried up. "What are you doing?" he demanded in a low voice, giving Rey and his longbow an uneasy look. "I don't think you should take part. You've already made it plain what you think of the dragon-calling. I don't want anyone upset."

"He's here to save us from the dragon," Amy retorted. "This is your fault. If anyone gets killed, it will be on your head."

Coster laughed nervously. "Yes, well, I hardly think—"

"Do you know what a dragon can do?" Amy shouted.

Someone in the crowd overheard and, thinking it was a joke, called back, "Make a fantastic barbecue!"

More laughter. They were in a festive mood, and not taking anything seriously. Frustrating as it was, Amy knew that a few days ago she would have been exactly the same.

"I've called the police," Coster said, cold now, more sure of himself. "They'll be here very soon."

Jez shuffled closer to Amy. "You know what this means?" he muttered.

"How can the police get into the castle," Amy retorted, "when no one here can get out!"

"With a helicopter." Coster smirked. "Yes, they believe it's *that* serious. So, I repeat, no more trouble, please. I'm aware that you've been deceiving me and my staff. This man," he nodded at Rey, "is no more a Hollywood actor than I am. Steven Spielberg, indeed! The police will sort it out. In the meantime, the dragon-calling will be starting soon, and I want it to go off smoothly."

"I hope the dragon knows that," Amy said, getting in the last word.

But Rey was tired of their talk. He set off with his long, no-nonsense stride toward the north tower, and Amy and Jez followed.

Thirty-two

Reynald was feeling dizzy. His head was spinning like that of a dog chasing its own tail, and his legs were heavy, growing heavier with each step. At first he thought that it was because of the tension of his predicament, then it dawned on him that this was part of the dragon's plot to best him. The apparition with the light, the fainting . . . they were all connected.

"Amy," he said, and his voice sounded dry and husky. Suddenly she was by his side, or perhaps she had been there all along. "Amy . . ."

She seemed to know what was wrong, because she slipped beneath his arm to prop him up, at the same time calling frantically for Jez. Then he felt Jez on his other side, supporting him, complaining about his size.

"You need to lie down." Amy was urging him to turn back.

"No," he shouted, or thought he did. It was probably little more than a whisper. "This is the dragon's doing. Just as before. Trying to stop me. I must go on. You have the longbow . . . ?"

"I have it," Jez assured him. "And the arrows."

"Keep going," Reynald panted. "Whatever happens. We must reach the north tower in time."

His head was spinning worse than ever, and he was spinning with it, around and around, back through the years. Back to that day in 1299, when all seemed possible.

"This is Angharad, Your Grace. My interpreter." He heard his own voice, as he introduced Angharad to his guests.

Angharad curtsied to the bishop, but he barely glanced at her. Important men like him didn't notice old women with gray hair and sunken faces, especially when they were peasants. No doubt Angharad had seen it all before. No one paid her much heed.

He was the only one who had ever troubled to listen to her and take her seriously. He was fond of her, too, a fact that amused her, although he didn't understand why. There were many things about Angharad that he did not understand.

"Great men," she said, when the bishop had moved on, "how can they understand the suffering of ordinary folk? How do they know how it feels to lose the one dearest to

you, or comprehend the suffering of having one's heart cleaved in two?"

"You have suffered such a loss?"

"My daughter," she said quietly.

"I am sorry for it, Angharad. But today you should put away your memories and celebrate. This is a great day for us all, a great triumph."

She said nothing.

"No more talk of dragons among the Welsh?"

"No more talk of dragons, my lord."

He nodded, and stared off into the distance.

"Do you know what they say, the Welsh? How to kill a dragon?" Her own words seemed to startle her, and she looked up into his eyes, her own dark and empty. Secretive.

Puzzled, he shook his head.

"An arrow, my lord, to that spot just below the breastbone. That is the only way to kill a dragon."

"I will remember it, Angharad." He smiled.

"The Welsh are expert longbowmen," she added. "Only a Welshman can kill a dragon."

He felt crestfallen, then he shrugged. "I am improving," he offered.

"Aye," she allowed him.

But the seed had been sown. He would fail when the time came. Her words would come back to him and his hand would tremble and his eyesight would blur. Angharad had poisoned him just as surely as if she'd offered him a cup of hemlock.

* * *

Reynald came to himself, and he knew. The doubts, the confusion, were gone, and the truth was as clear and remarkable as Amy's green eyes. He looked about him and realized he was leaning against the wall at the bottom of the stairwell, and Amy was touching his face as she spoke to him in a soft, worried tone.

When he blinked and shook himself, like a dog who's been swimming in a cold river, she gave a cry of relief. "Rey, what happened? We couldn't hold you up any longer, and Jez needed to get the spotlight fixed up. You've been out of it for so long!"

"How long?" He wiped a hand over his eyes, feeling the sweat on his brow. His body was weak and tired, but he refused to give in to it and let *her* win. Not now he knew she was responsible. Not again.

"It's five minutes to nine," Amy told him quietly.

So near to the dragon-calling!

"It was Angharad," he said grimly. "This is all her perfidy." He began climbing the stairs as fast as he could manage, with Amy at his back.

"Angharad? What do you mean? What just happened?" she said.

"I was . . . remembering, or maybe it was a dream. It was the day of the peace, and I was speaking with Angharad. She said things . . . I didn't realize then what she meant, but it was as if she wanted me to know."

"Know what?" Amy didn't sound as if she thought what he was saying was the most interesting thing she'd ever heard.

"Angharad was my enemy, damsel," he said grimly, and turned his head to giving her a piercing look over his shoulder. "She plotted to kill me. Revenge for some wrong I had wrought upon her. Her heart had been cleaved in two when someone she loved was taken from her."

"Do you mean she plotted with the dragon?"

"No. I think that she *is* the dragon."

"Oh God, you mean . . . ?"

"Aye, Angharad and the dragon are one and the same."

It made an awful sense. Angharad had pretended to work with him, when in reality she was working against him and seeking to take his land back. What better way for his enemy to triumph, than for her to enter his camp and pretend to be his friend?

Just like Morwenna with her dagger.

Morwenna and Angharad. Both his enemies. Both wanting him dead. In his head he heard Amy's voice, *Do dragons have children?*

"It is Morwenna the dragon is avenging," he said with absolute certainty. "Morwenna was Angharad's daughter—her beloved. Angharad sent her to me to kill me, and instead Morwenna died. That is why she hates me."

Amy drew a relieved breath as they reached the last step. "But how do you know this, Rey?"

"My heart tells me so."

She looked at him a moment, as if there were lots of things she would like to say, but there wasn't time.

"Amy!" Jez's cry startled him, and Reynald staggered, his head beginning to spin again. Amy's brother appeared before him, and held out a hand to Reynald, using his strength to help him through the door and onto the roof.

"I'm nearly finished," Jez said, panting with the effort. "Just a couple of adjustments. Sorry the light isn't as bright as we hoped, but it should do. You'll stand out, that's for sure," he added, straight-faced.

Reynald strode to the battlements, working hard not to appear anything other than his normal self, and peered over into the castle yard. It took him a moment to clear the clouds from his vision, but he could hear the guests laughing and chattering. Finally, when he could see again, he realized they were crowded together under an ornately draped roof of canvas, close to some braziers, while they waited for the show to begin.

His gaze lifted. The lights of the keep were blazing, and there was music coming from somewhere, a Christmas song that sounded suspiciously like "Jingle Bells." The snow had finally stopped, and although the night was bitterly cold, it was clear. Stars shone out in the midnight blue sky, and high above there was the flash of lights.

"Jesu, what is that?" he asked sharply, pointing up.

Amy followed his direction. "A plane," she said. Then, realizing who she was talking to, "It flies. Much quicker than a horse, Rey. Could be going to Paris or Madrid or Rome. People travel the world regularly these days, which makes it seem a much smaller place."

It was beautiful, he thought with surprise. He had been considering this time as inferior to his own, but suddenly he saw it through new eyes. He had learned much here. There were parts of this world he could apply to his own, and others he would be glad to discard, but nothing he had seen and done would be wasted.

Suddenly Coster's voice rose up from below, calling everyone to silence. "We are very lucky tonight," he began.

There was a sound approaching. Distracted, Reynald looked toward the gatehouse. The sound grew louder, a humming that seemed to vibrate in the stones beneath his feet. There was something coming, a dark shape, with red glowing eyes. Reynald felt his heartbeat begin to slow, felt his body preparing itself for the confrontation.

"It's a helicopter," Amy said loudly, above the noise.

"A police helicopter," Jez corrected her. "Damn him, I hoped he was bluffing."

"What is that?" Reynald whispered. "Is it the plane you spoke of?"

"Sort of. It's a . . . a flying machine," Amy explained lamely. "There'll be men in it, men who will want to talk to you, Rey. They may even arrest you and take you away with them. It's not good," she said, folding her arms tightly across her chest. "Not good at all."

"I cannot go," Rey protested. "The dragon is coming. Do they not realize that?"

"No. I don't think they do."

Jez clapped him on the back, and shouted above the incredible noise of the helicopter. "Don't worry, I'll head them off. Here, Amy, this is the control for the light. Just flick this switch down when it's time for lights on, and back up again when you want them off."

"Jez? Why are you—"

He grinned. "I want Rey to see my good side," he joked.

The helicopter was so loud now it drowned out all other sound, and the wind from the rotors made it difficult to stand upright as it passed close over them. It circled the castle and landed outside, on a flat piece of land beyond the moat. Anxiously, they watched as several men spilled from it and began to move toward the gatehouse and the drawbridge.

"How did Coster get so many of them here so soon?" Amy shouted. "Was he really so afraid that the complaints of a few minor celebs would cause him adverse publicity?"

She looked around, to see what Jez thought, but he was gone.

Now that the helicopter was silent, Rey could hear Coster again. He was introducing the dragon-caller, a smallish man in a white tunic that was decorated with a pattern of stars and moons. "This is Mr. Davies, a Druid, who has been calling dragons since he was a boy."

There was a titter of laughter.

"He must be freezing," Amy murmured.

". . . will not harm you . . ." Davies' voice rose and fell. ". . . do not be afraid . . ."

Then Davies produced a musical instrument of some sort—a whistle or a flute, it was too far away to tell—and began to play.

The sound was plaintive. Not really a tune at all, but an odd collection of notes, rising and falling, that somehow came together. At first it was slow, like a dirge, then it began to quicken, swirling and echoing around the walls of the castle, getting louder, calling out for the dragon to come.

"Will it work?" Amy whispered, shivering with more than the cold.

She saw that Rey was staring out over the darkened landscape with a sort of expectant stillness. *He is waiting*, she realized. The knowledge that it was really happening raised her fear level considerably.

The music had slowed again, and now it held a beseeching note. It really did seem to be calling.

"She is coming," Rey murmured.

Amy peered anxiously in the same direction, but she couldn't see anything. Certainly no loud engine noises, like the helicopter, or whirring rotor blades and flashing lights. All she could hear was the eerie sound of the flute, and beyond that a thick blanket of silence.

"Where? I can't see anything."

"I feel her."

Amy frowned. He was looking down over the ravine, which was as black as pitch, nothing like the green swathe of pine trees and bare deciduous trees you could see growing there during daylight.

She opened her mouth to question him again, then she felt it, too.

Something dark at the outer reaches of her mind, stirring, growing stronger as it drew nearer.

"Oh dear God," she breathed. "She *is* coming."

"Be ready with the light, Amy," he said urgently.

"Don't worry, Jez put it over there."

"When the light is on, you must run. I want you to run, Amy. That is an order."

"No."

"I order you to run," he said angrily, in the way he probably spoke to his garrison to make them do as he told them. But Amy wasn't afraid of him, and she had no intention of running anywhere.

"Tough," she said. "I'm staying. You need me. This is our big moment together, and there's no way I'm running off and leaving you to steal the glory for yourself."

He laughed. He actually laughed at her black humor.

And then she heard it. The flap of heavy wings. There was a tremendous roar, and fire spat across the dark sky. The dragon was momentarily illuminated, and it took her breath away. It was huge, much bigger than she'd remembered from their brief encounter in the tunnel. The head was long and square at the snout, while the tail was whip-like, narrow, with an arrow tip.

In the instant when it was lit up, she imagined she could see Angharad's black eyes staring back at her, and the wave of hatred that came from them, into her mind, paralyzed her with shock and trepidation.

A cheer went up from below in the bailey, and some of the crowd ran toward the drawbridge, while others climbed the steps onto the walls, to get a better view.

"Dear God, they think it's part of the show," Amy whispered hoarsely, the best she could do. "They'll stand there and clap until it comes over and incinerates them."

She'd hardly finished speaking, when the dragon spat out another gob of fire and smoke, but this time it spewed out for a greater distance, singeing the tops of a copse of trees in a field beyond the castle. Flames caught in the bare branches and flared, briefly, making a spectacular show.

Now there were a few screams from those who could see what was happening, and an uneasy shifting in the tightly knit ranks beneath the tent roof. "Be calm!" Davies was shouting, a high-pitched excitement in his voice. "It won't harm you!" And Coster, screaming, "Make it go away, you idiot, make it go away!"

The people down below had finally realized that this was no mock-up of a dragon, and it was certainly not computer-generated.

But they still couldn't quite believe it was the real thing.

The huge shape moved steadily toward the castle.

"Turn on the lights, Amy," said Rey, gathering together his longbow and one of his arrows. "We want to make sure she sees us."

Amy ran over to the cluster of equipment, checking that the spotlight was turned toward Rey, and reached for the control box Jez had left for her. But as she was about to switch it on, there was a scraping sound behind her. Distracted, she turned, just as Nicco darted out of the door to the stairwell and grabbed her around the throat.

Thirty-three

Amy let out a surprised shriek. The sound was only a tiny part of the chaos now being created above and below and all around them, but Reynald heard her. He launched himself toward Nicco, but then he saw the knife held to her throat, glinting in the light from the stairwell, and skidded to a stop.

"Ah, yes, very sensible," Nicco mocked. "I don't want my hand to slip . . ."

Amy cried out as the knife nicked her skin.

Reynald roared with fury. "Let her go!"

"You don't want me to slip again, do you?" Nicco asked coldly. It was that chill in his voice that convinced Reynald he was in deadly earnest.

"What are you going to do?" he asked, controlling his emotion with difficulty. A first for the Ghost, known for his cool and clear head in times of crisis. But this was Amy, this was the woman he loved.

"I thought I might kill her first, then you," Nicco confided in him. "And then I'll find Jez and kill him, too."

"You lackwit, can you not see—" Reynald began, furious, his hands clenching.

"See what?" Nicco demanded.

The sound of heavy wings beating grew steadily louder, then the dragon passed over them, blocking out the stars.

"The dragon," Amy whispered, as Nicco looked up. His mouth fell open. Then she'd caught hold of him and, with a twist of her hip, tossed him, and next moment he was lying flat on his back on the ground.

Above them, the dragon roared out another spurt of flame, and the flags flying from the top of the keep caught on fire, as well as some of the wooden roofing. People were running and screaming. Reynald saw that the tent was also on fire, and pieces of burning matter and embers were dropping down from above. There was a flicker, then a spurt of flame came from the pavilion, as it, too, began to burn.

Reynald stared about him, sickened, as his prophecy came to pass. This was every bit as terrible as he'd feared, and he could have stopped it if it wasn't for Nicco.

Furious, Reynald turned on his enemy. Nicco

was on his feet, staggering toward the stairwell, gazing around him in shock. Reynald pursued him, and Nicco didn't see the fist until it struck him brutally hard on the jaw. Nicco went limp, already unconscious before he hit the ground for the second time.

Amy was scrambling about, searching for the control box, which had been knocked out of her hand when Nicco grabbed her. "Yes!" She picked it up and looked triumphantly at Reynald. But by now the dragon had flown over the castle and was gone into the darkness beyond.

"We missed it!" she wailed.

"She will be back," Rey said with grim certainty. "She has only just begun."

Let Angharad come, and I will show her what sort of archer I am. 'Tis not only Welshmen who can kill dragons.

He found his longbow where he'd dropped it in his rush to get to Amy and nocked the first arrow, testing his muscles against the great strength required to draw back the bow. Aye, it felt good, although he was cramped with the steel plates and mail of his armor.

Reynald loosened the string again and took out the arrow, careful not to damage the goose feathers. He set his weapon down, and proceeded to remove his eighty-pound coat of armor.

"No, Rey," Amy was trying to put it back on again. "You need to protect yourself."

"I cannot fire the arrow properly if I am wearing this," he retorted, and, catching her hands, held them tightly in his. "Sshh, Amy. Listen to me. I need to be able to move freely."

She understood at last, and with an unhappy nod, let him finish. With the heavy armor off, he took up the longbow again, and this time when he tested his grip, he nodded with satisfaction. He was ready.

And then Amy spoke, her voice barely audible. "Angharad's coming back."

Down in the bailey it was madness. People were running and screaming, cowering under any shelter they could find and hoping it would save them. The flames from the burning buildings gave the scene a hellish quality, like a war zone, or the scene of some terrorist attack.

Jez knew he had never been this frightened, and yet at the same time he'd never felt so alive.

He found a secure place, inside the doorway of an old stone cellar, and he watched what was happening from there. He saw Miriam Ure and Davies, clasped in each other's arms beneath a table—there was a match made in heaven. Coster was in a huddle with the police from the helicopter. One of them, the tall one with gray hair, seemed to be in charge. Detective Inspector O'Neill. His nemesis.

O'Neill was organizing some of the guests into

groups, and his men were ushering them back inside the keep. Jez supposed that the thinking was the walls of the keep were so thick that even a dragon couldn't penetrate them.

Worriedly, Jez glanced up at the north tower and wondered what had gone wrong. He'd expected to see the spotlight come on as the dragon soared toward them, but nothing had happened. The top of the tower had remained stubbornly dark. Now he was torn between going back up there to help and staying down here where he could keep an eye on O'Neill and Coster.

There was a third option.

He could take off into the night with the Star of Russia and leave everyone else to cope with the mess. Jez was seriously tempted to do just that, but his conscience—what he had left of one—wouldn't let him. Amy was here, and she wasn't leaving Rey. Jez wasn't quite sure he'd made up his mind about Rey yet—it was a bit hard to get his head around the fact that the man was seven hundred years old—but he found himself liking him more and more.

No, he didn't think he could leave Amy and Rey just yet.

There was a movement from Coster, and he refocused. The pavilion was burning merrily, and there was some attempt at putting it out with a hose and what looked like an old-fashioned bucket brigade. Coster wasn't worried about the pavilion; he was pointing up. Jez followed the direction he was indicating, toward the north tower.

His spotlight was working after all. He couldn't help but smile as the light changed color from pink to purple, while white discs spun and twirled. It was the only spotlight he'd been able to find at such short notice, and it had been hidden away in a storeroom. It reminded him of disco ball from the eighties. He'd wondered at the time whether it was any good for attracting dragons. He supposed he'd know soon enough, as it shone out over the top of the tower and the figure of Reynald de Mortimer.

Others had seen, too, and there were gasps and relieved cries. It was as if the crowd saw in Rey the hero they desperately needed. Even Jez was impressed. Standing with his six-foot-six-inch longbow drawn, the arrow ready to fly, his muscles were locked, and he was ready. He looked like a fierce warrior of old, a man to be reckoned with. He looked like the paintings on the ceiling outside the great hall.

"You are a bloody marvel, Rey," he murmured, chuckling to himself.

Jez's gaze moved on, searching the lighted area. Although he could see Rey, he couldn't see Amy, and it worried him.

The dragon was coming back. He could hear its wings getting closer, making a whooshing sound through the air as it came. For the first time he noticed the odor, the same stench he'd been aware of in the tunnels. Rotten meat. Eau de dragon.

The creature must be able to see Rey, he told himself. Everyone else could. It was time for the Ghost to do his stuff.

". . . bloody idiot!" It was O'Neill's voice. Several of his men were running toward the doorway into the north tower, obviously planning to put a stop to Rey's heroics. Maybe they thought he was somehow responsible for the whole thing—Coster had probably tried to shift the blame.

Jez groaned as he realized he was going to have to do something heroic himself. For a moment he hesitated; his legs didn't want him to. While checking out the garage he'd found Coster's secret. He could still get out of here, head toward Shrewsbury and get back to London with the Star. By tomorrow he could be in some little cabin overlooking the sea in a much warmer part of the world. Somewhere where they didn't have dragons.

You can still take that third option.

Even as the words were running through his head, Jez had pushed away from the safety of the cellar door and was walking across the bailey, toward the group of men.

"Hey there! What are you going to do about this mess then, O'Neill?"

The tall man with the gray hair spun around. O'Neill's eyes narrowed and, despite the terrible situation, he actually smiled. "Jez Fairweather," he said, "as I live and breath. I'd heard you were here. I was coming to get you when I got the call from Mr. Coster here."

"In the name of God," Coster was gibbering. "That . . . that thing! What are you going to do about that thing?"

Jez shot him a scornful look. "You were warned," he reminded the manager, "but you laughed and went ahead with the dragon-calling anyway. Prepare to be sued."

Coster swayed, and with a moan collapsed against one of the policemen.

All the while the heavy flapping of wings was coming closer, then there was an almighty roar. Spurts of flame shot through the sky, some of them striking the castle wall. The smell of burning made Jez's nostrils sting and his eyes water. He coughed, shaking his head to clear it, and looked back up at the north tower.

The enormous dark bulk of the dragon was almost upon Rey, and then it slowed, hovering above him. The colored light had turned to a garish yellow, making the creature look even more nightmarish. It seemed to reach down with its two front legs, as though to take Rey in a deadly embrace.

Then it lashed with its tail, smashing glass, sending sparks into the air. The light went out.

Thirty-four

Reynald was concentrating so totally that when the light failed, he was disoriented. Behind him he could hear Amy yelling and Nicco cursing, but he couldn't turn to look. He must trust her to deal with the crisis on her own and not turn away now.

The spot he had been staring at was no longer lit, but in his mind he thought he could still see it. The soft flesh just below the breastbone, as Angharad had said so long ago. Did she want him to kill her? Or was it further evidence of her scorn for him?

Muscles screaming, arms aching, he bent the bow to its fullest extent.

Are you certain your aim is true? Are you sure you are good enough with the longbow to kill something as

*ancient as me? I do not think you can do it, Reynald.
You will never make a longbowman.*

Reynald ignored the doubts the dragon sent to
crowd his head, and loosed the arrow. It sang as it
flew from him. Like a machine, he was already
reaching for the second, already planning for the
next shot.

The dragon roared—he could not think of her
as Angharad. She threw back her head, sucking in
air as she prepared to douse him with flames.

He realized he was going to die.

His arrow must have missed. He'd failed again,
and Angharad was laughing in his head. He
glanced back for Amy, just as she knocked Nicco
over with a blow reminiscent of his own. The
Russian appeared to be tangled in the wreckage
from Jez's spotlight.

"Rey, do it!" she shouted, panting. "This is the
moment. Now, now! I know you can."

He knew he needed to loose his second arrow
before it was too late. He knew that this time he
must believe in himself, wholly and completely.
Just as Amy believed in him.

His eyes were growing accustomed to the lack
of Jez's spotlight, and he realized he wasn't in a
good position if he wanted to lodge his steel-tipped
arrow in the killing spot. Reynald ran along the
roof of the tower, moving closer to the dragon
rather than away from it, not giving it time to ma-
neuver itself about. Fire spewed from its mouth,

but only a small quantity, as it realized Reynald was no longer where he had been.

Angharad was confused—he felt her emotions now, just as she felt his. She turned her heavy body, but it was too late. He was directly beneath her. This time he didn't allow himself to think at all. Instead, he listened to the beat of his heart, shutting out everything else as he knelt on one knee, tilted his longbow upward, and loosed the arrow. All in one fluid movement.

His aim was perfect, and the arrowhead sank deep.

The dragon's roar turned into a woman's shriek, and it began to move erratically, struggling to stay in the air. A terrible keening sound rushed from its long throat.

Reynald knew then that this time he had done it. The dragon was dying, and as he watched, it began to fall. Losing its sense of direction and tumbling over, it struck the wall, making the whole structure shudder, then spiraled away into the darkness of the ravine. There was a splintering of branches, and finally a thud as it struck the earth.

Angharad was dead.

Amy felt as if her body were someone else's, as if her legs didn't quite work properly, as she stumbled forward to where Rey stood looking over the battlements.

She couldn't see anything as she joined him, only darkness. Everything was very still. The dragon had been so old, thousands of years old, and now it was gone. She felt sadness for the fact that such a unique creature was dead, but there was no question which one of them she'd wanted to win.

"You've done it, Rey. I knew you would," she said, and reached out to grasp his hand. His skin was warm but wet with blood. She held it closer and saw that he had torn his flesh during his battle with the dragon, and Nicco. With a distressed murmur, Amy began to tie her scarf around the wound.

He watched her, a tender look on his face.

"I love you so much," she said, swallowing the lump in her throat. She held his hand against her cheek and closed her eyes, trying to cram as much memory of him as she could into her head.

"And I you," he said, and wrapped his other arm about her, drawing her against him.

"It's over," she whispered. "You can go home now, Rey. You can start again. I know there's so much you want to do. I envy you that."

She sounded wistful, but she couldn't help it. They had been intimate lovers, and friends, and there was no point in telling lies to each other. Amy would miss him terribly and long for him every day of her life.

"I'll come here, sometimes," she said. "Then I

can feel close to you, even though you're seven hundred years away."

Someone was coming, she could hear the sound of footsteps on the stairs. She held him tightly a moment more, then released him, stepping back. Her arms felt empty, but she didn't let him see, as she turned to face the new arrival.

Jez sprinted across the roof toward them. "Well done, mate," he said, clapping Rey hard on the shoulder. "You really are a bloody hero. If I hadn't seen it, I would never have believed it."

"We have succeeded, all of us," Rey said.

"Yes, well, I only saw one man standing under that dragon with the bow and arrow. I think you're the one who should get the medal." Jez jerked his head toward the spotlight. "What happened?"

"The dragon smashed it, and before that Nicco was here."

Jez looked about and noticed Nicco's prone body. "What happened to him?"

"Nothing more than he deserved," Amy said. "He tried to kill me," she added indignantly, "so I had to throw him onto his back again, and then Rey knocked him out, and then I knocked him out. He nearly messed up everything. He knows you've got the Star of Russia, Jez, and he wants it back."

Jez put his arm around her and gave her a hug. "I'm sorry about introducing you to our friend Nicco. I didn't realize just what we were getting into there. Next time I'll be more careful."

"Jez . . ."

"I know, only joking." He fidgeted a moment. "I have to go, Amy. O'Neill is down there. I slipped away from him while he was distracted by the dragon and the fires, but he's probably looking for me right now."

"Where will you go?" she asked.

"Back to London at first, and then away. Don't worry, I'll be in touch. But I'll need to keep my head down for a while, until O'Neill finds some other poor bugger to harass."

"What about a car? They know yours."

"I have Mr. Coster's keys," he said with a smirk. "Did you know he had a snow scooter? I'm sure he won't mind me borrowing it, just for a day. He owes it to me, anyway, for what he's put us through."

"Will you be all right, Jez?"

"I have the ring, so yeah, I'll be all right." Suddenly he reached out and hugged her again. "You were right, you know. You don't need this. I'm proud of you for making your own life, and for telling me how you feel. Whatever happens from now on, you remember that."

She hugged him back. "Send me a postcard."

"Mr. Fairweather?"

The voice drifted up from the bailey. Amy looked over the wall and saw O'Neill, standing in a hail of ashes from the burning pavilion, looking up at them. To her dismay, she also saw his men stationed at the various exit points from the north tower. Jez said he had bolted the door that led to the stairwell, so they couldn't get in. Yet.

"What is it with that man?" Jez asked, with a mixture of bewilderment and anger. "Anyone else who'd just seen a dragon would be too busy to worry about me." He sighed. "Maybe I won't be going on holiday after all."

"Mr. Fairweather, will you please come down. It will make my life much easier if you do, and maybe it will help you on your day in court. I have a witness this time who will make a statement that you were staying here under false pretences. Movie producer? Wasn't that what you put down as your occupation? And I'm sure we'll find lots of other charges to add to the list."

He pointed at the man standing beside him, holding a handkerchief to his face. It was Coster.

"The slimy toad," Jez muttered.

"Jez, I'm so sorry. If I hadn't asked you to help, you'd be away by now."

He looked at her indignantly. "No, I wouldn't! You and Rey needed me. I wasn't going anywhere."

"Mr. Fairweather?" O'Neill was calling again. "One last chance to come down, or we're going to have to come up. You're nicked, sunshine."

Jez groaned. "I bet he's been wanting to say that for years."

"I won't let you go alone," Amy began, but Rey stopped her.

"Come with me," he said.

Jez glanced at him uncertainly. "I don't need my hand held, Rey."

"I am not holding your hand," Rey said wearily, "I am helping you escape."

Jez and Amy looked at each other.

"I thought you didn't approve of my way of making a living," Jez reminded him. "You were talking about chopping off my hand before."

"That was before," Rey retorted. "Come with me, before it's too late. There is a secret passageway that leads down into the wall, and then out into the keep." He was already leading the way. "Once you are in there, you will need to get out quickly. But you know about the tunnels. You can use them, if you have to."

Jez gave a shudder. "Let's hope I don't."

Amy laughed. Suddenly she felt as if everything was going to be all right, as far as Jez was concerned, anyway.

Rey had knelt on the stone surface near the door to the stairwell, feeling with his hands. Then he grunted and tugged at an iron ring. A stone slab lifted, disclosing a set of dark, cobwebby stairs winding down inside the thickness of the wall, just as Rey had said.

Jez peered into the space. "You've been in here, I take it?"

"Aye. It's safe. Do not get caught, and if you do,

do not say I helped you. I have my reputation to maintain."

Jez reached out to grasp his shoulder, saying a hasty thank-you, and then he gave Amy a quick final hug. He began to descend into the darkness, and Rey reached to close the door.

"I'm going to do it," Jez said, looking up, his face a pale blur. "I'm going to go straight, Amy."

And then the door shut and he was gone.

"Thank you for helping him get away."

Reynald glanced up. Amy was looking at him as if he was her heart and soul.

"I did not do it only for you, Amy. He risked his life, too, to defeat the dragon . . . Angharad."

He bent to retrieve his longbow and stood for a moment, inspecting the curve of wood and the linen string, thinking that it was amazing that something so simple, so beautiful, could be so deadly.

"She had to die," Amy said gently. "You were right when you said it was either her or us."

"I know. But still, I can't help but feel saddened. She betrayed me, and I understand why. She was fighting for her land and her life, just as my father did, just as I have and, please God, will again."

"Are you sure it wasn't just a case of revenge?" Amy was watching him, her green eyes bright.

"Morwenna was her daughter, after all. Her death was the reason why she hated you so much."

He nodded, not meeting her eyes.

"Angharad sent her daughter in human form to try and kill you. I think that she hoped that without an heir to his lands, your father would not be able to hold on to them, that they'd fall into disorder and Angharad would be able to take them back for herself. I suppose all of this country belonged to her, once."

"But Morwenna failed and was murdered by my father."

"I wonder if Angharad could have saved her? She was calling out. Maybe she didn't get here in time? How bitter that must have been for her."

Reynald nodded. "I see your point. She blamed me and my father for the girl's death, but she also blamed herself."

"Guilt is a corrosive brew. It can eat at you and drive you mad."

The voice came from behind them. When they turned, the eagle was sitting on the battlements, silhouetted against the stars.

Reynald felt confused. In one way he longed to see the witch and to be told he could now return to his home, but in another . . . It would mean leaving Amy behind forever.

"Do not feel sorry for Angharad," the eagle went on. "Believe me, Reynald, in your place she would have relished your death and feasted upon your flesh."

"What will happen now?" Amy said, meaning to Rey. He would go away and leave her, she knew it. Suddenly she felt bereft, and her new life no longer seemed like something to look forward to.

"I will take Angharad to the between-worlds," the eagle said. "She and her kind will be together at last."

"I meant, what will happen to Rey?"

"Why, is he wounded?"

The eagle was being purposely obtuse, and Amy glared at it. She'd had a rotten night; she didn't need to be spoken to like this by a bird.

As if it read her mind, it gave a chuckle, rustling its feathers.

Down below, O'Neill was supervising his men as they tried to break down the door into the tower. So far they hadn't managed it, but they were making a lot of noise.

"Rey has done what he had to do," Amy began, as patiently as she could. "He's completed the task you set him—"

"But this wasn't the task he had to complete," the eagle said coldly. "The dragon was incidental."

"I don't understand," Rey whispered, clearly shattered. "Have I failed, witch? Tell me now."

The eagle sighed. "No, you haven't failed. You have passed your lesson. The Ghost has finally learned to listen to his own heart and not the urging of other people. That was how you defeated the dragon, by believing in yourself."

Suddenly it hopped down off the battlements and moved toward them, and as it came it changed shape, morphing into a young woman with long auburn hair and a gray animalskin cloak about her shoulders. Her eyes burned blue, like neon.

She smiled, and Amy shuddered. There were things in her eyes, dragons in a cavern full of fire. For a brief moment she thought she saw Angharad together with a smaller dragon, then they were gone again.

"I think you have earned your second chance, my Ghost, but it is up to you. Will I return you to 1299, so that you can finally make your peace with your neighbors? *Without* Angharad's interference."

"Do you mean I have a choice?" he said, striving to understand.

"I don't know. Is there a reason you might wish to remain here?"

"There is Amy," he said.

"What of Amy?" the witch mocked. "I do not have long, Reynald. Speak to me. Tell me what is in your heart!"

He felt Amy's gaze on him, but he didn't look at her, not yet. His heart was too full.

"Amy and I are two halves of a whole, alike enough in mind and heart to have the same goals, but different, too, so that we challenge each other. I feel as if there is a chain linking us together, despite the seven hundred years that separates us."

The witch smiled but said nothing, while downstairs O'Neill and his men pounded furiously against the door.

Amy touched his arm, then his face, turning it toward her, forcing him to look at her.

There was an expression in her eyes he didn't understand. So sad and yet so brave. "It's all right, Rey," she said quietly. "I'm all right. I can manage here. This is what you want, what you need to do. Go back and do what you must. Create the world you've always dreamed of. Don't worry about me; I can take care of myself."

She didn't want him, he thought, bewildered. And then he realized that that wasn't it at all. She thought she wasn't good enough for him, and he'd let her believe it.

Reynald shook his head, pulling away, and with two strides was standing before the witch of the between-worlds.

"I cannot leave her," he said stubbornly.

"But she is tainted, isn't she, Reynald? She is everything that you would have avoided in your own time . . . a woman who lies and steals, who has lived the life of a criminal, who has slept with other men—"

"I do not care!" he roared. His chest was rising and falling, and each breath was painful. "I do not care," he whispered. He turned back to Amy; he felt as if he was being torn in two. "You are all to me, damsel. I see past what you did before, those things do not matter, because I see you as the woman you are now. Strong and beautiful, good and true. I love you, Amy, with all my heart."

She was smiling, tears spilling from her eyes. "Oh Rey, I love you, too. So much."

Behind him the witch laughed, and he staggered, struck by her power. "Now that's more like it, Reynald. You see, you are learning at last."

Confused, frustrated, he threw up his hands. "What more must I do, witch, to convince you?"

"You need an heir, Reynald," she told him.

"I . . ."

"Do you or do you not need an heir, Ghost?" It was a demand and not a question.

"Yes. But I do not see—"

"Of course you do not see! None of you mortals see. That is why I am here to guide you, and sometimes prod and push you, along the right road. You have an heir, Reynald, or you will have in nine months' time. Amy Fairweather is carrying your child."

He was stunned, but no more than Amy.

"Now wait a minute," she began.

"I do not have a minute," the witch replied. "Decide now. Will you take her with you to your own time? And, Amy, do you wish to go? Quickly."

Below them there was a splintering crash, as the

door finally began to give way. Voices rose in triumph.

"Yes," Amy said, shaking, crying. "Yes, I do, I want it more than anything."

Reynald laughed wildly, and pulled her into his arms. "Aye," he declared. "I want her with me. I cannot imagine my life now without her. I want her and our child." He felt tears burning his own eyes, melting the cold man he once was into the living, feeling man he would be in the future. Amy had done that.

"I love you, damsel," he said, kissing her face. "I love you with all my being."

"That's much better," the witch murmured, and folding her hands before her, began to chant.

Caught fast in Rey's arms, loved and in love, Amy heard the footsteps of O'Neill and his men, coming fast up the stairs, then the world began to spin, as if she'd had too much champagne, and only Rey was keeping her from falling.

Just as suddenly as it started, it stopped.

She blinked. It was daytime, and it was summer. A warm breeze fanned her face. She stared out over Rey's green lands, toward the Welsh hills, and saw the colorful canvas tents and the flags flapping in the wind.

"It is the same day I died," he murmured in wonder. "We are signing the peace, Amy. It is 1299."

"You have your chance to right the wrong," Amy said, shaking from head to toe.

Rey laughed aloud. "Life is good," he said, his voice deep and husky with joy.

There were voices approaching. For a moment she thought it had all been a dream, and it was O'Neill, but then a group of soldiers appeared from the stairs, clanking in their armor and chain mail, prickly with weapons.

"My lord!" the one in charge said, frowning at the sight of Amy in her strange clothing. Rey drew her even closer against him, and the men stood at a respectful distance, waiting to be spoken to, their eyes flicking only briefly in Amy's direction.

"Captain, is Angharad here?" he said sharply.

The man shifted, glancing back at the others.

"Answer me!"

"My lord, I know no one of that name."

"Who arranged this peace then? Who spoke with the Welsh?"

"My lord, 'twas you . . ."

Rey gave a deep, relieved sigh. "Good. That is well."

The captain shuffled again. "My lord?"

"Yes, what is it?"

"The bishop is asking for you, my lord, and your chaplain—"

"Julius?" said Rey. He looked down at Amy, his expression fierce and possessive with love. "I have some extra work for Julius. I want him to perform a marriage ceremony. If my lady is willing . . . ?"

But he knew she was. Amy laughed in delight,

taking his big, scarred hand in hers, and lifting it to her cheek. "Aye, my lord," she said carefully, "I am very willing indeed."

The soldiers stared, openmouthed, at the sight of their stern and serious lord holding hands with a woman. And then he laughed, too, and said, "Congratulate me. The Ghost is to be wed."

That caused them to send up a cheer that echoed all around the castle.

"Thank you," he murmured in Amy's ear. "You have done all of this, my lady."

"My pleasure," she whispered back. "Does that mean we get to sleep together tonight? In your bed?"

The Ghost smiled down at her, his gray eyes gleaming lasciviously. "Who said anything about sleeping?"

Epilogue

The Sorceress sat quietly. This room was one of her favorites, full of crystals and candles, so that the light shimmered and refracted. She felt as if she was floating in time and space, a small fragment within the greatness of the universe, but an important fragment nonetheless. Without her, time could not function.

She sighed, and the candle flames danced.

The Ghost and his Amy were alive and well in 1299. The world they created would be a remarkable one, and an inspiration to others for centuries to come. That was how it always should have been, if not for Angharad. As the changes rippled out through time, the castle that was now a hotel would become a home again, a place for the descendants of the de Mortimers to gather and remember their famous ancestors. For Amy's child would be one of five.

One of the tricks of being a Sorceress who could travel through time was her ability to visit different time periods and the people who dwelt there. Recently she had been checking up on her other two warriors.

The Black Maclean and his Bella were content in their home at Loch Fasail, Scotland, where their harsh life was warmed by the depth of their love. Maclean had always been a great man, but with Bella's help he'd forged a new understanding between himself and his people. They had begun their own family, too, with a boy and a girl. Although the authorities in Inverness had questioned him, they had more or less left him alone. Mainly because Maclean had become a hero to the Scottish people, and they were afraid to touch him in case it began another rebellion. Besides, he had important friends. Bella was busy writing a diary of her days, a book that would become famous down the centuries for the love story woven through it.

As for the Raven and his Melanie, they were happy living in Cornwall. Their life was busy and full, and Nathaniel had settled into his position as squire. He was admired and loved in the district, and the wild reckless streak that had once threatened to destroy him was channeled into breeding horses and the occasional race at Truro under his wife's anxious eye. Melanie had shifted faultlessly from London solicitor to Cornish lady, although she spent a great deal of time instructing her husband on his duties as magistrate, and it was said by some that it was Melanie and not Nathaniel who should sit upon the bench. Their love for each other was an inspiration to all, and the portrait Nathaniel had commissioned showed the two of them, together with their three children, standing before their home, Ravenswood. It would hang there long after they were gone.

Another triumph.

The Sorceress knew she had completed what she set out to do. These men, who had once been sleeping in the between-worlds, lost souls who had left shattered lives and broken dreams behind them, were now successful and happy. They would be an inspiration to those who came after. The universe would be a better place for the changes she had made.

Then what was the harm? Why not do it again?

But what if the next Immortal Warrior failed? What if her little hobby was discovered by the Lords of the Universe? They would be angry. She might even lose her position as Sorceress of Time. Maybe it was better to quit while she was ahead.

And yet . . . there were so many more deserving warriors awaiting their chance. So many almost heroes who could be helped. And each of them had a mortal woman who was a perfect match.

The Sorceress smiled, and her power caused the crystals to ring.

So, what was it to be? Would she awaken the next Immortal Warrior? Or would she stop now and play it safe?

After a moment she had made her decision. The Sorceress stood up and, with a wave of her hand, snuffed the candles. The crystals fell silent, as if they were holding their breath. Waiting to see what would happen next.

Next month, don't miss these exciting new love stories only from Avon Books

Surrender to a Scoundrel by Julianne MacLean

An Avon Romantic Treasure

Evelyn Wheaton swore she would never forgive Martin, Lord Langdon, for breaking her friend's heart. But Martin has never met a woman he couldn't charm and he won't give up until he's won Evelyn—for a lifetime.

Love in the Fast Lane by Jenna McKnight

An Avon Contemporary Romance

Scott Templeton thought he had seen everything during his racing career. But that was before the ghost of the legendary Speed Cooper appeared in his car. Now Scott's being haunted, Speed's family is up in arms, and Scott has to navigate the most dangerous track of all—love.

Wild and Wicked in Scotland by Melody Thomas

An Avon Romance

After being stood up at her own betrothal ball, Cassandra Sheridan escapes to Scotland. When she encounters a handsome and dangerous stranger on the road, she's intrigued—and horrified when she realizes he's Devlyn St. Clair, her missing fiancé! Now Devlyn must convince Cassie to forgive him before he loses her once and for all.

Desire Never Dies by Jenna Petersen

An Avon Romance

Lady Anastasia Whittig may be a spy, but she greatly prefers research to the more dangerous field work. But when one of her friends is nearly killed, Anastasia teams up with fellow spy Lucas Tyler to track the villain down. Little do they know that this mission will test the limits of their courage—and their passion.

Avon Romantic Treasures

Unforgettable, enthralling love stories, sparkling with passion and adventure from Romance's bestselling authors

DISCOVER CONTEMPORARY ROMANCES *at their*
SIZZLING HOT BEST FROM AVON BOOKS